P9-EEU-339

PRAISE FOR *THE SILENCE OF BONES*

PRAISE FOR *THE FOREST OF STOLEN GIRLS*

ALSO BY
JUNE HUR

The Silence of Bones
The Forest of Stolen Girls

THE
RED
PALACE

JUNE HUR

FEIWEL AND FRIENDS
NEW YORK

A FEIWEL AND FRIENDS BOOK

An imprint of Macmillan Publishing Group, LLC

120 Broadway, New York, NY 10271 • fiercereads.com

Our books may be purchased in bulk for promotional, educational, or business use. Please contact your local bookseller or the Macmillan Corporate and Premium Sales Department at (800) 221-7945 ext. 5442 or by email at MacmillanSpecialMarkets@macmillan.com.

Library of Congress Cataloging-in-Publication Data

Names: Hur, June, author.

Title: The red palace / June Hur.

Description: First edition. | New York : Feiwel and Friends, 2022. | Audience: Ages 13–18. | Audience: Grades 10–12. | Summary: While investigating a series of grisly murders, eighteen-year-old palace nurse Hyeon navigates royal and political intrigue and becomes entangled with a young police inspector. Includes author's note.

Identifiers: LCCN 2021021227 | ISBN 9781250800558 (hardcover)

Subjects: CYAC: Murder—Fiction. | Secrets—Fiction. | Criminal investigation—Fiction. | Nurses—Fiction. | Korea—History—Chosŏn dynasty, 1392–1910—Fiction. | Mystery and detective stories. | LCGFT: Novels. | Detective and mystery fiction.

Classification: LCC PZ7.1.H8645 Re 2022 | DDC [Fic]—dc23

LC record available at https://lccn.loc.gov/2021021227

First edition, 2022

Book design by Liz Dresner

Feiwel and Friends logo designed by Filomena Tuosto

Printed in the United States of America

10 9 8 7 6 5 4 3 2 1

To my husband, Bosco—

*"Friendship is born at the moment when one . . .
says to another "What! You too? I thought
that no one but myself . . ."*
—C. S. Lewis

1

F ollow me," Physician Nanshin whispered, "and ask
no questions."

Moonlight drifted as quietly as falling snow, illuminating the pavilion roofs and the animal-shaped
statues that lined the swooping eaves. Floor lanterns spilled
golden light across the frosted courtyards, and against the
latticed labyrinth of doors and windows. Silence reigned,
except for the distant ring of the great bell, echoing through
the capital and rumbling over Changdeok Palace. By the
twenty-eighth ring, the palace gates would be bolted shut
for the night.

As soon as the royal physician turned his back to us,
Jieun and I exchanged wide-eyed stares.

Isn't our shift over? she mouthed. *Shouldn't we be permitted
to return home?*

I flicked a nervous glance at the physician. *This is very
odd,* I replied.

But what did we know of what was odd or unusual? We were both new to our positions as nae-uinyeos, nurses handpicked to serve in the palace.

"There isn't a moment to spare." The royal physician sounded breathless as he quickened his steps, his hands gathered within wide sleeves. His blue silk robe billowed like waves in a storm, his long apron as white as foam frothing atop a crashing sea. "We must hurry."

Jieun and I hastened our steps accordingly. Our long shadows stretched out, of her holding a tray and me a lantern. We kept quiet this time, when normally we would have complained about our growling stomachs or our limbs tired from working all day. Things were different in the palace. No one acted like children here. Even royal children behaved like solemn and anxious elders.

In long and quick strides, we left the Royal Apothecary, located in the eastern corner of the palace, and traveled in a line from courtyard to courtyard, the sound of the great bell rolling after us. It tolled, slowly and repeatedly, for the twenty-sixth, twenty-seventh, and finally, the twenty-eighth time. I could almost hear the main gates rumbling shut; it would be impossible to leave the palace now. Uneasiness settled into my bones, and the warnings I'd been given echoed through my mind.

To enter the palace means to walk a path stained in blood, our medical teachers had whispered. *There will be bloodshed. I only hope it will not be yours.*

The further south we traveled, the more deserted it

became, until we were easily four li away from where I knew most of the royals dwelled. At least a half hour's walk.

The shadows swamping the empty pavilions grew darker and darker; the fall of snow was no longer pocked with blue footprints, but untouched. Then at last, we passed through a guarded gate and entered a courtyard illuminated by lanterns. In the center lay a square lily pond, its frozen water reflecting the round, luminous moon and the black ridges of the guardian mountain.

I'd never come this way before.

A grand pavilion stood before the courtyard, a building with a long row of hanji-screened windows, rows of towering pillars, and an elaborate black-tiled roof. The wooden plaque hanging under the eaves read *Joseung Pavilion*. The main house in the Donggungjun compound.

The residence of the Crown Prince himself.

I had never seen the Crown Prince before, but I had heard gloomy whispers about Prince Jangheon. When he was born, it is said that the king—usually known for his rigid stoicism—had nearly tripped over his robe in his haste to hold his son. A most beautiful son, and his only surviving heir. The king had fallen so in love with the child that he'd rushed to formally establish him as the Crown Prince—a status that had come with a price. At only one hundred days old, the infant prince had been pulled from his mother's embrace and moved to Joseung Pavilion to be raised completely by strangers in an isolated part of the palace. So far away from his parents that, after a while, he'd only seen them once a year. Now there were disturbing rumors about the neglected prince.

The time will come soon, I'd overheard a palace nurse say once, *when the Crown Prince will be put to death, either by the hands of the Old Doctrine faction or his own father.* Whispers that had immediately clamped into silence at the sight of Jieun and me, for we were new to the palace.

"Come."

I blinked, my attention returning to Physician Nanshin. He gestured at us to quicken our pace further. We did so, following him past a row of court ladies, unmoving like statues. One young woman, however, watched us from under her lashes. Our eyes met, then her gaze quickly dropped. And yet I still felt as though we were being watched by a thousand more eyes.

My pulse beat as I set aside my lantern. We made our way up the steps onto the terrace, then into the pavilion, where tiered wooden doors slid open one by one, drawn by servants who moved as quietly as shadows, ushering us deeper until we reached the inner quarter. We were met by a eunuch, his face pale and fraught with distress.

"I know your day is over, uiwon-nim," the eunuch whispered to the physician, "but it is urgent. The prince is in need of your assistance."

My head was bowed, hiding the shock that widened my eyes. Since entering the palace, I had attended only to women—princesses, concubines, and court ladies. I had yet to assist physicians as they tended to male royals.

"Please, follow." The eunuch hunched over as he accompanied us into a chamber enveloped in darkness, shadows lurking at the edges of glowing floor lanterns and candles. There were piles of books everywhere, haphazardly pushed aside. Two court ladies trembled before a finely woven bamboo screen; it hung from the ceiling, concealing a figure beyond it. At our entrance, they pulled the screen up, revealing a white-robed figure lying on a sleeping mat.

"Leave, both of you," said a commanding female voice.

As the court ladies left, I snuck a glance at a woman sitting near the wall. It was Lady Hyegyoung, the wife of the Crown Prince; they were both twenty-three years of age, bound to each other since marriage at the age of nine. She looked immaculate as always, garbed in a silk gown dripping with luminous gold-threaded dragon medallions, and her smooth hair shone in the candlelight, tied into a perfectly thick coil at the nape of her neck and held in place by a golden rod. I had encountered her several times before at Chippok Hall. She seemed to prefer spending most of her time with her mother-in-law rather than here with her husband.

"His Highness has been feeling ill the past two days, and it is getting worse," Lady Hyegyoung said, projecting her voice, as if she were not speaking to us but rather to those outside.

"Has His Royal Highness taken any medicine today?" Physician Nanshin asked.

"No. He seemed much better this morning, but then later in the afternoon, he fainted and has been indisposed since."

The physician bowed his head. "I will inspect His Highness now." He knelt before the young man, whose back was turned to us, and Jieun and I knelt behind the physician. The bedcover rustled, the sound of the Crown Prince rising into a sitting position with the assistance of his eunuch.

"Tell me, what is wrong with His Royal Highness?" Lady Hyegyoung asked. "He has expressed weakness and fatigue all day long."

I couldn't resist; I'd never seen the prince, not even from afar, for he spent most of his time training in the Forbidden Garden, honing his skills with sword and bow. Carefully, my gaze ran along His Highness's sleeping robe, his wrist held out to the physician, the frail column of his throat . . . then paused before a wrinkled and frightened face.

I blinked.

I squeezed my eyes shut, then looked again. Nothing changed. I wasn't hallucinating.

A wave of confusion struck me at the sight of an old man, a eunuch, dressed in the Crown Prince's nightgown and sitting in the Crown Prince's bed. He was *not* Prince Jangheon. Yet Physician Nanshin remained kneeling, nimble fingers on the imposter's wrist, as though the eunuch were indeed the future king himself.

"His Royal Highness is feeling weak because his ki is

weak." The physician glanced over his shoulder, revealing a crescent of his face, sweat dribbling down his temple. "Nurse Jieun, bring the ginseng tea."

Jieun remained frozen, staring ahead at the imposter prince. "E-Eunuch Im?" she whispered.

The physician shot a look at her, his face ashen. *"Silence,"* he hissed. Then he looked at me. "Nurse Hyeon, please bring the medicine."

At once, I reached for Jieun's tray, then rose to my feet, and to my horror, my hands were shaking. The tray wobbled, and I felt stares turn my way.

"You look flushed, Nurse Hyeon," came Lady Hyegyoung's lowered voice, "and rather flustered."

I gripped the tray tighter, but it continued to rattle. "Begging your pardon, my lady."

"I am told your birth name is Baek-hyeon."

"Yeh, my lady." I sounded breathless. "That is my name."

"A name usually reserved for boys."

I wanted to wipe my brow—never had a royal scrutinized me so. "When I was born, my mother's disappointment was so great that she nevertheless gave me a son's name."

Her eyes watched me closely, and the air around me grew tight and painful; even the slightest movement hurt my skin. Then she whispered, "You look almost identical to the prince's favorite sister, Princess Hwahyup. She is six years dead."

My limbs remained frozen, not knowing whether this

similarity was offensive to Her Ladyship or not. I didn't realize that my muscles had knotted painfully until she looked away and at once my shoulders eased.

"And you are Jieun," Lady Hyegyoung said, her voice still hushed. "Half cousin to the new police inspector."

"Y-y-yeh," Jieun stammered. "I a-am."

I set the noisy tray down and returned to my spot behind the physician, kneeling on the floor and burying my sweaty hands in my skirt. I wanted to glance to my side, where Jieun knelt, but trepidation kept me still.

"I have summoned you two specifically for a reason." Lady Hyegyoung slid a glance to the latticed doors as footsteps creaked on the other side of them. The silhouette of a court lady moved across, then disappeared. "Because you both share one thing in common."

I finally glanced at Jieun. We were the same in age, having both just turned eighteen. We were both daughters of lowly concubines, and thus servant girls of impure blood, belonging to the cheonmin class—the lowest of the low. Only, Jieun's father acknowledged her as his daughter, whereas mine considered me as irrelevant to him as his house servants.

"You are both newly selected palace nurses," Lady Hyegyoung explained. "And before that, you were Hyeminseo nurses favored by Nurse Jeongsu. I trust that woman."

I gripped my skirt tight. Jieun had to be as confused as I was.

"Nurse Jeongsu is a family friend. And Royal Physician

Nanshin's family is tied to mine. I hope I can trust you two as well, Jieun and Hyeon, for your mentor assured me of your trustworthiness." Then a somber note dusked her voice. "I hope no one has recruited you as their spies already."

"No, indeed not, my lady!" Jieun blurted out. "We would not dare—"

Her Ladyship placed a finger to her lips. "In the palace, you speak with a loud voice only when your words are public words; you must whisper when speaking private words. Everyone is listening in the palace. Everyone is spying for someone." Her gaze then moved away from us and settled on the imposter prince. "Can I trust you, then?"

"Yeh," Jieun and I replied together.

"Then continue to tend to His Royal Highness, and should the king summon him, you are to tell His Majesty that his son is indisposed still."

She wanted us to lie—to the king himself?

This could mean our deaths.

It was difficult to breathe, but I bowed my head, and so did Jieun. It was our duty to obey. I continued to stare at the floor, listening to my thundering heartbeat and to the sound of silk rustling as Physician Nanshin tended to the imposter prince, performing for our silent audience.

The court ladies. The eunuchs. The spies.

I could almost imagine what they saw: a shadow play of silhouettes against the hanji-screened door, in the shape of a physician and two nurses moving around the prince in the candlelit darkness.

How long we were expected to perform, I was unsure, and the tense hours that followed dragged on enough that the sharp sense of fear—fear that we had unwittingly fallen into a deadly game—dulled into a thrumming headache. As more time stretched on, the oppressive silence trimmed away even the headache and left only a single question:

Where had the real Prince Jangheon disappeared to?

The question danced around in my skull, and I slowly surveyed his chamber. My gaze brushed across a gleaming porcelain vase on display, across lacquered furniture with mother-of-pearl inlay, and came to rest on a scattering of books nearby—occult books, judging from the rumors I'd heard. His Highness was obsessed with Taoist scripture, magic formulae, and teachings on how to command ghosts and spirits.

Perhaps the palace had grown too ordinary for a prince fond of the unconventional. Perhaps he had wandered outside, even though that was forbidden—no royal was permitted to leave the palace without the king's permission.

My mind roved around the books and furniture, searching for something to latch my thoughts on to, to keep me alert. Hours passed in such a way, stagnant and quiet, as though time had fallen into an unending loop. Physician Nanshin sat as still as a rock, and Jieun spent her time counting the acupuncture needles in her norigae chimtong—a small silver case decorated with elaborate knots and tassels that hung from the waist strings of her uniform, something all uinyeos carried around. And Eunuch Im, the imposter prince, stifled a yawn. I pinched my skin hard, but the numbness continued to deepen. Fear had never felt so tiring as it did today; I was exhausted. I could no longer tell whether one hour passed, or several.

I pinched myself again, hard. *Stay awake.*

And then my thoughts cut loose, drifting out of the royal chamber, out of the palace, and to the nearby public medical office, the Hyeminseo. It was the place where Jieun and I had studied to become nurses since the age of eleven. We'd spent our days there, our time split between caring for commoners and studying furiously for our medical exams, determined to achieve the highest marks—every year, two of the most excellent students were recruited to work for the palace. For this dream, I had learned to survive on little sleep. I would study late into the night to catch up to the other students in the beginners class, all servant girls around my age, between ten and fifteen with brilliant minds. We would spend the whole day in our pink jeogori jackets and blue skirts, our hair neatly braided, our heads always bowed over books or raised to listen to lectures led by stern teachers. Once, when a teacher had rebuked me for falling asleep during a lesson, I'd learned to stay awake no matter what by pinching myself so hard that the skin would peel.

Kohpi. That was the nickname my peers had given me, for my nose would always bleed from exhaustion, from pinching myself awake when I'd slept no more than three hours. Nurse Jeongsu had even given me small strips of cloth to keep in my pocket, to plug my nostrils with whenever they leaked red.

I was supposed to be excellent at keeping myself awake. Yet sleep had never felt so irresistible.

At one point I must have nodded off, for I startled awake to the deep, booming echo of the great bell. My hazy mind teetered, and it took me a moment to realize the bell was announcing the end of curfew—it was five in the morning.

I rubbed my eyes and looked around.

The chamber was still dark. And in the shadows, Lady Hyegyoung was awake, still sitting with her shoulders slightly slumped forward. Sweat gleamed on her broad forehead as she waited, straining her ears for the sound of the king's footsteps. Soon the whole palace would awaken to find the Crown Prince missing. This could not bode well for her.

Or for any of us.

Doors behind me slid open, so abruptly that I shot a glance over my shoulder. Before us was a young eunuch, panting as he tried to straighten his black cap.

"Eunuch Choe," Lady Hyegyoung said, her voice cutting. "Where is His Highness? I told you not to return until you had found him."

"I—" He breathed hard, wiping his brows. "I entered the palace as soon as the gates reopened, my lady. The prince is on his way here, right this instant."

Her Ladyship tilted her head back for a moment, eyes closed, relief straining against the edge of her brows. "Go tell His Highness to use the back window of his chamber, to avoid the court ladies seeing him. I have left it open." She waited, but the eunuch remained where he was, gripping his hands tightly together. "Well?"

Eunuch Choe wrung his hands, then said, "A great misfortune has struck the capital, my lady. A m-m-massacre. There was a massacre."

I held my breath, chilled by his words.

"What do you mean?" Lady Hyegyoung asked.

"I was escorting His Highness back when he told me he'd just witnessed a most gruesome sight. The Crown Prince was very much shaken, so he is"—Eunuch Choe glanced at the door, then hurried to Her Ladyship's side—"he is in an *unstable* mood. I would leave the pavilion at once, my lady, and return to your residence."

I frowned. Was Her Ladyship in danger?

As though sensing my question, Lady Hyegyoung's eyes darted my way, and she seemed almost surprised to see us still kneeling in the chamber. "The palace gates are open now. Leave. And tell no one of this if you value your lives."

We bowed, then retreated, our steps quiet. I couldn't wait to talk with Jieun; we always gossiped about the palace goings-on while walking to our respective homes, hers near the northern district and mine near the fortress gate.

Just as the doors slid shut behind us, Eunuch Choe's voice slipped through. "My lady, four women were murdered. At the Hyeminseo."

My heart tensed around that one word. *Hyeminseo.* A medical office to many, but to me, it had been my first and only true home. The place where my dreams had blossomed, of becoming a nurse and rising above my station. Of being more than just Hyeon, the illegitimate daughter, the vulgar commoner.

I hoped I'd misheard, but when I glanced at Jieun, at her horrified eyes and gaping mouth, I nearly tripped down the stone steps into the row of court ladies. I tried taking a deep breath, but choked on what felt like shards of ice.

Hyeminseo nurses . . . dead . . . *murdered*?

Before I knew it, my steps had staggered into hurried strides.

"Nurse Hyeon," Physician Nanshin called, "you mustn't run in the palace—"

"Uiwon-nim, I must go." And with that, I bolted across the yard, jumping from stone step to stone step, skidding across the hardened layer of snow. It took a moment to realize that Jieun was right behind me, both our hearts beating to the same plea.

Please let the eunuch be wrong. Please. Please. Please.

———

Blue mist drifted over the snow-dusted main road, its biting cold nipping at our ears and cheeks as we hurried down Donhwamunro Street, past the sleeping market stalls. The sun had not yet risen, and shadows lurked deep at every corner. My teeth were chattering by the time we approached the Hyeminseo, a vast walled-in compound that held the medical office and its spacious courtyards.

"Wait." Jieun touched my elbow as we came to a standstill. A small group was gathered at the gate's entrance, guarded by a police officer, his face reddish-orange in the torchlight. "Isn't that Palace Nurse Inyeong?"

"Nurse Inyeong? Why would she be here . . . ?" My

gaze arrested upon the familiar face in the crowd. It was indeed Nurse Inyeong, wrapped in a straw cloak, her face pale and her eyes staring ahead. When a gust blew by, she tugged her sleeves down low, then shivered as she held the cloak closer to herself. I barely knew her, only that she was a few years older than me. "Maybe she can tell us what occurred," I whispered.

We hurried over, weaving our way through the spectators, who hummed with whispers. Once we were near enough, I reached out to tap Nurse Inyeong's straw-cloaked shoulder, but she ducked and disappeared deeper into the crowd. A moment later, I saw her slipping into an alley, leaving me alone with my question.

Who had died?

I turned, craning my head to look past the officer guarding the gate, spear flashing in the torchlight. Four bodies had been laid out in the courtyard on stretchers, one next to the other, motionless under straw mats. I crossed my arms, holding myself tight against a surge of panic.

I was only a few steps away from the gate, and I moved to get even closer.

Jieun caught my sleeve. "Where are you going?"

"I need to see who was killed," I whispered.

"But it is a crime scene, Hyeon-ah!"

"Perhaps we could be of help. We were once Hyeminseo nurses."

I took another step forward, and at once the police lowered his spear to block my way.

"Stand back!" he bellowed.

Jieun at once retreated, but I stayed still, dread thickening in my blood as I stared into the courtyard.

"Stand *back*," he warned again.

Words formed and floated from my lips: "But I am a nurse. I wish to examine the corpses."

The police officer looked me over, and I knew what he saw—a young woman in a pale blue silk jacket and a dark blue skirt, wearing a long white apron. My hair, tied into a coil and secured by a bright red ribbon, and a garima, a black crownlike headpiece made of silk.

"A Hyeminseo nurse?" he asked.

"No." I presented my special identification tag, one that allowed me entrance into the palace grounds. "I am a nae-uinyeo."

The officer tilted his head to the side, his brows furrowing. The police didn't need me; they had plenty of skilled servants to examine corpses, namely damos—nurses sent to work at the police bureau as punishment for their bad grades. And yet the officer moved his spear aside and asked, "So you were sent for?"

Without a moment's hesitation, I lied, "Yes, I was, sir."

"Go on in, if you can stomach the sight. What kind of dog would do such a thing." It wasn't a question, but a statement.

Taking in a steadying breath, I walked into the courtyard and at once felt my heart grow cold. I had seen death before, but never like this. Despite the straw mats covering the four bodies, I could see the tops of their neatly brushed hair, the tips of their still fingers, the hems of their uniforms.

I flinched at sudden movement. A halo of light moved behind the hanji-screened windows, likely the police officers examining the main office. The light paused—illuminating a streak of blood splashed across the screen—then poured into the courtyard, burnishing the straw gold.

My breath whooshed in and out in nervous gusts as I crouched before the four bodies. My hands trembled as I grasped the edge of the first covering and pulled. The sound of gooey blood sent bumps down my skin, like I was peeling off a layer of thick, slimy film that had grown over the dead. I tugged again, revealing a long forehead, a narrow face with staring eyes, and a mouth parted as though in a silent scream.

It was nineteen-year-old Bitna, a student nurse. Memory of her voice tinkled in my ears. *Hyeon-ah! Can I borrow your notes on* Injaejikjimaek?

It took me several reeling moments to regain my composure. Once I did, I pulled the mat further down and stopped at the sight of two bloody slashes, one across her throat and another longer one across her chest. Her fingernails were lined in red. She had put up a fierce fight.

I had to close my eyes, steadying myself against the icy flash of horror, waiting for my pulse to slow, for my breathing to find its natural depth. I then proceeded to examine the next two corpses.

First was twenty-year-old Eunchae, another student nurse I'd worked with at the Hyeminseo, and who was betrothed to be married next month. Ripped hair clutched in her fist. Her nose bruised purple, blood pooling under the skin. A stab through her stomach. Then the same slash across the throat as Bitna.

Next was elderly Head Nurse Heejin, one of the few senior nurses who took the time to tutor the nurses who were falling behind in their studies. She'd recently told me about her infant niece and what joy she'd felt in holding her. A child she would never hold again. The old woman's back had been slashed, perhaps when she had turned to run. And again, the same slash across the throat.

By the time I reached for the last mat, I was blinking cold sweat out of my eyes, sitting on the ground because I couldn't hold myself up any longer. I took in deep gulps of air to press down my whimpers. I knew who the fourth victim was, even though her face was still concealed: It had to be Nurse Jeongsu. Ten years my senior and like an older sister to me. She often tutored students in the early morning as well.

I took in a shuddering breath, then pulled down the straw cover.

For a moment, I stared in confusion. This wasn't my mentor, but a woman dressed in the dark blue uniform of a musuri, a lowly palace servant.

A sharp ache pounded behind my left eye as realization dawned; I knew who this was. It was Court Lady Ahnbi. I'd seen her before, serving one of the king's concubines, Madam Mun. She was around my age. But what was a court lady doing here, dressed as a servant? How had she ended up dead outside the palace? Court ladies were considered the "king's women"—forbidden to marry and forbidden to leave the palace walls. Any indiscretion on their part was severely punished, often by death.

A loose strand of damp hair fell over my face. I shoved it aside and examined Ahnbi closer. From what I could observe, she had been stabbed in the chest. Her wound was less bloody than the rest, inflicted by a smaller weapon. She'd then been killed by a single stab to the throat. There was no sign of an altercation—at least, not at a quick glance.

"So, you mean to tell me that you witnessed nothing," a deep, booming voice rumbled from within the medical office. My gaze flew up. The halo of lanternlight outlined the silhouette of a powerfully built figure on the screened door. "You are certain of that?"

I hurried up to the building, then went around to the backyard, out of view from the officer guarding the gate. I stepped close to the side of the latticed window, making sure not to cast a silhouette against the hanji screen.

"I must have fallen asleep, Commander Song."

My brows knotted. *Nurse Jeongsu?*

"Asleep?" the commander said.

"While Head Nurse Heejin tutored the students, I was so tired I went to rest in another room. I was exhausted from assisting with two childbirths yesterday."

"Childbirths." There was a snarl in his voice. "Why any mother would trust *you* is beyond me. You are careless with the lives of others—"

"Commander," she tried again. "I would not harm any of the other nurses. We are all on good terms, and I assist

19

them in their studies. We do this often, meeting either late at night or early in the mornings for extra lessons. Please be calm and think. I, too, want justice for my dead students."

"I am most calm," he hissed. "And I will find everything you are hiding from me. I *know* you are hiding something." His silhouette took a threatening step forward. "You hid secrets from me twelve years ago, and I'm sure you are doing it again."

I wanted to push past the hanji screen and tell Commander Song that he was wasting his time. Ask anyone in Hanyang—the capital of Joseon—and they would declare Nurse Jeongsu to be benevolent and kind. Even Lady Hyegyoung had spoken fondly of her just this morning. The real killer was still out there—

My thoughts froze. The skin on my back tingled, the feeling of being watched. Slowly, I glanced over my shoulder, hoping that I would see only the sky, a grayish-blue over the otherwise black landscape.

Instead, my gaze slid up against a pair of straw sandals, then a dusty white pair of trousers, then a patched jacket. My pulse thundered as I stared at a quiet face sculpted in shadow and streaks of mud. The oblique sweep of his brows was crisp against his tanned skin, his dark hair tied into a topknot. He was tall, lean, and half-starved, judging by the hollowness of his cheeks. A peasant, perhaps come to the Hyeminseo for medical treatment.

"What do you want?" I whispered.

His gaze rested on mine, as steady as his voice. "This is a crime scene."

He must work for the police bureau, I thought. *A servant, perhaps.* At any moment, he might call out that a suspicious person lurked in the backyard.

"I am a nurse, and the guard allowed me in," I said, holding his gaze. "You may ask him if you wish."

"You are a Hyeminseo nurse?"

"A palace nurse," I clarified. "But I was once a student here."

A line formed between his brows. "Do you know the suspect in that office?"

I flinched at the word *suspect.* "She is my mentor."

"Your mentor . . ." His gaze slid beyond me to the place where only a thin screen separated me from Commander Song. "The commander will not be pleased to know that the prime suspect's student is eavesdropping."

"I wasn't eavesdropping," I snapped. "I meant to leave. I was just wondering where the voices were coming from. Besides, the police guard *let* me in. You may ask him yourself—"

"Tie her up." Commander Song's voice shot out from within, rattling my nerves. "And secure her in the prison block. She will be questioned later in the morning." Then his silhouette turned to Nurse Jeongsu's. "If you cooperate with us, the questioning will be brief, and you will return to the Hyeminseo within a few days. As I said, it all depends on your cooperation."

There came the sound of shuffling fabric, and no sound of resistance; Nurse Jeongsu was allowing herself to be arrested. Footsteps creaked, then withdrew from the office, followed by Commander Song's voice thundering from somewhere on the other side of Hyeminseo. "Officer Gwon, continue to question all witnesses. The rest of you will continue to search for the murder weapon."

I glanced at the police servant. "I think I should leave now."

"I think you should follow me to the main courtyard."

"I think not." I made an attempt to leave, but he side-stepped so suddenly that I found myself staring at his chest, my nose nearly brushing up against his filthy attire. "Let me pass. I am a *palace* nurse."

"Everyone related to this crime scene, in one way or another, must be interrogated."

"I am not related to this crime scene in any way," I assured him. "I *just* arrived."

"Well, you can explain that to the commander—"

"Wait," I said, my mind racing. I dug into my apron pocket, pulled out a coin, and proffered it to him. "Here, take it."

His lashes lowered, his stare on the gleaming coin. "Bribery is a hanging offense."

I breathed out slowly, withholding a curse. "What do you want, then? You must want something, surely."

"Evidence," he said simply. "That is all."

He was an upright servant, then, likely loyal to the commander. "Will you let me go if I tell you something significant about the case? You can tell the commander you figured this out yourself."

"I don't think whatever you have to say will be of

significance . . ." The garima billowed, and I watched as his gaze followed the black silk dancing around the crown of my head. He gathered his hands behind his back, apparently changing his mind. "Very well. Tell me what you know."

I shoved the coin back into my pocket, and while pausing to collect myself, I mentally flipped through the pages of all the medical case reports I'd read and memorized. I then glanced to the side, keeping an eye out for the commander or other officers as I said, "Stab wounds always look messy, typically with several strikes and cuts around them. But when I saw the fourth victim in the dark blue uniform, I immediately noticed what was missing: defensive wounds. There was just one stab to the throat—a very practiced stroke. The killer knew precisely where on the body to attack to inflict the deadliest damage. I find that very telling. Also, that same wound was inflicted by a weapon smaller than the ones that killed the other victims."

I paused in my line of thought, realizing that the police servant hadn't uttered a single word, nor had even blinked as he watched me, his gaze as intense as his eyes were dark. I tried not to look away.

"How do you know all this?" he asked quietly.

"I am a nurse," I reminded him.

"You are a nurse," he repeated under his breath, "not an investigator."

"Uinyeos are investigators of the human body—"

Footsteps crunched across the snow somewhere nearby.

"What?" Commander Song's voice echoed through the chilly dawn air. "You let a woman onto the crime scene? Where is she now?"

My heartbeat spiked as I glanced at the police servant. He could choose to turn me in to the commander with one word—

"You should leave now," he whispered instead.

At once, I bolted toward the stone wall that enclosed the Hyeminseo, a wall that was too high for me to climb. Flicking a glance over my shoulder, I gave the police servant a sheepish look. "Please, could you help me reach the top of the wall?"

He tensed. "How?"

"You could offer me your back."

"My back . . . to climb on?"

"Hurry," I whispered. "He's coming!"

He remained still.

Letting out a huff, I murmured, "I'll climb over myself, then."

Wiping the clamminess from my palms, I ran and leapt, and my hands latched on to the top of the icy, tile-capped wall. With all my might, I heaved myself up, my knees chafing in the attempt to scale the surface. But my fingers slipped, and I was on the ground again.

"A *palace* nurse?" Commander Song's voice drew closer. "What did she look like?"

I needed to get out. *Now.*

I gathered myself and took another leap. Holding on

to the top of the wall, I pulled myself up and managed to glimpse the other side. Sweat dampened my forehead as I tried to muster up more strength. My arms trembled and my fingers ached. Suddenly, a pair of hands clasped my waist and hoisted me up with ease, high enough that I could hook a leg over the wall. And as I hung onto the tiles, I glanced back at the serious young man, my eyes locking on to his somber gaze.

"Stay away, if you can." His voice hovered between a warning and a challenge. "If you don't want your life ruined, I had better not see you lurking around a crime scene again."

A frown drifted across my brows. I wasn't sure what he meant.

"Of course," I whispered back. "I highly doubt our paths will ever cross again."

Catching a glimpse of Commander Song's police hat, I pushed myself over and landed on the other side, then pressed my back against the wall, my heartbeat pounding in my ears. The commander and his servant exchanged low-voiced murmurs, which were followed by the crunching of their receding footsteps. A sigh of relief escaped me; I was safe now. Yet in the ensuing silence, the crushing weight of reality returned.

Four women had been murdered.

The ripped hair in one hand, the blood lining another's nails. Whispers of their desperation to live, yet still they had been killed.

Who could be this cruel? This *evil*?

I ran a hand over my face, then looked around. Everything looked the same as before: The sea of clay huts with snow-covered straw roofs, the dirty roads threading through the capital, the dark ridges of the mountains guarding us within their basin. And yet it was as though I had climbed over the wall and had fallen into a nightmare instead. The air here was taut with the scent of terror, and the faces of the dead leaked into my eyes and washed the sky in a reddish-blue.

What will you do now? The thought of Nurse Jeongsu echoed after me. *What will you do?*

I walked, stumbling a little each time my knees buckled. I searched for Jieun, and when I couldn't find her, I walked homeward toward the eastern gate. Everything seemed out of order, strange, and too sharp. When I passed a butcher slamming his knife down on an animal's flesh, I flinched and found myself on the brink of tears.

Who had killed those women? What could have possibly pushed the killer into murdering them? Through the blur of my vision, I stared at the faces of the people I passed—grimy and carved in lines, men and women and children darting their beady black eyes my way.

I had stepped into a world that seemed to be hiding terrible secrets from me.

2

The wick had burned all the way down. It was just after dawn, so I didn't want to stumble out of my chamber and disturb the entire household in search of another candle. My five-year-old brother Dae-hyeon was likely fast asleep, and as for Mother . . . Well, I always avoided her, reluctant to witness her tense stillness as she waited for Father. He rarely visited, preferring to split his time between his wife and his new concubine. Mother was unimportant to him.

Quietly moving my low-legged table closer to the window, I whispered to myself my mantra: "I will never be like Mother."

I would not love, unless I was loved first and loved the most.

I would be nothing at all, if I could not be first.

I would not sit silently wasting away as the world passed me by, like Mother. I was determined to be heard, to have my thoughts considered. So I continued to write my letter to Commander Song, black ink slithering across the skylit paper, my writing neat and small. I kept my wide sleeves rolled up so as not to leave a smear.

I was on my fourth page, testifying to Nurse Jeongsu's kindness of character and incapacity to kill, and I found myself stepping further and further into the past. I was eight again, shivering outside the Gibang House, left there in midwinter by my mother, who believed I could have no future other than that of a gisaeng, a female entertainer. She'd told me to wait until the madam—who'd turned me down—would reconsider and take me in. But the doors to the house had remained shut, and no one had come for me, until Nurse Jeongsu had crouched before me and cupped my frozen face.

"I am an uinyeo," were her first words to me. "You aren't alone now." She'd carried me all the way to the Hyeminseo.

Nurse Jeongsu had only been eighteen then.

I was eighteen now.

After pausing several times to massage the aches cramping my fingers, I finally glanced at the window to find that the sky had brightened. It was my day off today, as I only worked every other day at the palace, like many of the nurses employed there. I'd have time to watch the police interrogation that would take place today, while the testimonies were still fresh.

I took a sip of my barley tea, now cold, and wrote down the final line in my long letter to Commander Song:

If you knew her as I do, sir, you would be convinced of her innocence.

I waited for the ink to dry before folding the letter up. After quickly freshening myself and changing out of my uniform, I set off at a brisk pace. Within a half hour, I arrived before the fortress gate.

A guard inspected my identification tag as I gazed up. High above on the fortress parapet, a red-robed soldier made his rounds, and I wondered what he saw from up there, whether the kingdom appeared different after such a bloody night.

The guard returned my tag. "You may pass," he said, a cloud of steam forming in the cold air.

I strode through the gate at once, my senses sharpened and alert. Somewhere within this place, a killer still lurked. On either side of me stretched an endless line of huts, populated by tired-faced and hungry-looking people garbed in white robes as they smoked their pipes. Children shoved me aside as they ran by. I passed women with baskets on their heads and babies wrapped across their backs, some with an older child following them, laden with bundles of straw.

"Make way!" servants announced. "Make way for my master!"

It was protocol to kowtow in the dirt to passing nobles. So I took the Pimatgol alley, a narrow path people like myself used to avoid bowing and dirtying one's clean skirt. Once I was near the police bureau, I slipped back out onto the main road, then paused.

A crowd swarmed in front of a public wall, catching my attention. It was difficult not to notice the whispers buzzing in the air, fingers pointing at a handbill plastered there. Anonymous handbills were only pasted on public walls when the oppressed wanted a voice. When they knew that speaking openly would result in an execution.

"What does it say?" a peasant asked.

"I don't know," the other replied. "I cannot read."

"None of us can read! What does it say?"

I wove through the human cluster and looked. It was written in Hanja characters, writing meant only for the highborn, for the powerful. But I knew how to read classical Chinese, and so I took a few steps closer, and froze.

The Crown Prince killed—

The crowd suddenly split. Screams and gasps erupted as flashes of black hats and black-robed figures barged in, swinging their clubs. The police had arrived. One shoved me aside so hard my teeth clacked as I slammed into the wall. Yet I felt no pain, numbed by the words I'd read, and numbed by the sight of fear lighting the eyes of the police as they tore off the handbill.

I sunk against the wall as my legs turned to water. The Crown Prince's dark chamber flooded into my mind, a chamber that had whispered of his absence. His Highness had left the palace in secret and had returned as a witness to a massacre.

The Crown Prince killed . . . whom? Whom had he killed?

I rushed into the police bureau to see an empty interrogation chair placed before the pavilion. At the center of the raised wooden terrace, Commander Song was seated.

He was a great, growling old man with a wispy white beard. His elbow perched on the arm of the chair, his finger tapping against his cheek. He was waiting. The crowd of spectators, circled around the interrogation chair, were all waiting.

"You look ill."

Startled, I glanced around to meet a pair of deep-set, hooded eyes. It was Nurse Inyeong, the palace nurse I had seen at the crime scene. She was a tall and slim young woman in her mid-twenties, with a face as pale as moonlit petals, or perhaps it was the jibun powder she wore thicker than usual. But as delicate as she looked, when she pulled me aside, away from a passing police officer, I felt strength in her grip.

"How long have you been here?" I asked.

"Since the start of the interrogation."

"It's already begun?"

"All the witnesses have spoken, including family members of the *suspect*."

She said the last word like she also didn't believe Nurse Jeongsu was guilty. "You think my mentor is innocent?" I asked hesitantly.

"Your mentor?" She let out a breath, then shook her head. "I was a witness. I was the one who reported the crime scene."

My brows shot up. "What happened?"

"It's a long story," she murmured. "Before curfew lifted, I realized my drunkard father was missing and went to fetch him from the gambling den he frequents. I didn't want him to gamble away what little he has, as he is always prone to doing. But these days with the ongoing famine—" She shook her head. "I fetched him, and he was angry, so he walked off on his own. That's when I saw her—Court Lady Ahnbi, running down the street. She looked terrified, constantly glancing over her shoulder and not stopping to ask the patrolmen for help."

"And then she ended up dead," I said, half to myself. "I suppose the police know that she was a court lady, and not a mere palace servant?"

"Yes, I told them so . . ." Her voice trailed off, as did the focus of her gaze, like she was looking back on the pre-dawn hours. "I followed Court Lady Ahnbi, as I knew it was forbidden for her to be wandering outside the palace walls. But then I lost her, and I searched for a short while before deciding to head home again. Which was when I heard a woman scream."

Inyeong let out a shuddering breath. "It was quiet by the time I arrived. The gate was open, so I looked in. That was when I saw—" She looked about to faint as she pressed the back of her hand against her mouth. "I have never seen anything so horrific in my life."

Right then, the crowd burst into a frenzy of whispers. I followed their stares, and my gaze locked on to Nurse Jeongsu being pulled into view, no longer in her uinyeo uniform but in a plain white dress. Curls of snowflakes fell as quietly as her footsteps. Time slowed as I tried to recognize the woman who had mentored me for half my life, the woman whom I so looked up to. When I was a child, she had reminded me of a fairy maiden who had descended from the clouds—her face luminous as the moon, her eyes as bright as the stars on a cloudless night. But today she looked withdrawn and withered.

Tension gathered in the air, pressing against us, as everyone seemed to wait with bated breath. Two floggers stood on either side of her, thick wooden clubs held at the ready as she was tied to the interrogation chair.

I wanted to close my eyes. Police torture was notorious—so notorious that even King Yeongjo was always advocating to prevent the reckless beating done by police officials. His Majesty had tried to limit flogging to thirty strikes, and torture could not be repeated within three days. But it was common knowledge among us lowborns that the police did not follow His Majesty's commands, and often beat suspects to death.

Please, I prayed to the heavens, *protect Nurse Jeongsu.*

"A little before curfew lifted, in the pre-dawn hours," Commander Song's voice rumbled from the raised terrace, "different witnesses claim to have heard screams coming from the Hyeminseo. The mothers of two of the murdered victims claim their daughters had left early to receive extra lessons from Head Nurse Heejin, who was also found dead."

He turned now to Nurse Jeongsu. "You say that you, too, had gone to the Hyeminseo to assist with their studies?"

"Yeh," Nurse Jeongsu replied, her voice strained. "That is so."

"At what time?"

"We often open the Hyeminseo doors to student nurses an hour before curfew lifts."

"So at four in the morning, during the Hour of the Tiger?"

"Yeh."

"Then why is it that three neighbors claim to have seen you leave home at midnight and never return? Where did you go?"

Nurse Jeongsu stalled, her face pale. "It is no crime for a woman to be out late at night."

It was true. Women were permitted to roam the streets during the curfew hours; only men were forbidden, for men were considered a danger to the capital at night. She had done nothing wrong.

"I repeat my question," Commander Song said, his voice clipped. "Where were you between midnight and when you claim to have gone to the Hyeminseo, at four in the morning?"

She hesitated again, and this time for far too long. "I . . . I went for a walk."

"For four entire hours?"

"I had much weighing on my mind, sir."

The commander's elbow remained on the arm of his chair, his finger still tapping his cheek. "Perhaps you spent those four hours planning the murder. Perhaps you met with your partner in crime, who was to assist with the massacre."

"You have an abundance of imagination, sir, to believe

this." Her voice wavered, and I wasn't sure whether it was from outrage or terror. "But I have no motive—"

"You were covered in blood when we found you," Commander Song said. "Your hands were soaked red. If you are innocent, then tell me: Do you have an alibi that might confirm your testimony at any point during midnight to four in the morning?"

Her red-rimmed focus never wavered from the ground. "I do not."

Nurse Jeongsu, I silently begged my teacher, *defend yourself!*

"I had no reason to kill the student nurses," her voice rasped. "I was good friends with the head nurse. And as for the young court lady, I've never seen her in my life."

"You are a liar, Nurse Jeongsu," Commander Song snarled. "You are hiding something from the police. You claim to have fallen asleep, yet how does one remain asleep when witnesses from all corners of the capital heard the screams?"

A murmur of agreeing whispers rippled through the crowd around me.

"Officers collected evidence on scene, and one thing they found was a yakjakdu." The commander gestured, and a clerk stepped forward, holding out a long, straight blade with a wooden handle—an herb cutter broken off from the cutting board, covered in blood.

"You could not have possibly killed those four women alone. And someone must have helped you lure that eighteen-year-old court lady out of the palace," Commander Song continued. "Who was it? Who assisted you?"

Nurse Jeongsu clenched her teeth, a muscle working in her jaw. "I did not—" Her voice broke, as did my heart. "I harmed no one."

Commander Song leaned forward, his hands on his knees, as though he were peering down at a little girl. "In a few days, if you continue to not cooperate, I will have the floggers beat you until you can no longer stand, until your bones splinter into pieces." He added, softly, "You will speak then. The rogues brought before me always speak in the end. But it is up to you, how you tell the truth. Will it be by your own free will? Or through torture?"

"What is the point in speaking?" she snapped, at last raising her chin, her eyes as sharp as blades. *This* was my mentor. "I suspect you will not permit me to live long." Fear flickered in her eyes and shook her voice, yet her hands, which were tied behind the chair, gripped into determined fists. "If I shall be remembered for anything, I long to be remembered for this. For *this*," she repeated, her voice strangled.

What was she referring to? I had so many questions, yet Commander Song dismissed her with a sharp wave of his hand. "Get her out of my sight!"

Once the interrogation ended, I slipped into the servants' courtyard and looked for a familiar face, someone trust-worthy, whom I could task with the delivery of my letter to

Commander Song. I initially looked for the police servant, describing him to others as "the young man with glowering brows who dresses like a peasant," but after the strange looks I received while inquiring after him, I instead turned my attention to the damo stepping out of the kitchen. Her name was Sulbi; she was a student I had studied with at the Hyeminseo, and like all damos, she was here because she had failed her tests three times.

"Sulbi-yah," I called out.

She turned, a strand of hair dipping across her ghostly face. "Hyeon-ah," she said, blinking at me, seemingly dazed. "I can't believe I had to lock Nurse Jeongsu in a cell. Nurse *Jeongsu*, of all the people."

A burning ache tightened in my chest. "Do you think she is innocent?"

"I do," she whispered. "We know her. She wouldn't do such a thing."

"That is my precise thought—"

"I am worried for her, though, Hyeon-ah. The commander has a personal grudge against Nurse Jeongsu."

My stomach sunk. "What do you mean?"

"Many years ago, Nurse Jeongsu failed to save his wife and son during labor. He's never forgiven her for that. He has especially not forgiven her for attempting to deliver an infant into the world with so little experience."

"But we all begin with little experience," I said.

Sulbi nibbled on her lower lip, then shook her head. "She lied to the commander that she was more skilled than she was. She wanted to prove herself to her peers."

"But this was *murder*," I breathed. "Surely the commander wouldn't let personal feelings get in the way? He couldn't possibly want the real killer on the loose."

"Or perhaps he does."

My brows knotted. "Why would he want that?"

Sulbi wiped her damp forehead, then glanced around. "Don't tell anyone I told you this. Will you swear it? I trust you; I've always wanted to be your friend, knowing how . . . how perfect you are in all things," she whispered, leaving me shifting awkwardly on my feet. "You never make mistakes."

That was my life's goal, to never err. My life had been a mistake—born a girl, and on the wrong side of wedlock. I had no room to make more errors.

"An anonymous handbill was put up all over the capital," she said. My brows lifted, the memory of the crowd and the police flickering awake. "It claims the Crown Prince killed the women at the Hyeminseo."

I held in a gasp, barely keeping my face composed.

"This cannot be true, of course," she said in a matter-of-fact voice. "Most outside the palace do not even know what the prince looks like. So how could he be recognized?"

But Court Lady Ahnbi, a palace woman, died in the Hyeminseo, I thought. Her death, surely, would leave a trail of blood leading into the palace somehow.

"Someone is trying to stir up a conspiracy, I'm sure." Sulbi nodded, sounding convinced by her own words. "That is how it always is in the capital. Someone is always trying to bring someone else down. Maybe it's a rival from the Old Doctrine faction. Besides, the prince is not permitted to leave the palace alone. It is forbidden, isn't it?"

"It is," I whispered, lowering my gaze to hide what I knew: The prince had indeed been missing from the palace on the night of the massacre.

I pressed my fingers into my eyes and let out a quiet breath, trying to ease the growing sense of foreboding. The Hyeminseo massacre now carried with it the sickly scent of a terrible royal scandal, one that would easily sweep Nurse Jeongsu to her death. I shook myself out of the unease and handed my letter to Sulbi. "Please, do me a favor and deliver this to Commander Song—"

"Baek-hyeon." An icy, terribly familiar voice slid up behind me. "Deliver what?"

Sulbi's eyes widened with panic—the same panic I felt—and when she bowed low and rushed off, I wished I could disappear with her, too. I did not need to look to know whose shadow it was stretching over me. My father, the person whom I was forbidden from actually calling "father." In our kingdom, illegitimates belonged to the mother, not the man who had sired them.

"Lord Shin," I whispered, slowly turning.

My father was garbed in a silk robe of deep crimson, his head crowned in a tiered gauze hat. It oughtn't to have surprised me, seeing him here; he served in the Ministry of Justice—it was his duty to ensure that justice was properly administered.

Bowing low, I remained frozen.

"I saw you sneaking off, and so I followed you." His voice drifted down to me, cool and edged with a hint of curiosity. "What are you doing here, so far from the crowd?"

"I . . ." My mind scrambled for the right answer. "I was searching for a servant to deliver a letter to Commander Song. I wish to assist Nurse Jeongsu," I said, hoping to present myself as a loyal student. "She is innocent, my lord. I know it. If the commander truly knew her character, he would not—"

Father's outstretched hand appeared in my periphery. "Give it to me," he said quietly. When I did, his hand and the letter disappeared, and I listened to my heart pounding in my chest.

The morning chill crept into my bones as he perused my writing, and I dared not move. I was too afraid to even blink. Father frightened me more than a tiger. A tiger might eat me, but Father could crush my very soul.

And it had been five years since I'd last spoken with him.

I had spent those years catching glimpses of him around the capital; he, always on horseback or carried around on a sedan chair as his servants called out for us to make way for Lord Shin. Peasants would bow to him on the streets, including myself, mud flicking onto me in his passing. And it was fathers like him that ruled this kingdom. Men like him determined who was worthy and who was not.

At last, Father returned the letter to me. I waited, holding my breath. Did he approve of my words?

"This is not evidence." His words pierced me. "The commander will only be persuaded by evidence, and what you have written is an abundance of emotions, crude and unintelligent."

Gripping the letter tight, I wanted to rip it apart, to make it disappear from Father's sight.

"There are far more important things for you to focus on," he said. "I hear you've become a palace nurse."

Beating down the hurt from my voice, I managed to say, "I have, my lord."

"I will play your father this one moment, then, and give you a word of advice." A breeze stirred his robe, red silk billowing around his leather boots. "Stop worrying about Nurse Jeongsu's fate. She is not your mother. She is not your sister. You are not responsible for her life."

I kept my stare pinned to the ground, my heart bruised and my stomach knotting at his words.

"You are a vulgar commoner, but have become a palace nurse. It is a golden opportunity for you, a one in a thousand chance. Do not let yourself be distracted. Do not meddle in police affairs. If you do, it will endanger your future."

"Yeh," I whispered.

Father turned to leave, and then paused. He gathered his hands behind his back, and I could sense his frowning gaze peering down at me. "Promise me you'll keep your head low. Let the commander do his job, and know that there is nothing you—a mere girl—can do to assist him."

I remained bowing until Father left. As soon as he was out of sight, I coolly tore the letter up and threw the shreds on the ground.

I had ached to be faultless before Father, a yearning that had driven me to look at young nobles as my competitors. It was why I had studied all the required books. In fact, if I'd been born a boy, I could have passed the civil service exam with ease. *The Great Learning, Doctrine of the Mean, The Analects,* and *Mencius.* I still tried to memorize those texts whenever I had spare time, to fill my mind with the knowledge that filled theirs, to be as like them as I possibly could.

To be a girl worthy of Father's attention.

But today, I'd shown him only how inadequate I still was. *This is not evidence,* he'd said.

Then what was?

I didn't intend to find the killer; all I wanted was enough proof to steer Commander Song's wrath away from my mentor. And I would show Father that I was capable. I could not wait for love and acknowledgment to come embrace me. I had to go find it myself, to earn it through hard work.

I rested my hand on the side of the gate, looking around as I wondered where the prison block was, the shadowy place into which Nurse Jeongsu had been dragged. She knew something, that was for certain. But whatever the truth was, she was willing to die to keep it hidden. Hidden, perhaps, even from me.

3

The next day, I visited the Hyeminseo on my way to the palace.

Everyone seemed on edge. The scent of death was too fresh in the early morning air, the blood-stains still present on the snow. A shaman had been discreetly summoned to perform a ritual to exorcise any lingering evil spirits.

In the midst of the chaos, I managed to take Nurse Oksun aside. We'd studied together since we were eleven, and I knew her to have a good head on her shoulders, always calm, no matter how dire the circumstance.

"When you have time"—I slipped a piece of paper from my travel sack and gave it to her—"could you ask around to see where Nurse Jeongsu went last night at around midnight? I've written down all the details."

"The streets are usually empty during curfew," Oksun said, glancing down at my note. "I doubt anyone would have an answer."

I hesitated, but I knew Oksun admired Nurse Jeongsu as much as I did. "Please, try at least. *Something* is better than no information at all."

"Hyeon-ah . . ." She flicked a glance up at me. "Are you leading an investigation?"

"No, of course not," I said. "I'm simply collecting a few pieces of evidence. I only need to find enough to prove Nurse Jeongsu's innocence. Only that, and then I will be done."

She watched me with doubt-filled eyes, like she didn't believe me. "I know you, Hyeon-ah. I know you too well. You get obsessed with tasks." She hesitated, then murmured, "But you are a friend, so I'll ask everyone I know. Discreetly."

"Thank you," I whispered.

The market stalls were just opening by the time I left the Hyeminseo. Rolls of precious Chinese silk laid out to tempt the wealthy. Brassware gleaming in the wintry morning light. Stacks of straw hats and baskets shivering in the mountain breeze. A new day had begun, and my shoulders felt heavy with the new danger it came with.

When I finally arrived before Changdeok Palace, I presented my wooden identification tag and entered through Tonghwa Gate. I half expected guards to drag me away, to tie me to an interrogation chair where I'd have to confess the prince's whereabouts on the night of the massacre. But they paid me no more heed than usual.

Father's warning steadied me. *Keep your head low. Let the commander do his job.*

Clutching the travel sack against my chest, I strode into the Royal Apothecary, a large courtyard with several stately pavilions. Black roofs undulated like the mountain ridge and eaves flared with majestic colors. Walls and beams were painted red, with bursts of jade green latticed windows. The building I was heading toward, in contrast, was lackluster and tucked at the far back. I stepped into a vast quarter where three other nurses were quickly changing into their uniforms. They were young women with sharp black eyes and subtly rouged lips. They didn't like me, for they thought themselves above me.

Keeping my eyes lowered, I bowed and offered them a greeting before moving to a corner, then proceeded to change into my own uniform. I pretended to mind my own business, but as they whispered, I listened closely.

"Did you hear?" One nurse dipped her finger into a small pot of honey and dabbed it on her hair, to control loose strands and add a bit of gleam. "About the massacre in the Hyeminseo?"

The second nurse shrugged into her apron. "Nurse Inyeong was the first to stumble upon the scene, apparently."

"I heard she was a damo for years." The third nurse smoothed out her blue skirt, the silk whispering under her touch. "She became a palace nurse only last year or so, and she is twenty-five years of age! Ancient, if you ask me."

They walked off, still gossiping among themselves. After waiting a moment, I stepped outside and made my way to the medical office, my mind circling around what I'd overheard.

I didn't know Nurse Inyeong well, but I felt sorry for her. No one seemed to like her. Palace nurses often shunned

45

those who had worked as a damo first, a demeaning position for a nurse to be in. Damos were extensions of the police, mostly dealing with dead female bodies and violent female criminals, since male officers were forbidden by law from touching women unrelated to them. It took only three failed tests for a nurse to become a damo; anyone could easily become one. I, too, could have become one had Nurse Jeongsu not taken the time to tutor me.

Not everyone had a Nurse Jeongsu in their life.

At last I arrived before the office, a grand and stately pavilion. A male voice echoed from within, likely Physician Nanshin delegating the day's tasks to the nurses.

I hurried up the stone steps and strode inside. All the palace medical personnel were clustered in the main hall, hands gathered in their sleeves, heads bowed. I quickly joined the row and breathed in the earthy scent of dried herbs, stored in the drawers of large medical cabinets and suspended from the ceiling in white pouches. Normally the scent put me at ease. I'd spent seven years breathing in this aromatic smell while studying, assisting with patients, and giggling and gossiping with my peers.

Today, however, I couldn't help but wonder what horrors hid beneath the familiar.

"You all must have heard about the incident that occurred the night before last," came Physician Nanshin's voice, startling me to attention. "And you may have heard of a dangerous rumor being tossed around. But I advise you to keep your silence. Anyone who indulges in this rumor will have to answer for it with their life."

I bit my lower lip. He was speaking of the anonymous handbills. The accusation about the Crown Prince. I shook my head; I didn't want to think of it anymore.

"Now!" His voice lifted, like the crisp turn onto a fresh new page. "Today will be a busy day."

He proceeded to delegate the duties. Nurses were divided by the three specialties—pulse reading, medicine, and acupuncture. Pulse readers like myself were in charge of assessing and determining the level of balance in the mind and body; this was done by examining the symptoms, by making inquiries, and by checking the pulse in accordance with the Royal Medical Bureau manual. The medicine maker was responsible for reporting the symptoms to the physician, discussing possible diagnoses with him, and, once a treatment was decided upon, spending hours preparing the concoction with great care before administering it. As for the acupuncturists, they were the most respected among us, for they were highly skilled nurses who knew how to alleviate illness and pains using the body's pressure points. They understood the intricate constellation of ki flowing through the body, and knew exactly where and how deep to apply the needles.

"There is one last task," Physician Nanshin said, once everything else was delegated. He cleared his throat, as though in distaste. "I need one pulse reading nurse and one acupuncture nurse to inspect the health of Madam Mun and her infant."

I glanced to my side at the rest of the nurses. No one volunteered. No one liked Madam Mun, the eighteen-year-old who had gone from being a mousy kitchen maid to the haughty concubine of the king. But I knew her better than anyone here, and she had always been arrogant, even as a child.

At one time, long ago when we were both eleven, she had been my friend . . . of a sort. She was the daughter of one of Mother's friends. When I first met her, she had introduced herself as Mun Seohyun, but had ordered that I call her *Mun-ssi*, Madam Mun. It had been her way of flaunting her surname—for a lowborn to have a surname was indeed a great and rare honor, no matter how it had been obtained or salvaged. And so I had acquiesced to calling her Mun-ssi—secretly jealous that I was not granted use of a family name—as she ordered me around in all our excursions and mischief-making. A tyrannical friend she had been, but a friend nonetheless.

"I will go," a female voice abruptly offered. It was Nurse Inyeong.

"Good." Physician Nanshin cleared his throat again. "We still need a pulse reader."

I had intended to help Jieun brew medicine today. I'd often help her with the work when there was no patient to tend to. But at the sight of Nurse Inyeong, the urge to speak with her grew strong.

"I will go, too," I said, my voice clear and determined, even as the other nurses stared at me, their lips turned down with distaste. Inyeong, too, looked my way with a stunned glance. I kept my voice steady, and said, "I will help, uiwon-nim."

———————

Under Confucian law, men and women could not touch each other if they were not kin, and this custom was enforced and followed by highborns. We, the uinyeos, had therefore been formed after a series of unfortunate—and preventable—deaths among female royals who had refused to be touched by male physicians. In the eyes of most, we were merely assistants to the royal physicians, forbidden from making any decisions of our own.

A young physician therefore led the way, to supervise us. He walked ahead, while Nurse Inyeong and I followed behind. We passed by patrolling guards in red robes and eunuchs scurrying about carrying messages. But once we were alone on the snowy path between courtyards, the physician glanced over his shoulder at us. His face was young despite the facial hair around his mouth.

"What did Physician Nanshin mean?" he asked, his question puffing before him in a white cloud. "What rumor?"

I said nothing, remembering the physician's warning toward silence.

But to my shock, Nurse Inyeong answered. "Anonymous handbills were found around the capital. They claimed that the Crown Prince is responsible for the Hyeminseo killings. I don't believe any of the rumors, of course."

The physician looked a shade paler. "Of course, of

course." He then faced forward and quickened his pace, as though to escape the answer to his own question, leaving me momentarily alone with Nurse Inyeong. I glanced at her powdered face, and I wondered if she knew what other nurses were saying about her.

"You stare," she said, as I quickly looked away. "Is there something you wish to say?"

I hesitated a moment. "Some say . . . you were a damo for a very long time."

Her face remained still, stoic. "You mean the other palace nurses." A mirthless smile tugged at her lips. "You ought to think twice before talking to me. If you wish to fit in well with the other nae-uinyeos, you had better not be seen associating with me again."

Hostility was not new to me. I'd grown up with it, shunned by my father and his legitimate children. At a young age I'd discovered ways to cope with disfavor.

"Uinyeo-nim," I said politely, for she was older than me, "I came into the palace to prove my worth, not to make friends."

She looked at me again, a long, considerate gaze, like she had missed something before and noticed it now. "I was simply a witness to a crime, as you know, so it has drawn unwanted attention my way. Those palace nurses are always so eager to mention my history, to find any way to put me in my place."

She fell silent when a guard passed by, and once we were alone again, she added, "This is what happens when young uinyeos are promoted to palace nurses. They think they are better than everyone else, especially those like myself. A lowly damo who became a palace nurse later in life."

A beat passed, and then I asked, "How long were you a damo, uinyeo-nim?"

"Nine years."

Stunned, I examined her again. Nine years meant she had failed every attempt, every month, to reclaim her position as a nurse. So how had she suddenly managed to become a palace nurse after nine years of failure?

As though reading my mind, she said, "I chose to fail those exams."

Another jolt of surprise. "You *chose*?"

"I wanted to continue serving in the police bureau out in Gwangju. The commander there—a mentor to me, as Nurse Jeongsu is to you—was investigating a murder case, and I was swept up in it. For years we searched, and I couldn't stop thinking about the injustice, the cruelty involved. An *entire* family was murdered in one night, and only a little girl survived. She'd hidden in a chest and had been forced to listen to her mother being butchered alive."

The hair on my skin rose. "Was the killer ever caught?"

"Yes." Her voice rasped, her jaw clenching. "But not until long after we discovered that one of the witnesses had falsely testified. The commander tortured the witness to death. And once the investigation was over, I wanted a fresh start, to forget."

"Tortured to death . . ." I whispered. This mentor she spoke of was nothing like Nurse Jeongsu.

"I decided that it was time to move on when another tragedy struck my life. My mother died, and her dream had always been that I become a palace nurse. So I passed every monthly test until I finally managed to receive the highest collective mark by the end of the year. I wanted to enter the palace, for her." A shake of her head, and she mumbled, "I also needed the money, and palace nurses are paid well."

I remembered what she'd told me a day ago. "Your father's gambling . . ."

"My hair will turn gray early because of him. But how can I fault him? He has gone through a lot in life." Real emotion strained her voice, a ghost of a shadow crossing her face. "It seems there is always someone in the family determined to drive us mad."

Like my father, I thought bitterly. *And mother.*

Before I could respond, the young physician cleared his throat. He was no longer so far away, and I realized that we'd arrived at Madam Mun's residence. We both sealed our lips as we walked into the pavilion.

———

A smug look brightened Madam Mun's face upon our entrance. Her stare followed me, as though to ask, *Do you still envy me, Hyeon-ah?*

I lowered my head, but I couldn't stop staring at her from beneath my lashes. *I do.*

Her skin glowed like a drop of dew, her lips blossomed like a pink rose, and her eyes were as bright as sunset. She wasn't simply one of the king's many concubines; she was one of His Majesty's four highest-ranked royal consorts, a concubine with the privileges of a wife.

"Madam." The young physician stumbled forward. "We have come to ensure your well-being."

She lifted a finger. "Proceed."

Pushing down all my emotions, I wore a polite face as I knelt before Madam Mun and inspected her, asked her questions, and checked her pulse.

"She needs her energy level restored," I concluded to the young physician, after sharing my findings with him. He nodded in agreement.

Nurse Inyeong proceeded to apply her acupuncture needles to Madam Mun. Looking for a distraction, I turned my attention to the infant, whom the wet nurse transferred into my arms.

"How old is the agisshi now?" I asked, using the honorific for young princess.

The wet nurse scratched the side of her nose. "Two weeks old."

"How many times has the agisshi drunk from the breast today?"

"One time."

"Did she have any bowel movements?"

"Once."

"Good." I would have to jot this information down later—every few hours other nurses would have to come again to record the health progress of both the mother and child. But for now, I gazed back down at the infant and could feel the weight of Madam Mun's disappointment in my arms. She had wanted a son so badly. From what I'd heard, she had prayed and made offerings to Samshin Halmoni, the Seven Stars spirits, the mountain spirits, Buddha, and to certain rocks and trees considered to be sacred. She had even eaten all the right foods. Still, the heavens had given her a girl.

I let out a slow breath to ease the ache in my chest. *I hope your mother will love you one day,* I wanted to whisper to the child. *More than my own ever did.*

After I had been born, Mother would set me on the floor to play with dirt. But when my brother was born, she'd always carry him around. When I had grown older, she'd left me to be raised by a servant. But when my brother had grown older, she had surrounded him with tutors and rare honey-fried biscuits.

The unfairness of it all had festered in me, and I could feel it rearing its head even now. An anger that would burst into little fires. I'd blamed her for being born a bastard. Mother's cherished jade ring, I'd hidden under a large cabinet. My brother's study notes, I'd thrown out into the pouring rain. And my half sister's valuables, gifts Father would pamper her with, I'd stolen and thrown into a stream. I'd broken and destroyed, trying to ease the hurt.

Anger like this never truly went away, but Nurse Jeongsu had kept it from devouring me.

"The shape of who you are is an image of heaven and earth," I whispered to the baby, Sun Simiao's words quoted in a book Nurse Jeongsu had gifted me with, an encyclopedia I still perused every year. It was called

Dongui Bogam, by the legendary physician Heo Jun. "Your round head resembles the heavens, and your flat foot resembles earth; you have four limbs as the universe has four seasons, you have two eyes as the universe has the sun and the moon." I dabbed her drool away. "Always remember who you truly are, agisshi—"

"Did you hear?" Madam Mun said, and I felt her gaze on me, as sharp as a dagger held to my throat. "There is an anonymous handbill circulating the capital, and a dangerous rumor. Have you heard it? Do you think it is true, Nurse Hyeon?"

I blinked at her, still holding the infant. "Yeh?"

"From what I was told, you and another nurse were serving the Crown Prince that night. Was he indeed in his chamber the whole time?"

From the corner of my eye, I watched as Nurse Inyeong and the young physician exchanged nervous glances. To gossip about a royal family member with the king's concubine was more than inappropriate; it could result in rolling heads.

"Well?" she asked.

An icy sheen of sweat formed on my brow. "The Crown Prince was in his chamber, madam. He was feeling ill all day, and so we were called to attend to him. There was concern for his well-being overnight."

"Indeed? There are usually other nurses for such duties. You are not an overnight nurse, are you?"

My fingertips grew cold. "I am not, madam."

"Then why were *you* summoned?"

I paused, wondering if I should spin up a lie. Instead, I answered with the truth. "I'm not sure."

With a wave of her hand, Madam Mun snapped, "Everyone leave except for Nurse Hyeon."

Uneasiness coiled in my stomach as I handed the baby off to the wet nurse and waited. Once we were alone, the madam propped an elbow on her knee, a look of determination hardening on her face. "Are you sure you do not know?"

"I am," I said, with more conviction. "I do not know, madam."

A long pause. "I believe you. But I have spies in every corner of this palace. If you are lying to me, I will find out and inform His Majesty." The weight of her stare prickled against the top of my lowered head. "You do know I could tell the king anything about you, and he would believe me."

A drop of sweat slithered down my back. Madam Mun was the same age as I was; I should have no need to fear her. Yet I felt a twinge of apprehension—*she* might not frighten me, but the king certainly did.

"But," she added lightly, "I will make sure to let nothing happen to you, if you become my eyes and ears. If you hear anything about what happened at the Hyeminseo, you are to tell me." Her voice lowered. "Especially if it has anything to do with the Crown Prince."

My heart froze. "I will try, madam."

"No, not *try*," she corrected. "You *will* do so."

"Yeh." I gritted my teeth as I bowed my head. "I will."

It was a lie, of course. Lies are the only defenses the lowly have against the powerful.

"Well." She sat impeccably straight and raised her chin, a smile on her lips. "Then you are dismissed."

I rose to leave, eager to escape her presence, then paused. If Madam Mun had spies around the palace, she might have an answer to one of the many questions that had been bothering me.

"A court lady died outside the palace walls," I said, slowly. "Do you know of anyone who might have wished her ill?"

Madam Mun's smile dropped. "You do not speak unless you are spoken to," she hissed.

"Madam," I tried again. "I am a mere servant, but we were once friends. If you have any fond memories of our childhood at all, couldn't you please answer me this?"

At her prolonged silence, I peered up from under my lashes. A shadow of dread had paled her countenance; she looked almost perturbed. But the expression vanished, replaced by a gleam of ill-disguised thrill.

"One of my servants saw Court Lady Ahnbi and Royal Physician Khun—the one who works in the medicinal garden—arguing the day before her death," she said. "Apparently at one point he held her shoulders." She tsked. "How indecent. Perhaps he is the monster you hunt." Madam Mun then dismissed me with a wave of her hand.

As I stepped out of her residence, my thoughts drifted, lingering on the web of names being woven in my mind.

Court Lady Ahnbi, Physician Khun, Madam Mun . . . and the Crown Prince.

The more I pondered, the more troubled I became. I couldn't help but fear that some hidden truth would soon be unveiled and sweep through the kingdom. A violent storm that would leave nothing untouched.

4

I t will be a simple task, and then it will all be over," I whispered to myself as I hurried through the capital, welcoming the snowflakes melting against my heated cheeks.

I'd spent an hour inquiring after Physician Khun's whereabouts, an hour scorched by several disapproving looks and questions as to why I wanted to visit the home of an unmarried man.

Regardless, I'd been too stubborn to stop. I was convinced that Physician Khun knew the truth behind the murders, one that would unravel the mystery and free Nurse Jeongsu from the commander's wrath. After all, the woman Physician Khun had argued with in the garden had turned up dead. He could be, for all I knew, Court Lady Ahnbi's sweetheart. They were similar in age; he was nineteen, and she was eighteen.

I stopped in my tracks. The possibility that Physician Khun might have killed her suddenly struck me hard. Men often chose to kill their victims with knives, a pattern I'd noticed while tending to the wounded at the Hyeminseo. Moreover, cases of women murdered by their husbands or lovers were not few and far between.

I could see it clearly: Physician Khun slipping a note into Court Lady Ahnbi's hand, a note luring her out of the palace, threatening to never see her again if she did not. And out in the shadows, he had stabbed her in the chest, only for her to escape into the Hyeminseo. He could have chased her in and then stabbed her in the throat, finishing her off. Physician Khun would have then realized that he had witnesses, a study group of two student nurses and their teacher. And so he had killed them all as well.

A moment later, though, my head cleared and my pounding heart slackened. Physician Khun couldn't be the killer. He was a healer, a protector of life. Surely he was not capable of murder.

A group of soldiers charged by, and I nearly dropped the note detailing Physician Khun's address, given to me by another physician. "Find him!" the leader bellowed. "He mustn't get away!"

I stared after them for a while, then continued on my way, down the crowded road that led up to a massive fortress gate. The guard waved me through after I presented my identification tag, and I stepped out of the capital, onto the path where I'd sometimes encounter Physician Khun as we both walked home from the palace.

Quiet and reserved, he reminded me of the plants that grew in his medicinal garden. So lost in his thoughts, he wouldn't notice the curious glances I cast his way. His dark eyes would always remain fixed ahead. His long legs would hurry past me until he was striding over the Cheonggye Stream bridge, disappearing into the distance. I would usually continue down the road that would take me to my mother's home, but today I instead crossed the bridge.

I followed the directions on the note, which I'd only needed to study once. Memorization came easily to me; I could memorize an entire page without much more than a glance. After making my way around the village, I came to the edge of a forest. The directions led me down the woodland path of bare trees and snow-coated rocks. It was difficult to walk—the path was overgrown with branches that snagged my ankles as I passed.

Eventually the forest opened onto a clearing. In the center stood a lone hut with a straw roof and crumbling clay walls, sliding screened doors, and a brushwood gate encircling it.

I paused in my tracks.

Physician Khun's home was so secluded—I had imagined that his hut would be situated within the hamlet, that we would speak outside while nodding to passing villagers and curious onlookers. I didn't trust him—or any man—enough to be alone with him in such an isolated place. I had turned to leave when a twig snapped somewhere nearby.

A shadow moved beyond the thicket.

The hair on the back of my neck rose, and I fell very still, counting my shallow breaths as I waited.

A few moments later, a man appeared; he was wearing

a black gentleman's hat and a long dull coat. A poor scholar. The man remained standing in the shadows, and I could tell he was watching Physician Khun's hut. He stood there for so long that a cloud moved in the sky, and I watched a shaft of light split through the branches and onto him.

My eyes widened as they rested upon a familiar face, handsome without all the mud smears from last time. A striking pair of dark eyes. An aquiline nose and a chiseled jaw. Hollowed cheeks that spoke of hunger, though nothing that a few hearty meals couldn't fix. It was the police servant, the quiet and stern young man who'd helped me escape from the crime scene.

But what was he doing here, now dressed as a scholar?

He did not move a limb as specks of snow drifted onto his face, a stillness I couldn't imitate. A branch was digging into the back of my thigh. I glanced around, pushed it aside, then looked ahead again.

He was gone.

I floundered a moment, confused. Then at the sound of sliding doors clacking shut, I hurried forward. I snuck around the side of the hut until I found the back door and slid it ever so slightly open. Peering in, I saw an empty room. I continued following the wall, then carefully cracked open the rickety window that looked into another room. Empty as well. Where had the police servant gone? I turned to inspect the other rooms, only to slam into something solid.

"You again," came a deep, bemused voice.

I stared up into lucid brown eyes. Snowflakes clung to his dark lashes. My lips parted, but I wasn't sure what I meant to say, my words stolen by the intensity of his stare. I blinked quickly, then I glanced down to see that he'd drawn a dagger. He sheathed it now—clearly he didn't see me as a threat. I wasn't sure whether to be offended by this.

"Why are you following me?" he asked.

"I was here first. Why were *you* inside Physician Khun's home?"

"Because he was not in."

It took a moment to decipher his words. He must have come to snoop through the physician's belongings—but to search for what? "So the police sent you here, I suppose."

"No."

"Then why . . . ?"

"I thought I said I never wanted to see you again."

"If I remember correctly," I said in an overly polite tone, "your precise words were *I had better not see you lurking around a crime scene again*. But *is* this a crime scene?"

The young man stared at me as though I were a strange creature, as though no one had spoken to him like this before.

I shrugged at his continued silence. "I simply came to speak with the physician. That is all."

His bewildered expression did not ease. "Why?"

"I have a very interesting explanation, and if you wish to know it . . ." I looked at the empty hut, wondering where Physician Khun had gone. "First answer my questions. Why are you disguised as a scholar?"

"To blend in with others."

"And why are you here if the police didn't send you?"

He paused, and quietly asked, "Are you interrogating me?"

"No. We are having a conversation—"

"I unfortunately don't have time for this," he said, turning from me.

Before I could stop him, he disappeared into Physician Khun's hut—the home of a man who might return at any moment.

Just leave, Hyeon-ah, a voice in my head warned. I didn't want to get involved, but there was something about the police servant that piqued my interest. My gut told me he had information, and I wanted it, too.

I stepped into the hut and found him hastening from corner to corner, opening drawers and chests and checking under folded blankets and between the pages of books. My gaze lingered on one book he'd flipped through and set back down—a military book.

"This isn't allowed," I said. "You can't just barge into someone's home and rifle through their things."

He continued on as though he hadn't heard me. Each item he inspected, he returned to its exact position: the porcelain vase, the document box, the candlestick holder. He picked up a small jar with a lid, opened it, and glanced inside. A speck of wariness flit through me at the sight of a white powdery substance. But then he closed the lid, set down the jar, and moved on, and I realized he still hadn't answered me.

"*Ya!*" I called out rudely. My patience was running thin. "If you don't want me to report you, then answer me. Why are you here if the police didn't send you?"

Letting out a sigh, he flipped through another book. "I have good reasons to involve myself in this investigation. Trust me."

"Why should I trust you? I don't even know you."

"You trust me enough to be alone in the woods with me. And it seems you are here for the same reason as I: Physician Khun is suspicious." He set the book aside and examined the next item, a little box.

"So you *do* know something," I whispered to myself. Then to him, I said, "I heard rumors about Physician Khun. He was last seen arguing with Court Lady Ahnbi." Secretly I hoped that if I offered him intelligence, he might return the favor. "He was holding her shoulders, apparently, and that detail made me wonder if they were sweethearts. If they were, then surely Physician Khun would know something about what had happened to her. That is why I am here."

A muscle worked in his jaw. "It took me the whole of yesterday to find what you learned in a moment's time. Then another half to track down Khun's residence." He glanced at me with a strange gleam in his eyes. "I suppose, since you work in the palace, you must know things that the police will never find out."

"It is true," I said.

"And would you tell the police?"

"Only so much as to lift suspicion from my mentor. I wouldn't tell the police everything, though." I walked over to the door and looked out for Physician Khun's return. "There is a saying among us who work there: *Palace secrets must never get out, or else inevitably there will be blood.*"

I waited for his response, but none came. The air fell so still I felt alone. When I looked over my shoulder, I saw the police servant reaching for the top of the bookcase. He was tall enough that he didn't need to rise onto his toes. Then withdrawing his reach, he walked off toward a window and lifted a small item to the light.

"Found it," he whispered.

I waited, my skin pebbling against a tingle of anticipation. Perhaps he had found evidence that would resolve the Hyeminseo massacre. My muscles tightened as he walked over to me. He stood close—very close—as he held out his hand, revealing a thick silver ring.

"A single garakji?" I said. Usually these rings came in pairs, the double rings worn by married women to symbolize the harmony between husband and wife. Traditionally wives were to wear them up until their own death. "Why were you searching for it?"

"Court Lady Ahnbi wrote to her family and mentioned Physician Khun several times. He was the only man mentioned in her letters," he explained. "Then during her autopsy, a damo servant found a single garakji ring hanging from her necklace. A ring with a plum blossom engraving."

He raised the ring between us, allowing us both to inspect it closer. To my surprise, etched into the silver was a delicate plum blossom.

"A married woman wears a double ring throughout

her lifetime," I said. "But in death, one is buried with her and the other is returned to her spouse. Does this mean Ahnbi and Khun were secretly married?" I glanced up and found my face alarmingly close to his. At once I took a step back.

His gaze followed me as he said, "Precisely."

Clearing my throat loudly, I forced my attention back to the ring. Ahnbi was a palace woman—to be married at all was considered adultery against the king. "I don't understand. Why weren't both rings in her possession? Why was her body found with only *one* garakji?"

"That is what I wish to know as well." He turned to glance out the door. Snow had stopped falling. "He might return at any moment now."

"Do you know where he went?" I asked.

"I sent him a note saying I was Ahnbi's brother, asking him to meet me at the inn. That way I'd be able to search his home without . . ." He glanced at me, something like a wry smile tugging at his lips. "Interruption. He's probably realized the note was a ruse by now. Come. We should leave."

———

As I followed the police servant, stepping out of the forest and entering a field of reeds that reached over our heads, my mind scrambled to make sense of the garakji. Physician Khun had the second ring. Had he taken it before or after Court Lady Ahnbi's death? And did the truth behind these two rings somehow connect to the massacre?

"You asked earlier what I was doing here," the police servant said, pulling me from my thoughts. The brittle grass and untouched snow crunched loudly under our feet. "I spent a year working in Pyongan Province, and a similar triple murder occurred there . . . one involving a loved one. When the Hyeminseo massacre occurred, it led me to wonder if the two incidents were related."

"How were they similar?" I asked, then had to add, "Don't you think that is too much of an assumption? There are mass killings that occur all the time, carried out by corrupt magistrates or nobles or soldiers."

His expression turned to stone, just for a moment. "I have my reasons."

I wiped a loose strand of hair away from my brow as I fell a step behind, my stare unwavering from the police servant's back. His shoulders were broad, and he stood as high as a mountain peak.

"What is your name, anyway?" I asked.

His gaze remained fixed ahead, never once turning to look at me. "Seo Eojin."

I waited for him to ask for mine. He did not. "My name is Baek-hyeon. But I prefer being called Hyeon." His strides were so long, I had to half run to keep from falling farther behind. "What will you do with the ring now?"

"Hold on to it."

A current of annoyance rippled through me. Commander Song needed enough evidence to wield justice properly *now*. "You should tell the commander," I said.

"Not yet."

"Why not yet?"

"To allow Khun the opportunity to give his account. Without torture."

"Eojin," I said, unable to hide my incredulity, "you are only a *servant*. You can't decide this on your own."

He halted so suddenly my hands reflexively landed on his back—a broad and strong back, I couldn't help but note—to keep from crashing into him. I wrenched my hands away and retreated as he turned, his eyes falling on mine. "A servant?" he repeated.

"Yes. You are a police servant," I said. "And it is not your place to do as you wish. You have found evidence, so now you must submit it to the commander—"

Shaking his head, he slipped the ring into a pouch tied to his sash belt, and the sight of evidence disappearing left my face burning. Any day now the police commander could choose to torture Nurse Jeongsu in an attempt to make her confess. Images filled my mind in a haze of red. Of flesh split open. Bones shattered. Blood soaking her clothing and dripping onto the dirt. And I would have to live with the guilt of knowing that, perhaps, I could have prevented such brutality if only I'd presented the commander with the ring.

My hands moved of their own accord, darting to the pouch. My fingers grazed the fabric, but before they could clamp on to the string, Eojin firmly caught both my wrists and held me still. He looked as startled as I felt.

"What are you doing?" he asked.

"If you will not submit this evidence," I said, my voice strained, "I will."

His grip loosened, but the restraint remained, his tanned fingers wrapped around my pale wrists.

"Listen to me." His voice was a low murmur. "I know the commander. Once he thinks he knows the truth, nothing will change his mind. He will not help you save your teacher. There is only one who can."

The red haze slowly cleared from my mind. I had trouble finding my voice, but once I did, I managed to whisper, "Who?"

"The true killer. A full confession will force Commander Song to reconsider. Or," he added, as he gently let go of my wrists, "the fourth nurse. If she is still alive, her testimony will be key."

I stared at him in surprise. "What fourth nurse?"

"A woman came to the police bureau, swearing that her daughter—a student nurse—had left early for the Hyeminseo on the night of the massacre and never returned home."

"What is her name?"

"Minji. Only twelve years old. Perhaps you knew her?"

My heart thudded heavily inside my chest, my mind scrambling. "No . . . I don't think so." I didn't know too many of the lower-level nurses, and at twelve years old, Minji was likely a chohakui, a beginner student. "What do you think happened to her—"

"Wait." Eojin raised a hand, and I fell still, the feathery reeds swaying against my face. His eyes widened as he stared at something beyond my shoulder. "I hear something."

I turned my ear and listened. At first, all I heard was the crisp winter silence.

Then came the faint sound of scrambling footsteps and a wheezing gasp for air.

At once, Eojin waded around the reed field, and I followed him out onto a road. A terrified peasant was running our way, his clothing blood-soaked and his skin blue-tinged. One hand was clutching his wounded side, and the other hand was holding on to a roll of paper. When he was about to run past us, Eojin reached out and caught his shoulder. A cry burst from the man as he immediately crumbled to the ground.

"What happened?" When there was no answer, Eojin crouched before the trembling man and gently tried again. "Who did this to you?"

"I—I—" The man pressed his lips together, trying to form a word, yet failing with each attempt. At length, he stammered, "I—I don't know w-what I did wrong."

"Tell me," Eojin said. "I can help you."

I stepped past Eojin, trying to get a better look at the wound. "I am an uinyeo," I said reassuringly. "Let me see if I can stop the bleeding."

The man stared up at me, and tears welled in his eyes, as though he was relieved at the sight of me. "I was paid to paste these up around the capital today, as d-d-discreetly as possible. I can't even read it." His voice broke into stutters, but as I knelt before him, he composed himself enough to speak on. "I needed to feed my children so I agreed. I was pasting it up, and then a soldier attacked me and I ran out of the fort."

Eojin took the handbill from the man and unrolled it. As he read, his expression darkened.

"What is it?" I asked as I worked. The man's flesh had been cleanly split, down to the ribs. A wound inflicted by a sharp blade.

"It is the same anonymous handbill from the day before," Eojin said gravely, "accusing the Crown Prince of the murders."

My blood turned cold. The peasant's eyes went wide with shock.

"Who told you to post this?" I asked him.

"I don't know!" His voice was shrill.

"What did the person look like?" Eojin pressed. "Man or woman? Height, any unique traits, any description at all."

The peasant glanced over his shoulder, at the empty road. "N-now I realize why they wanted to kill me. I had no idea—no idea I had committed such a great crime—Oh gods, I don't have time to talk." He shakily struggled to stand. "I need to get away—"

The land trembled beneath our feet. Eojin grabbed both of us and dragged us deep into the reed field. I craned my neck and saw glimpses of horsemen in dark red hats adorned with two plumes, pointed like tiger ears.

"Royal guards," I whispered.

Eojin pulled me down and ducked over me, his chest covering my back and his arms shielding my head. He hissed at the peasant to duck as well. But the man just grew paler, his eyes wider and wider until they stared ahead like two open graves.

"Heavens help me," the man whimpered, backing away despite Eojin's attempts to grab him. "I need to go."

The peasant turned and stumbled away, pushing aside the grass like he was swimming through it, glancing over his shoulders constantly until he disappeared from sight. But I could still hear him, the whipping of grass as he ran. For a precious moment, escape seemed possible for him.

And then came the thundering of hooves.

I pressed against Eojin as the reeds thrashed around us, the air roaring as riders sped past, the smell of horseflesh whipping by. Eventually the feathery plumes above us fell still as the hooves pounded into the distance.

Turning my head ever so slightly, I found my face close to Eojin's, his eyes sharpened under dark brows. We exchanged nervous glances, then I watched as his gaze tilted up.

The whistle of an arrowhead sliced the air.

My entire body jolted at the sound of the arrow striking a solid, fleshy object, followed by a scream. The peasant. Shot down like a wild animal. His scream turned into pleas for mercy as I heard a forceful snarl: "You dare slander the Crown Prince of this kingdom? You defamed the seja-jeoha, a crime punishable by death."

"P-p-please! I did not know—"

There was the sharp ring of metal, and then I heard the wet sound of blood spurting.

My lips fell open to scream in horror. Eojin clamped a

hand over my mouth, his heart racing against my back. He was as afraid as I was.

"Take the corpse and bury it in the hills!" the soldier ordered. "And you, find the traitor's family and arrest them. The king will deal with the rogues as he pleases. The rest of you, continue to tear down the remaining handbills. Not a single one must remain by nightfall."

I could hardly breathe. I had never witnessed a human life taken so callously, so swiftly, with not even a tremor of remorse. It struck me then that investigating the Hyeminseo massacre might very well get me killed.

Run away, then, a warning voice whispered in my mind. *Nurse Jeongsu is not your blood family. Run away. Save yourself.*

I stared into the swaying grass, panic rising within me. I was too young to ruin my life, my future too ripe with possibility. I could turn my eyes away from Nurse Jeongsu's suffering, and no one would blame me. No one at all.

But I must not, I thought, more a plea to myself than a decision. I could never call myself a nurse again, not in good conscience, if I turned my eyes away from such injustice. *I must do something.*

5

We waited among the thicket of reeds until crimson bled across the sky. When we were certain that we were alone, Eojin slowly rose to his feet. My limbs were numb and tingling as I hobbled through the field, following him out. I didn't so much as ask where we were going—I didn't particularly care, as long as it was away from here.

"If you need to talk . . ." Eojin said, glancing my way.

I couldn't form a single word. As we walked in silence, no matter how hard I tried to forget, I couldn't stop hearing the whistling of the arrow, nor the awful thud of the arrowhead slamming into flesh. The sounds ricocheted inside my skull until I thought my sanity would surely slip.

Eojin, however, had quickly recomposed himself. He had the anonymous handbill unfolded before him and was studying it with intense focus.

"I want to go home," I finally said. I didn't want anything to do with the handbill, or Physician Khun, or any of this at the moment. "I'm leaving now."

"Are you certain you wish to leave now?" He glanced down at me. "I'm not sure you want to return home just yet."

I followed his gaze and saw that my fingers were stained in blood, my sleeves were red, and even more blood was smeared on my torso from when I'd tried to stop the man's bleeding. A dizzying wave rushed through me.

"You should clean up before you return home. Here." Eojin took off his long white overcoat and draped it over me. The fabric still held his warmth, offering me a strange sort of comfort. "So you don't draw too much attention."

"Where are we going?" I whispered.

"A place travelers go for a warm meal."

We arrived at an inn outside the fort, its walls bursting with laughter and overflowing with boisterous folk. Men drank on raised platforms or on the cold ground in small groups around tiny tables. Female servants scurried around with trays full of wine and steaming meals. Across the crowded scene, kitchen steam billowed, filling the courtyard with the scent of the sea and herbs plucked from the mountains.

In this moment, I was very glad that we had come to the inn. A place of overwhelming smells and sounds that left no room for the memory of whistling arrows.

"We'll get a room for you to change in, and to talk," Eojin said as he folded up the handbill and slipped it inside his robe. He turned and called out, "Jumo!"

A woman with a scarred mouth stalked over, a tray balanced on her hip. Her eyes darted from Eojin to me, then back again, before her face split into a wide, chipped-tooth grin. "Ah, what a handsome couple you two make. Newly married?"

Eojin cleared his throat, his skin flushing.

It was scandalous to be out this late together as we were, unmarried. It would be unwise to draw the attention of the gossips, so I rushed to say, "Yes. We were wed just today."

The tips of Eojin's ears burned even redder. "We are in need of a room, and a hot meal," he murmured, his usual stoic voice flustered.

"Of course you are, my dears." The woman arched a knowing brow. "Follow me."

We wove around floor tables and over the arms and legs of drunkards, nearly tripping a few times, until at last we arrived before a small room.

"Would you be so kind as to bring me a bowl of water?" I held the overcoat closed, my hands tucked inside the sleeves so as not to reveal my bloody fingers. "To . . . freshen myself."

"Right away, my dear!" The servant slid the hanji-screened door open for us and lit a candle inside, for the day was growing dark. Then she brought in a bowl of water for me. "I shall return shortly with your meals."

Eojin paid her, and as soon as we were alone, he sat down behind a low-legged table, bringing out the anonymous handbill again.

I turned from him and dropped my gaze to the wooden bowl. The faster I cleaned myself, the faster I'd wipe away the memory of murder. My wide sleeves rolled up, I dipped my hands into the water, rubbing and scraping my fingers; blood had worked its way into the grooves of my skin.

Once washed, I faced the wall as I untied my sash belt and slipped my arms free from my stained apron, which I then stashed in a corner. I inspected myself once over. There were still small red smears on my clothes here and there, but this would have to do.

I tucked loose strands of hair behind my ears, smoothed out the wrinkles in my skirt, then joined Eojin on the floor, the rickety wooden table between us.

"You asked before to see the handbill," Eojin said, his voice low. "Do you wish to see it still?"

Do not hide. Do not run away. I nodded. "I do."

He turned the crinkled paper over to me, the sheet splattered and smeared in blood. Chills prickled down my spine as I heard again the whistling arrow, the thudding of death. I closed my eyes a moment until my mind cleared, and when I opened them, I saw before me Hanja characters, ink dripping in vertical lines:

The Crown Prince killed me.
The Crown Prince killed the four women.
The Crown Prince will kill again.

I held my hands together tightly. There was a sinking sensation in me that I might end up dead for having covered up for the prince. My only hope was that this handbill was a lie. Surely people lied about royals all the time.

"The commander is being pressed for a quick conclusion," Eojin said. "I wasn't sure why before, but now I understand: The royal family is likely trying to suppress the rumors about the Crown Prince."

"Why would—" My voice cracked. I tried again. "Why would the royal family do that?"

Eojin stayed still, deep in thought, and then spoke under his breath. "The prince could be the killer, or he might not be and is being framed. Either way, the palace would consider this a family matter, not one to involve the police in."

A simple task, and that will be the end of it, I remembered promising myself that very morning. But the truth was not simple at all.

Eojin leaned closer to the handbill, which I'd set down before me. "It seems the person who wrote this did so in a manner that is unnatural to them. Perhaps in an attempt to mislead investigators."

I glanced at him in bewilderment. "How do you know all this?" *Him*, a police servant.

We both jolted as the door rumbled open; the scarred-lipped servant scurried in with a tray loaded with food and drink. Eojin slipped the blood-stained handbill from the table as she set out our meal—two steaming bowls of jang-gukbab, side dishes, a white bottle, and drinking bowls.

"I brought our newlyweds something special." The servant grinned, tapping the bottle that smelled of soju. "A little treat."

Strong alcohol was banned in our kingdom, but everyone secretly drank. I often caught commoners selling and drinking soju in the back alleys of Cheongjin-dong. I'd never taken a sip before, but today I found myself staring at the bottle, wondering if a sip would erase the memory of blood. Wondering, but I had no intention of doing so. Not with a strange and suspicious man in my company.

"Aigoo! What a lovely sight you both make." The servant winked at us and made one last comment about the "throes of young love," but her words flew over us. Eojin and I stared at the table, waiting. As soon as she left, I immediately asked again, "How do you know the writing was unnatural?"

Eojin set our meals and drinks aside, and flattened out the handbill again. "I examined the letters as we were walking. This handbill is written in ink, but if you look closely, you can see faint charcoal markings, like an underlying tracing of the words. There are also unusual brush lifts, where the writer may have continually stopped to check their handiwork. Everything about the handwriting is uneven, with odd brush pressure and tremor markings. It looks like a forgery, like this person was trying to imitate someone else's writing style."

He then ripped the handbill in half, the hiss of paper startling me, and surprised me further when he handed me a piece. "You work closely with palace people. If you want to save Nurse Jeongsu, inspect their writing. See if there are any that match this handbill. We may not find the truth about the Crown Prince, but finding whom his accuser was trying to imitate might give us some answers."

"You are . . ." I sounded a little breathless. "You are asking me to join you in a private investigation."

"Yes, I am."

I stared at the ripped paper, waiting for a thousand excuses to rise in my chest. I had just watched a peasant be killed by the royal guards. The Crown Prince himself could possibly be involved in the Hyeminseo massacre.

Instead, I felt awake for the first time in years. Worry about my studies, about how I'd raise my status, about Father's approval of me—all of it vanished. Perhaps it was the night air, chilly and crisp with the pure scents of snow and pine. There was a freshness, a vigor to this moment that made his offer irresistible.

"Why me?" I asked, part of me still desperate for a reason to say no.

"Tell me something," he said quietly, holding my gaze. Candlelight flickered in the dark of his eyes. "When you said that the lack of defense wounds on Court Lady Ahnbi was very telling . . . what did you mean?"

I hesitated, then said, "It means the victim allowed the killer to draw close."

"How do you know?"

"Humans are resilient. We don't want to die," I continued. "We have a very strong instinct to fight and survive. So there are almost always defensive wounds on stabbing victims, unless the victim was incapable of fighting back."

"What you're saying is that Court Lady Ahnbi likely trusted whoever killed her. She allowed the killer close enough to her, thinking herself safe, and so had no time to fight back when she was stabbed twice."

"Exactly," I whispered.

"The damos examined the corpse. They reported that there was a single stab to the lungs and the throat, and no bruises or cuts."

I frowned. *No sign of a struggle.*

"They mentioned no other observations. Nothing they found led to your conclusion. That is why I have asked you. You see things others do not see. Things *I* don't see." His earnestness cracked his otherwise reserved facade. It was like watching a pathway appear at low tide, connecting the mainland to a faraway island across the sea. "I can't find the truth alone," he added, his voice and expression raw, "and I think you have something to offer. I think you know it, too."

My pulse thrummed with fear and anticipation, the same way I'd felt when Nurse Jeongsu had asked me whether I would like to become an uinyeo, whether I was willing to follow the call to put the lives of others before my own needs. And this time, I felt as though I were being called to join in a dark adventure greater than myself.

A lull fell over our conversation, my indecision strong. The thrill was intoxicating, along with the thought that *I* could save Nurse Jeongsu. Yet I was not so naive as to think that by lifting the noose from her throat, it would not end up around mine.

"I know you said the commander can't be trusted." I

tried again to find a reason to say no. "But surely he can be convinced to see the truth. Surely he wants to find the real killer as badly as you do. He is a *police* officer."

Eojin shook his head, his expression taut. "If the royal family is involved, he will make sure to bury this case."

"How can you be so sure?"

He replied with one word: "History."

I waited for him to explain, tension creeping up along my spine.

"We must remember the past as a warning." He picked up his torn half of the handbill, and turning it around in the warm glow of light, he said, "Nearly twenty decades ago, Prince Imhae killed female entertainers and escaped punishment with ease. It is an unspoken rule that the police do not go against the order of things, especially not over the death of a few lowborn women. To investigate a royal family is not only difficult, but impossible. Whether or not the Crown Prince is the killer, it doesn't matter. He has been implicated, so the police will be looking to close this case immediately, and by any means necessary."

I looked at Eojin, at his tall, dusty black hat and white robe with bloodstains smeared on his sleeve—the peasant's fingerprints. Eojin, the young man with whom I had witnessed a man's murder, who was now asking me to join him in a search for the truth.

"Perhaps I ought to tell you now." He set the ripped handbill down, gazing blankly over my shoulder. "I couldn't quite find the right time before . . . to tell you who I am."

"Who you are?" I repeated, frowning.

"The police bureau appointed a new jongsagwan." He spoke simply, like he was telling me the hour of the day. "I am Police Inspector Seo."

A wave of ice-cold shock washed through me. Then a whisper slipped from my lips: "Liar."

He stayed still, as though he hadn't heard me.

"*Liar*," I repeated, this time with intention. "Why did you lie to me?"

He reached into his robe, withdrew a brass medallion, and slid it across the table. I took it and found myself staring at a mapae—the token high-ranking police officers and royal investigators carried, permitting them the use of government-owned horses while on assignment. On the front was an engraving of five horses, and on the other side it read *Official Seal of Personnel Authority*.

"I thought you were like me . . ." I whispered. A servant. A cheonmin. Someone who could commiserate with being unwanted, an equal to pursue this incomparable adventure with.

But he was different from me. He was my better.

Then a burning memory surfaced to mind. *Inspector Seo.* I knew that name, and knew of him well. He was Jieun's cousin. He was also the young man I'd overheard Father mention to Mother not long ago—the new inspector who had passed the civil service examination at a young age, so young the king had held off on passing a position down to him for two years. Father had even said he'd wished this prodigy had been *his* son. Envy had dug so deep into me on hearing this, envy over a young man I'd never met and wished I could be.

"So, you disguised yourself to fish palace intelligence from me." Although what I really wanted to say was, *How could you make me feel so small?*

"Not intentionally . . . at first," he said.

Knowing now I was in the presence of a highborn, I waited for the usual fear to settle into my bones. But instead I felt resentment. I looked at Eojin, and I still saw the police servant from the other day, his face bruised, his cheeks hollow. It seemed like a cruel trick that *this* was the young man Father preferred over me.

"You say you're an inspector, but you can't be more than twenty," I said.

"It isn't unusual to obtain the jongsagwan position at twenty. Many do." He paused. "But I am not yet nineteen."

My stomach sunk further. "We are barely adults, you and I."

I pushed into his hand my ripped half of the handbill and the medallion—and with them, the burst of thrill and sense of purpose. Cold reality settled over me now: This was a dangerous official investigation he was speaking of, and I was only eighteen. I'd always felt older than my years until today.

"I am sure you can solve this on your own, nauri." I addressed him by the proper honorific. As was protocol. "You have an entire police bureau to assist you."

"Do you know what Commander Song told me this

morning?" Eojin pressed, his voice edged with a desperate note. "He said that *only* four women were slain—not enough of a reason to stand up to the royal family. He told me to think of my reputation, of my family, of everything I would lose if I continue to investigate."

"Perhaps you should," I replied, even as I regretted my words. "Perhaps you should think of your reputation and your family. That is the first and foremost concern of all the other yangban aristocrats I've met."

Eojin did not so much as flinch. "I told you I had a personal reason for wanting to find the killer," he said, and a shadow of hesitation passed over his face. I could have, in this moment, walked away. But I wanted to know.

"Last year in Pyongan Province . . . one villager by the name of Hongchul was found slain. Witnesses saw a rider carrying off a sword and a woman's decapitated head. I later found that head in a forest . . . along with my father, stabbed to death."

The sharpness in me faded, and I felt myself grow pale before him.

"I don't tell you this to guilt you into joining the investigation. I tell you this so you know that I'm not afraid to lose everything. I'll take the blame should anything go wrong." He pressed the ripped half of the handbill back into my hand. "You have more to lose than I, so you must choose for yourself. Decide fast, though. You don't have long to save Nurse Jeongsu."

6

Eojin escorted me home in silence, and later that night, I lay buried deep beneath my blanket. Each time I fell asleep, I woke up in a cold sweat, remembering the decision awaiting me. A dangerous private investigation, and Nurse Jeongsu's life on the line.

By morning, stress had risen to my skin in the shape of hives looking like massive clumps of mosquito bites. I remained in my room the rest of that day, writing out a list of all that I had at stake.

Palace rules are strict.
Crown Prince a suspect.
The dead peasant.
My nursing practice at risk.

It went on and on, then finally I wrote:

Disapproval.

My attention lingered there.

What I dreaded most wasn't defaming the Crown Prince or even losing my life. My fear was quieter than that. I dreaded Father's disapproval, and disapproval from those like him—the powerful and highly respected. I'd somehow come to believe that if only Father would acknowledge my worth, then it would be like a badge of honor that the rest of the world could see, too.

And perhaps because of this desire, Father had become like a ghost to me, haunting the corners of my mind. Perhaps it had begun the day he'd visited the Hyeminseo five years ago. *The professors here speak highly of you,* he'd said. *They say you might even become an eo-uinyeo one day, the highest-ranking nurse; a woman whom even the king himself trusts and respects. I could hardly believe them, but perhaps you will surprise me.*

A smile had glimmered in his eyes, and I'd never forgotten that look. It was this yearning for a second such glance that haunted me, the fear that I would never receive another warm recognition from him. A fear that sometimes dipped into anger.

I grabbed the paper and crumpled it in my fist. Nurse Jeongsu's life was at stake, and here I was worrying about Father's approval. It seemed so trite, so selfish. I did not want to be like this, a girl too afraid to do what was right for fear of what others would think.

And I did know what was right. I recognized it as clearly as I did the sun in the sky.

The next morning, I changed into a fresh new uniform. I usually carried it to the palace and changed there, to avoid dirtying the skirt on my journey, but today I didn't want to expose my hive-ridden skin. Once the bumps were hidden—my sleeves pulled low and jibun face powder applied to my welted cheeks—I slipped out of the house with quiet steps, hoping not to wake my little brother, and emerged into the early morning. White mist hazed the landscape; the scent of budding green filled my nostrils. Winter was coming to an end.

Picking up the hem of my skirt, I ran down the road to shake off my restless edge. I ran until my lungs were on fire and my forehead beaded with sweat. I arrived at the fortress gate in no time, and when I was halfway toward the palace, I caught a glimpse of Jieun walking with her shoulders tucked in, clutching her travel sack.

"Jieun-ah!" I called out.

Jieun flinched and jolted around, dropping her sack as her face drained of all color. "Oh, it's you!" Relief whooshed out of her as she placed a hand over her chest. "You scared me for a moment."

I picked up the cotton sack, which I knew held her uniform, and gave it to her. "What is the matter?"

"I haven't been sleeping well." Then she flicked a glance my way. "I didn't get a chance to speak with you at the palace two days ago. I wanted to ask how you were faring. About the killings. My cousin told me it was awful, what happened to those girls."

The warmth I'd felt at the sight of Jieun immediately

cooled, replaced by the memory of Eojin and the urgent decision awaiting me. It was difficult to believe that my path had tangled with his, the young man Jieun had spoken about for years. She had never referred to Eojin by his name, though. She was illegitimate, and so would always refer to him as "my cousin" or "Young Master Seo" or "Inspector Seo" ever since he'd come to live with her father to study in the capital.

"What is it?" Jieun asked.

I must have stared blankly at her. "Your cousin is Seo Eojin, is he not?" I asked, a part of me still suspended in disbelief. "The one you called a rare prodigy?"

Jieun nodded as we made our way to the palace. "Have you met him? Perhaps you saw him that day at the Hyeminseo. He'd just returned from a long travel." She shook her head. "I think he was investigating something in the countryside, and he arrived dressed as a *pauper.*"

"But . . ." I still couldn't get over his age, and the pinch of jealousy. "He is so young to be a jongsagwan."

"The previous inspector was only twenty-one," Jieun said with a shrug. "Inspectors are often young; No one minds their age, so long as they are from a good family."

I fell silent, my brows furrowed as I tried to understand how an eighteen-year-old could possibly lead a police investigation. Once we arrived at the palace gate, we presented our identification tags and were admitted.

"I'm going to visit the bookshop after work," Jieun said, the barest hint of color returning to her cheeks. She looked less like a ghost now. "If you'd like, we could go together?"

When Jieun and I had served in the Hyeminseo, Mr. Jang's bookshop had been our favorite place to spend our breaks, and the place Jieun escaped to whenever the days grew too dark.

"I'm hoping to finally get my copy of—" Jieun glanced around, then whispered, *"The Tale of Unyeong."*

A faint smile tugged at my lips. The story revolved around the illicit love affair between a palace woman and a young scholar. Ever since Jieun and I had entered the palace, she'd spent all her time looking for a copy.

"But then again . . ." A shadow passed over Jieun's countenance. Her smile slipped into a nervous twitch. "Perhaps *The Tale of Unyong* is not an appropriate read at the moment. I think it'll remind me of that dead palace woman. What was her name again? Court Lady Ahnbi?" Her voice faltered as she glanced up.

It was then that I sensed a pair of eyes watching us.

Physician Nanshin stood ahead, a slight frown wrinkling his brows, his hands gathered in his sleeves as his robe billowed in the chilly breeze. For a moment I feared he'd overheard us and would rebuke us for either talking about the scandalous book or about the Hyeminseo incident. But then, he looked more troubled than he did upset.

"Nurse Hyeon." He uttered my name with a heavy, foreboding note. At once my shoulders tensed. "Lady Hyegyoung wishes to speak with you at her residence."

Why? I wanted to demand. But I had learned that in the palace, one must bite one's tongue and obey. One must never ask questions.

Clutching my fingers tight, I bowed my head low. "Yeh, uiwon-nim."

"But you had better wait. Do not go yet." His worried gaze weighed on me as I remained bowed. "The Crown Prince is there, and it would be wise not to cross paths with the seja-jeoha." Then he added under his breath, "You look too much like his deceased sister, Princess Hwahyup. It might . . . upset him."

It wasn't the first time someone had remarked on our similarity. Lady Hyegyoung herself had pointed out, two days ago, that I looked like the Crown Prince's dead sister.

As I waited for Jieun to change into her uniform, I stared into a puddle of melted snow. My reflection rippled on the surface—or perhaps it was the reflection of Princess Hwahyup. Precise features within a powdered white face, a sharp contrast to the dark eyes fringed with midnight-black lashes, and hair the shade of a moonless night.

But what did it matter if I looked similar to Princess Hwahyup? What reason had I to be afraid of the Crown Prince? He had favored his seventh sister, so was this not a good thing? I'd heard once before that Princess Hwahyup had been the Crown Prince's only true companion. For among all the king's children, they were the most hated, and must have been companions in their shared misery.

After a moment's hesitation, I shrugged off the physician's advice to wait and instead picked up an empty tray from a nearby storage room, so as not to appear aimless as I wandered. This could be my only chance to ever lay eyes on the prince. And I wanted to see for myself:

Who was this prince everyone whispered about?

Was he a killer, or an innocent young man being framed?

I hurried out of the Royal Apothecary and made my way toward Lady Hyegyoung's residence, facing the guardian mountain that loomed in the distance, a silent observer to whatever lay hidden within these walls. Once I slipped into the compound, I stopped next to a pillar to wait. Time passed slowly, and then I saw it, a flash of blue silk, a robe radiant with silver dragons.

The Crown Prince.

I kept as still as stone as I watched him, unable to blink or breathe, unable to look away. He was a handsome young man of fair complexion, a strong profile, and expressionless black eyes that absorbed the empty palace around him. He moved with the grace of a deer but was built like a military general. I tried to imagine him with a sword, slaying the Hyeminseo women, but instead I found myself conjuring myths about gods and immortals, stories handed down since the beginning of time.

I could almost understand why Commander Song dared not investigate, dared not disturb the seja-jeoha. As I stared at His Highness stride past me, his attendants streaming behind him, it was like watching a man who was the kingdom itself. No one else could compare to the length nor breadth nor height of his existence. He was our future.

Suddenly, a puppy scampered out from Lady Hyegyoung's residence. The little ball of fur rolled through the slush, skidded across the dirt, then tumbled into His Highness's robe with a yip.

The attendants froze. My back tensed as the Crown Prince crouched and reached out, and I half expected him to crush the creature for dirtying his hem. Instead, his expressionless black eyes turned gentle as he raised the pup before him, and he did not sneer upon receiving a slobbering lick across the mouth.

"It is cold out, Geon-ah." His Highness's deep and smooth voice coursed out like spring water. "You should return inside, little one." He gestured at an attendant, then passed the pup over to her. "Bring him back to his mother."

He then rose to his feet and disappeared through the gate. I felt a forceful tug of curiosity, a tug that drew me out of the compound. Surely the Crown Prince's gentleness to animals meant he felt gentleness toward mankind as well . . .

Keeping several paces behind, I followed the prince and his string of attendants as he made his way further into the heart of Changdeok Palace. When they arrived before a large pavilion gate, I snuck up to the back of the line so that the guards let me through without a second glance.

Once inside, I finally lifted my head and glanced around. A long building—with rows of red pillars and jade green windows, and a roof that rippled like a black dragon with a green underbelly—wrapped around a square courtyard. A solemn quietude pervaded within the walled-in space.

Then I saw the sign hanging below the eaves. My blood turned cold.

HUIJEONGDANG HALL. The office of the king.

You shouldn't be here, a warning voice in my head hissed.

I glanced over my shoulder, and my gaze slammed into the guards who were watching me. I needed to leave now before I drew too much attention, yet my feet wouldn't move. I realized that I was waiting for something to summon me deeper into the courtyard. I wanted, so very much, to know what whispers were uttered within the king's office. Perhaps it was the center of all secrets. And perhaps I would know, once and for all, whether investigating this place and these people was a lost cause.

I took in a deep breath and tried to look composed.

I walked slowly, aimlessly, listening for a sign.

Two crows perched on the flared eave, their screeching caws filling the air. Pine trees creaked in the wind. Then I heard voices. I followed the sound to the back courtyard, where at least a dozen hanji-screened windows marched down the wall. There was a small hole punctured into one of them. A hole made by a spy? I peered in.

Inside knelt rows of scholars garbed in silk robes, heads bowed. The Crown Prince knelt among them. Across the room was the white-bearded king in his red dragon robe and black cap, sitting upon a low-legged platform. He sat isolated against a painted background of the sun and moon and the peaks of mountains. A painting that symbolized him: He *was* the sun, moon, and mountains.

"I read this when I was young, and I can still recite it."

The king held up a five-stitched book. "Yet you can't even recite one line from it. That is why you can't explicate it. If you want to understand, you must memorize."

"I am not the son you wish me to be, and I am sorry for it." The Crown Prince's voice was even, toneless almost, and his face was blank. "I have also been too ill these days to study, abamama."

King Yeongjo heaved out an impatient sigh, his gaze flicking over the scholars. "You always lie to me. You simply do not *like* to study." His Majesty's words were cutting—just like my own father's, so similarly heavy with disappointment that my chest tightened and a flash of heat seared my back.

"You never seem too ill to play military games in the Forbidden Garden," the king continued, "and like a child you spend the remainder of your time *drawing*." He spat out the last word, then he gestured with his hand. "Bring it here!"

A flustered eunuch scurried over with a sheet of paper on a tray.

"While you avoided your lectures due to *illness*, it was brought to my attention that you instead used that time to paint. You—the future ruler over a suffering kingdom in need of a wise father—" His Majesty paused against a tight strain in his voice, his brows knitted over a distraught face. "You instead spend your time painting dogs?"

The king snatched up the paper and tore the painting down the center, the sharp rip sending goose bumps across my skin. Piece by piece, the painting turned into a shredded mess. The Crown Prince remained kneeling, his back stiff, the tips of his ears red.

"Get it out of my sight," the king snarled.

The eunuch gathered the pieces and tossed them out the window. The wind blew a few pieces my way; I set down my tray and collected a handful, gingerly piecing the shreds together. As I did, His Majesty's voice continued to ring in my ears.

"You are my son, yet you are nothing like me. I worked hard to be worthy of the throne, to become a good king to the people, yet you live so comfortably. Pampered like a mutt. You always dismiss your studies, unlike your own son, who wakes up at dawn and studies until late, right by my side, able to recite everything he learned without stumbling on his words like a fool. How are you less capable than a six-year-old? *He* would make a better king than you."

Crown Prince Jangheon stayed quiet, his eyes rimmed with red like flames. Not a word of defense left his lips.

The king clucked his tongue, sharp—the sound of utter disdain.

"Confucian learning allows for one to grow in virtue and to cultivate human goodness." A shadow of defeat sunk his features. "Yet you do not study the ways of Confucius, and therefore you do not grow in virtue. It is because you are not cultivating virtue that the heavens punish the people with this ongoing famine—"

"It is the anniversary of my birth, abamama," the Crown Prince whispered.

Everyone tensed. I could feel their eyes widening, the blood draining from their faces, their pulses spiking until I could feel their dread pounding in my own chest.

"Every year on the day I was born," the prince continued, his voice wavering, "you summon me here to rebuke me before your officials. I can never pass the day in peace. I am your son, y-yet . . ." He paused to calm himself. "Yet nothing I do ever pleases you. How can a father despise his only son so much?"

The king's white beard trembled, outrage contorting his face. Reminded too much of Father, I snatched up my tray and bolted away. I left the shreds of paper where they lay, what was once a skilled watercolor illustration of a father dog, his back turned to his two pups clamoring for attention.

Once outside the compound, far away from the guards stationed by the gate, I heaved out a shuddering breath and closed my eyes.

Fathers were terrifying.

I knew how to keep my heart calm in the face of death and dying, screaming patients, and yet one sharp word from my father, and I turned into a fragile child. Before him, I never knew how to keep myself from crying—the type of crying that left me in a heap of violent shudders and gasped attempts to speak—no matter how much he resented the sight of it all.

I wanted so much to be accepted by him.

And I hated this feeling; I wished it to go away.

At last I arrived before the lattice-screened doors of Lady Hyegyoung's chamber, my hair slightly disheveled, my uniform damp from sweat. Two court ladies slid the door open for me.

Hoping that she hadn't noticed my prolonged absence, I knelt before Her Ladyship. She was dressed impeccably as always, sitting on a floor mat, her heavy silk skirt pooled around her. Her face was gaunt, tired, yet her expression was impassive.

"I hear you are an excellent reader of the pulse," she said.

My mind scrambled to read between the lines of her words, trying to understand why she'd sent for me. I barely managed a reply. "I—I am honored to be considered as such."

"Let me see for myself." She lifted her arm, revealing her bare wrist, threaded with the faint blue of veins.

I took in a few quiet breaths, calming my bewilderment. Shuffling closer, I reached out, placing three fingers on her wrist to take her pulse. Chon, gwan, and cheok. Three different points that offered different threads of one story, the pulse like a language of its own.

I stayed in complete silence, bowed over her wrist, letting the sensitivity of my fingertips listen to the story of her pulse. Sometimes pulses were slippery, choppy, hesitant, or hollow. Reading her pulse was like listening to and deciphering a secret. And the longer I listened, the more I understood Her Ladyship. She was different from how she presented herself. She could lie to everyone, but her pulse could not. For a woman who was only three and twenty, her pulse was tight. She carried the pulse of a grief-stricken fifty-year-old with the propensity to worry, to be beaten daily down by waves of thoughts, the weight crushing.

I slowly removed my hand, and under the steady surveillance of her stare, I dared to present the truth. "You are filled with apprehension every day, my lady." And I knew why. Seeing what had occurred between the king and the prince, I could hardly imagine how terrified Lady Hyegyoung must be whenever she met with her husband—surely she would be on the receiving end of the prince's anger, his lashing out. "You feel besieged on all sides, and often feel so overwhelmed."

As though I had touched a bruised spot, Lady Hyegyoung's eyes watered, and a drop slid down her cheek before she quickly dashed it aside. Her face veiled, she asked, "Did you tell anyone that the prince was absent that night?"

A jolt ran through me. "Absolutely not, my lady."

She watched me for a long time. "Do you think Nurse Jieun did?"

I shook my head fiercely. "No, my lady. We are too fearful of our lives to expose this."

"I believe you." She remained still, her lips pale. "Recently, one of my court ladies caught Madam Mun's informant spying on the prince. Her name is Nurse Aram. Do you know her?"

"No, my lady," I whispered. "She likely works on the days I am not at the palace."

"I see."

I waited, wringing my cold hands.

"Well, I questioned the spy—with a whip to her calves. And she confessed to me that Madam Mun is hunting for information about the Crown Prince's whereabouts on the night of the massacre. I'm not sure how that *Mun woman* even came to suspect his disappearance."

I bit my lower lip, then felt bold enough to ask, "Begging your pardon, my lady, but why do you think Madam Mun is so determined?"

Lady Hyegyoung expelled a tired sigh. "She is ever determined to defame the prince, to turn the king fully against his son. She is a greedy concubine determined to have His Majesty all for herself. The palace is full of her spies—Court Lady Ahnbi was one of her spies, too."

A gasp escaped me.

Lady Hyegyoung massaged her temples, then she looked at me, her eyes sad. "You must be devastated about your mentor," she said.

My head was still spinning from the intelligence she had just shared. Court Lady Ahnbi, a spy? But I recomposed myself and finally answered, "Yes, my lady. I know she is innocent."

"Of course she is. Nurse Jeongsu is dear to my family. My youngest sister grew up motherless, dispirited and sickly. Nurse Jeongsu recommended that my sister learn how to read while young, convinced a healthy mind would lead to a healthy body. It proved to be true, and I came to respect her a great deal."

I bowed my head, not knowing what to say.

"So, when I learned that two of Nurse Jeongsu's students were to enter the palace, I summoned her and asked about you and Jieun. She praised you both, and especially you. She said you are like a crane among wolves." She turned her gaze to the latticed window, and a look of determination furrowed her brows. "You are intelligent and strong-willed, and I'm sure you care for Nurse Jeongsu very much. I know you are looking into the murders."

My stomach dropped, a free-falling sensation that left me light-headed. "My lady, I wouldn't dare—"

"Madam Mun's spy informed me of this as well. She said the madam recruited you to privately investigate."

I shook my head and blurted, "I only agreed to it because I was already looking for answers. I had no intention of revealing anything important to her—"

"A crane among the wolves," she said quietly. "I know that is what you are. You have no ill intent toward me. I only hope you will be as loyal to the Crown Prince."

I dug my nails into my palm, hard. "Of course I will, my lady." And I meant it, yet a question loomed over me: *But what if he is the killer?*

As if hearing my thoughts, she said, "I have heard the rumors. This anonymous handbill circulating, suggesting the Crown Prince is guilty of murder and should be convicted . . ."

A pause ensued. Trepidation prickled under my skin as I waited.

"But do you know, Nurse Hyeon? The anonymous writer does not know what he asks for. To convict the prince is to incriminate our entire family—along with our only son, the only grandchild of King Yeongjo. Neither a convict nor a convict's son can inherit the throne. So there would be no heir. No future. A conviction would upheave this dynasty." She reached out and touched my hand, and an overwhelming sensation expanded in my chest. "But I will not try to stop you."

"Yeh?" I sounded breathless. She was a royal. She could order that I leap off a cliff, and I would have to do so.

"We are women," she continued, "and nothing short of death stops us from doing precisely what we wish to do. That is what the laws and restrictions binding our lives breed: determination and cunning. The likes of you will not obey me. You will tell me that you intend to be as still as a rock, and yet I know you will dart from shadow to shadow like a fish." She dropped her voice to a whisper. "Now, look at me. And listen carefully."

I did so. My gaze lifted onto a pair of sincere eyes—so sincere that whatever she was about to say had to be the absolute truth.

"When Prince Jangheon returned to the palace that night, his robe was not tarnished. I saw no blood on him, not even a scratch. I need you to believe me. He is innocent, Nurse Hyeon."

A sigh almost escaped me. He'd had no blood on him, which was impossible if he had indeed been the killer. I had seen the messy wounds, the flesh lining one victim's nails, the clump of hair in another's hand. The killer would have borne obvious marks of violence. The prince was indeed innocent.

"You may come speak to me whenever you need, Nurse Hyeon. And in the meanwhile, do all you can to save Nurse Jeongsu; she is a good woman in need of a good friend. All I ask is that you do so without disturbing four hundred years of history."

7

A strange flutter filled my stomach after I left Lady Hyegyoung's residence—the sensation a bird might have, perhaps, when flying out of its cage. I realized that the thought of palace rules had bound me to silence, restraining me from assisting the young inspector. But Lady Hyegyoung was a royal; she *was* the palace, and she had permitted me to search for the truth. As for the four hundred years of history, I was not concerned. What could I possibly do to cause chaos up high? How could a mere servant girl imagine disturbing the universe?

A wild laugh escaped me as I hurried back to the Royal Apothecary. I could help find the truth without my life crumbling around me. If I investigated discreetly enough, Father would never find out, either.

My heart felt light as I proceeded with the rest of the day, and it was a quiet day at that. There were few ailing royals and concubines to attend to, and so I was assigned to assist with the cutting and drying of herbal plants. And there were many; the baskets from the medical garden were overloaded with leafy green plants with nutritious roots. My wrists ached by the end of the workday, stinging from the hours spent slicing plants and hanging them up to dry. A sting I hadn't noticed while I was working, busy as I had been thinking about my investigation and realizing that I hadn't seen Physician Khun all day. The most suspicious man in this case. As nurses and physicians had coursed in and out of the apothecary, I'd asked them for the whereabouts of Physician Khun, but not one had seen him. He hadn't come in for work that day.

Once our shift was over, I quietly walked with Jieun out of the palace, still thinking about Physician Khun all the way to the bookshop. I wanted to ask Eojin what he knew, and needed to give him my answer as well—but I had to do so in secret if I was to assist him with no one the wiser. Perhaps I could meet him somewhere outside the fortress. But first, I needed to relay the message to him . . . and his cousin stood right before me.

For some reason, my cheeks burned as I attempted to bring him up. "Jieun-ah . . ."

"Eung?"

"I . . ." I cleared my throat. "I need to speak with your cousin."

"My cousin?" She shot me a confused sort of half smile. "You know each other?"

I massaged my wrist, anything to keep myself occupied. "Eung."

She didn't respond as we stepped into the bookshop and

browsed the open shelves, stacked with five-stitched books. But I could feel her mind turning, trying to fill in the gaps in her knowledge. I cleared my throat awkwardly and flipped through a few books, only to return them to the shelf. Nothing caught my interest; my mind was too preoccupied.

"Are you fond of each other?" Jieun suddenly asked.

"No, no, no," I said, horrified. "We crossed paths at the Hyeminseo, and there are a few things regarding the . . . the massacre . . . that I wish to speak to him about. Discreetly. I don't want my father to find out." I glanced at the open shop door, at the still-bright sky. "Would you ask him if he is available before nightfall?"

"I could speak to him, tell him where to meet you." She folded her arms around a book, and her smile sharpened with mischief. "Now that I think of it, my cousin has never fallen in love. He's never met his match. But you . . . If you married him, would you become my cousin-in-law?"

I nearly choked on my surprise, though it should not have been surprising at all. Jieun was a romantic. When she wasn't studying, she was matchmaking.

"No such thing will happen, I assure you." Then I quickly added, "You could join us. We could search for the truth together." This thought suddenly seemed very alluring. "Yes, you *should* join us! We can meet at the inn, all three of us. And once the discussion is over, you and I can take our meals together. I'll pay for it. Then you could stay over at my home, and we could study together for our upcoming exam . . ." My voice trickled away, disturbed by Jieun's dead silence.

"I will not," she whispered. "Do not ask me to join."

I blinked. "But why not? He is your cousin, and Nurse Jeongsu is also your mentor. You adore her."

Jieun stayed quiet. Her arms remained folded, though now she looked as though she were trying to wrap herself up tight, like the air had suddenly grown too cold. "I want nothing to do with the investigation."

The fear in her eyes was unmistakable. "What happened?" I asked gently.

"I lied to you." Her voice cracked as she looked away. "I didn't wait outside the Hyeminseo. Apparently, there was a burglary earlier in the night, and patrolmen ran by saying they'd finally found the man. The guard got distracted, so I slipped inside to fetch you. I saw the covered-up corpses. I should have left them covered up, but . . . I looked." Her face went white, as pale as it had been this morning. Now I understood why she had looked so frightened. "Whoever killed those women . . . he is still out there, and if he finds out that we are searching for him . . . it'll be *us* under the straw covers."

"Jieun-ah." I tried to hold her gaze, but she avoided my eyes. "That is why I intend to go about this very discreetly. No one needs to find out. We can—"

She shook her head. "I don't want anything to do with this. I'm sorry if this upsets you."

I stared at my friend—my *only* friend. I'd spent years looking at Jieun, at her round face and dainty chin, her bright eyes and her ever-smiling lips. We had done everything together. But I remembered once more that this investigation was not a game. No matter how careful we were, our safety was not guaranteed.

"I'm not upset. Not at all." I reached out and held her hand, her fingers so icy that I immediately felt very sorry I'd asked her in the first place. "I won't press further on this. I promise."

"Thank you," she whispered, then finally meeting my gaze, she added, "I will speak with my cousin, though. I'll relay your message to him. He did tell me that later today he intends to visit Mount Bugak. I think to question a few more of Minji's relatives, who live near there."

The missing fourth nurse, I thought.

"Perhaps I'll tell him to meet you somewhere nearby?"

I nodded, still holding her hand. "Pretend that this message has nothing to do with the investigation."

She nodded. "I will just pretend that I am . . ." A pause, and then she gazed down at the book in her arms. She'd picked *The Story of Chunhyang* off the shelf, a love story about a lowly gisaeng's daughter and a young nobleman. A weak smile passed over her lips. "That I am setting up a romantic tryst between you two. I'll tell him to wear his most becoming robes that go best with a moonlit encounter."

My face flushed again, heat spreading down my neck and across my chest. But I was glad to see her smile. "I shall meet him tonight under the moonlight, then. Perhaps at Segeomjeong Pavilion."

"Segeomjeong Pavilion," she whispered, light returning to her eyes. "I will tell him that."

"No, I only said that in jest—"

Jieun set the book aside and walked off, her steps determined; I had planted a ridiculous idea in the head of a girl who spent all her earnings on purchasing romantic literature.

"I was only jesting," I repeated as I quickly followed behind her.

I crossed the small bridge that arched over Hongjewoncheon, a stream of more large, flat rocks than water, and at once caught sight of Segeomjeong, a black-roofed pavilion resting at the foot of Mount Bugak. The storied place where warriors would rest to clean their swords at the stream, where lovers would meet so that no one but the mountain and the frogs could see. A nonsensical place to meet with the young inspector, and I hated being nonsensical. But Jieun had relayed my message, and he'd agreed to meet me here a little before dusk.

I heaved out a sigh. What had been done had been done. There was no point worrying about a matter I could not change.

Stepping onto the deck, I tilted my head back. Brown pillars surrounded me, supporting elaborately flared eaves that were painted jade green and patterned with primary colors. A faint breeze blew by, and I took in a deep breath, filling my lungs with the scent of ten thousand trees.

It was no wonder that I'd read of Segeomjeong Pavilion so often in literature and poems. The pavilion was nestled under a forested mountain and next to a trickling stream that sparkled in the setting sun, casting a spell over one's mind with the thought that everything was well with the kingdom. There was no famine. There was no horror, no pain. There was no grief. There was only water, earth, and trees.

This featherweight feeling lasted only a moment.

Leaning against the low lattice fence, a thought burrowed into me: Everything was *not* well, and so far, the truth seemed impossibly out of reach. On my way here, I had stopped by the Hyeminseo to speak with Nurse Oksun, to see if she had any news. She'd shaken her head, explaining that she'd asked everyone she could think of, but no one knew where Nurse Jeongsu had gone at midnight, hours before the Hyeminseo massacre.

I was so lost in my thoughts that I didn't notice the passing of time until I heard the distant thudding of horse hooves. I glanced over my shoulder. The sun had set midway, burnishing the sky and snow-damp earth with a golden glow. I recognized the fast-approaching rider as Eojin.

Dread sunk into the pit of my stomach, but I beat it aside, straightened my back, and folded my hands before me. I had made a decision, and I would stick to it.

I would do anything and everything to help Nurse Jeongsu.

Eojin leapt off his horse, tethering the reins to the bridge, then crossed over to my side. In a few long strides, he was standing before me, bringing with him the scent of mist, pine, and a hint of sweat—as if he had rushed here. At the sight of him in his police uniform, I felt like I was staring at a younger version of Commander Song, with his black hat and beads running down in a loop around his face. His robe of blue silk, sleeves studded with silver. A sword secured imperiously to his side.

A cool discontent fell over me as I pulled my gaze low. "I apologize for making you come all the way to this pavilion, nauri."

I waited for an awkward round of small talk, or perhaps even an embarrassing comment about the location I'd chosen. Instead, he simply asked, "Have you decided?"

"May I be so bold as to ask—"

"You are bold, so be bold with me," he said, his voice so firm it surprised me. "There is no need for politeness."

I turned his request over, then muttered, "I suppose there is nothing polite about murder."

"Precisely," he said. I could hear a smile in his voice.

Emboldened, I raised my gaze a notch higher. "Then tell me, nauri. Tell me everything you know about this investigation, and I will disclose all I know."

He leaned against the lattice fence and slipped out a small journal, flipping it open. "We interviewed every witness who was near the Hyeminseo that night."

I ran a finger along the collar of my uniform, then timidly joined his side, staring down at the page he was pointing to. I saw neat Hanja characters, listing names. The first was *Nurse Inyeong*.

"Palace Nurse Inyeong, a former police damo, was the first witness," Eojin said. "She claims to have followed Court Lady Ahnbi to warn her about the palace rules against leaving the premises, only to lose her. Then she heard screams, which led her to the crime scene."

A shiver coursed down my back at the memory. "Where were the bodies found?"

"Court Lady Ahnbi was found lying near the gate."

An image of her dripped into my mind, cold and red. *The clean stab to her lungs and throat.*

"Head Nurse Heejin, she was found at the bottom of the steps, right outside the office."

A slash across her back, then her throat.

"The two student nurses were found inside the office, Student Eunchae sprawled near the doorway, and Student Bitna curled up against the wall."

Bitna, with her blood-lined nails. Her throat and chest wounded. Eunchae, with the broken nose and a fistful of hair. Stabbed in the stomach, then finished off by a strike to her throat.

"All victims had one thing in common," I whispered, "the wound to the throat."

Eojin nodded. "During her second examination, the damo measured the stab wound that punctured Court Lady Ahnbi's lungs and neck," he said. "They were made by a weapon that was approximately four chon and two pun in dimension."

I frowned. "But the commander thinks the murder weapon was an herb cutter. The measurement is far too narrow, I should think, for it to be a yakjakdu. The herb cutter is more like a sword in length. With that measurement, I'd be more convinced that a . . . a long and *very* thin blade had stabbed her."

"I thought so, too. But besides Ahnbi's, the other wounds match the herb cutter."

I folded my arms and paced the deck, trying to envision the bodies myself, a closer examination of the stabs and slashes than the quick once-over I'd had at the crime scene. "Would it be possible for me to examine the corpses?"

"They're gone."

"What?" I whispered. "It's only been four days."

"Commander Song said the victims were decomposing too fast. I tried to convince him to keep them longer, but on the third day, he had all four women buried."

My surprise only grew. A murdered person's body often spoke for them, their wounds able to tell such detailed stories. And to have such evidence buried in a matter of only four days?

I would have to rely on what Eojin and the damo had seen. "You mentioned that Court Lady Ahnbi was stabbed in the lungs. The lungs are protected under the ribs . . ." I let my thoughts linger on this point, trying to find another tale the dead were trying to tell me. I frowned and glanced up at Eojin. "How easy is it to stab someone in the lungs?"

"Not easy at all, if one knows nothing about the human body. One would have to slide the blade between the ribs—that is the only way to enter the lungs easily." A line formed between his brows. "In a medical sense, what happens when one is stabbed in the lungs?"

The breeze had grown stronger, and no matter how

often I tucked my hair behind my ears, it came flying out again. "Massive blood loss, difficulty breathing, but death usually isn't instantaneous—" I brushed aside another strand, then gave up, leaving it to twirl across my face. "It would take a few hours to die from such a wound usually, hours for the lungs to fill up with blood."

"Perhaps that is why the killer chased after Ahnbi for the second strike: He knew she wouldn't die quickly enough. Perhaps she'd lost too much blood to defend herself, and thus the wound to the throat you noted."

"What did the damos discover about that one?"

"They confirmed the wound was deep enough to have been fatal, that the stab had severed a large blood vessel in her throat."

This confirmed the uneasy feeling I'd had when I'd first seen the wound. Had her attacker known exactly where the large blood vessel was?

"The killer either accidentally found the spot on the victim that would instantly kill her," I said, "and knew he'd found it with one strike, because he didn't strike again. Or he has a lot of military or medical training."

Physician Khun, Nurse Inyeong, and the Crown Prince came to my mind. The first two had spent all their lives studying the human body, and the latter was known for his military prowess. "Who are the suspects?"

Eojin heaved out a sigh. "At the moment, there are too many that we will need to eliminate."

"Like whom?"

"Physician Khun is the most obvious one."

"He didn't come to work today," I said, suddenly remembering his absence. "No one has seen him. Have you?"

"I went to speak with him recently. He's holed up in his hut, too grief-ridden to even get out of bed," he said, and when I waited for more, he spoke on. "I questioned him about his relationship with Court Lady Ahnbi, and he denied everything. He even denied that the ring belonged to him. And yet he certainly seemed to know much about her. He told me that it wasn't *him* I should be questioning, but Madam Mun."

My brows lowered at her name. "Madam Mun?"

"He told me that the madam had made Court Lady Ahnbi's life miserable, though he wouldn't reveal the details. He said she could have hired assassins to carry out her dirty deeds—to end Ahnbi's life." Eojin looked at his notebook. "So Madam Mun is a suspect as well, though I don't know why she'd target a court lady."

I fell still, gripped by a restless sensation, a sense of knowing. I knew the answer to this. Then a thought surfaced like a gasp. "Court Lady Ahnbi was Madam Mun's spy."

Eojin glanced up, looking startled. "How do you know this?"

"Lady Hyegyoung told me—"

"Lady Hyegyoung, the Crown Prince's wife? But why would a royal family member confide in you, a servant?" he asked, and I realized I'd said too much. Under his scrutinizing gaze, the memory of that night stirred awake, and I feared that if Eojin looked too closely at me, he'd see it—the palace secret that could result in heads rolling. *My* head.

"Is there something I should know?" he asked quietly.

"I am a nurse, and those I tend to often confide in me," I said, then quickly changed the subject. "I *do* know that Madam Mun tasked servants to spy on the prince. I hear she is trying to turn the king against his son, to isolate His Majesty. To have him all for herself."

Eojin continued to examine me, and perhaps he noticed anxiety flushing my face. A line formed between his brows as though he was realizing something, and my panic spiked. Desperate to divert his attention, I glanced down at his notebook. "What about Minji?" I pointed to her name on the page. "She's the one that escaped the massacre, correct? Have you found her yet?"

"I haven't finished listing the suspects." There was a wary edge to his voice. "The Crown Prince is also a suspect."

"It's getting dark." I looked everywhere but at Eojin. "I should leave before the night descends. It'll take me at least two hours to reach home."

The light had bled from the skies, a reddish-purple glow pooling over the horizon, casting shadows across the landscape and over half of Eojin's face.

"I still have more questions to ask," he said in a low voice. "I'll escort you home."

Without waiting for my protest, Eojin strode over to his

horse, and I followed, thinking of ways to evade his interrogation. When we paused before his black steed, I was certain he'd make me walk. I was a servant, after all, born to trudge through the mires. At least the weather was nice today.

Eojin adjusted the saddle, glancing at me for the briefest second. "You can ride the horse," he said. When I gaped at him, too confused to respond, he rubbed the back of his neck, looking unusually discomposed. "Are you . . . afraid of horses?"

"No, of course not," I said, pushing away my surprise.

I marched up to the horse and struggled to hook my feet into the stirrup. I tried a few more times, then my heart lurched with surprise as Eojin grasped my waist and easily lifted me onto the saddle. His hands withdrew without lingering, yet the memory of his warmth remained on me. He was of noble birth; he wasn't supposed to touch me. It was the rule, a part of Confucian morality, and those from Eojin's class intensely guarded their public reputations for proper and virtuous behavior.

I sat perched on the horse, too bewildered to move, and Eojin led the creature toward the road; it took a few long moments of riding through the evening breeze for my face to cool. By that point, I'd forgotten entirely about our earlier conversation until Eojin finally brought it up, snapping me back into reality.

"Lady Hyegyoung is very protective of her husband, from what I've heard," he said, a note of caution in his voice. "She wouldn't have confided such sensitive information in you without reason. Without a circumstance binding you to secrecy."

The shadows of Prince Jangheon's chamber slid into my mind again. "I really do not know why she confided in me," I lied. "But I assure you, the Crown Prince is innocent. Her Ladyship said he returned with no blood on his clothes."

His steps slowed. *"Returned?"*

My breath caught. I had slipped, badly. "I mean . . . He was in the palace all day. So how could he be the killer?"

Eojin paused, and the horse ambled to a stop. He looked up from under the brim of his hat, his eyes looking so deeply into mine that I couldn't look away. "I need to know," he said. "I won't let harm befall you for telling the truth."

My lips remained clamped; my pulse thundered.

"I need you to trust me," he said slowly, steadily. "We are quite alone in this investigation. I need to know that I can rely on you. One lie, and everything unravels."

I gripped the saddle tighter, my indecision a deadweight in my chest. Then it occurred to me that Eojin had trusted me with sensitive information. He'd opened his investigative journal for my perusal. It was only fair that I tell him the truth . . .

After a long pause, I whispered, "The Crown Prince was not in his chamber on the night of the massacre." A shadow of surprise passed over his face, as well as a flicker of horror. "You must swear not to tell anyone of this."

He seemed unable to find words, so I pressed. "If you tell anyone, it will mean something horrible for me."

He held my gaze, his brows drawn low with concern. "I promise. I promise on my father's grave that nothing you tell me will ever be turned against you."

And in that moment, I felt a strange feeling.

I trusted him.

8

A murder investigation is like a game of janggi: The moment one picks up an octagonal piece, time stills and the world falls away, leaving only strategy, tactics, and questions. I felt myself under such a bewitchment conversing with Eojin about our next moves.

But as soon as Eojin stilled the horse and asked, "Is this your home?" the spell broke.

A murder investigation or no, I would always return to this house. The dirty and cracked walls stared at me. The broken tiled roof leaked with memories of rain dripping onto my sleeping face. Mold spots creeping within. Father's growing disinterest in Mother—in us—scarred our home in a visible way.

"What is the matter?" came Eojin's voice, quiet and deep.

I realized that I was clenching the saddle harder. "Nothing," I whispered, then corrected myself. "Nothing is the matter, nauri."

I climbed down from the horse before he could offer to assist. "You should go now," I said, "before the fortress gates close for the night."

After a moment of hesitation, he swung onto his horse, and I politely bowed my head low to bid him farewell, as I would to any other noble. I suddenly remembered my smallness, my insignificance.

"We're both of the same age," he murmured, steering his steed around. The creature's muscles rippled under a velvety black coat. "There's no need for such formalities."

I ignored him, the weight of my home on my shoulders. Once he departed, I drew myself up and approached my family's residence. The gate had been left wide open, and I saw Servant Mokgeum with a broom, idly sweeping here and there. She paused at the sight of me, then at once put her broom aside and sidled up to me.

"Who was that handsome young man, agasshi?" she asked, eyes gleaming. "Your sweetheart?"

"It's not what you think, ajumma," I mumbled.

"And that is how every love story begins." She chuckled. "Ah, and look! You look better. The lumps from this morning are gone."

I'd forgotten about those. I unconsciously touched my face as I made my way into the courtyard, heaving out a sigh.

Mistaking my sigh for something else, Servant Mokgeum cast me a worried look. "Your mother put your brother to sleep, and she's been waiting for Lord Shin ever since." She chewed on her lower lip. "Do you think His Lordship will visit today, agasshi?"

"Likely not. He's found a new concubine, I hear."

With that, I gave the servant a faint smile and stepped into my home. Silence and shadows swarmed around me, heavy with Mother's grief, the one wound I couldn't stitch up. A wound that made me feel so helpless I wanted to run away from it—but I was her daughter. We were family.

Turning, I made my way toward her room, and just as I reached it, my brother's door slid open. Dae-hyeon must have heard the sound of my footsteps, and now he came out, sniffling and rubbing his teary eyes.

"Noona," he whimpered, "I had a nightmare."

"Again? Come here." I scooped him up into my arms. "Aigoo, our Dae-hyeon is growing so big I can hardly carry him."

"No, I'm not." He stuck a thumb into his mouth, as though in protest.

I brought him back to his room and settled him on his sleeping mat. With a washcloth, I wiped away his tears and snot, then pulled a blanket over him.

"Go to sleep, Dae-hyeon-ah," I murmured, patting his shoulder as I waited for him to drift to sleep, watching as his eyelashes fluttered shut.

For years, I'd been unforgivably cold to him, so cold that Jieun had once asked, *Do you despise your brother?* Perhaps I had hated him a little, resenting him for the privilege he'd been born into, born as a boy. To be a boy opened doors that would never open for me, shielded him in a way where my own status as a woman had stripped me naked.

123

But I'd given up on disliking him.

No matter how hard I'd tried to shake him off, Dae-hyeon had clung to me like a piece of sticky rice. He'd grown on me over time. Now I spent most of my days off work with him, studying while he rolled around munching on honey-fried biscuits. Though, with the investigation I'd agreed to assist in, Dae-hyeon would have to take his honey-fried biscuit to Servant Mokgeum. I doubted that I'd have much time to spend with him, let alone to even study.

Once my brother's chest rose and fell evenly, a sign that he was fast asleep, I carefully retreated from his side. I stepped out into the hall and faced the darkness once more, the echoes of Mother's sadness ricocheting against the lonely walls. Along with my own sadness, too. She thought I didn't know what kept her up at night, and why she remained lying on her sleeping mat for half the day when the sun was out, and why she had trouble eating and digesting her food. She thought I didn't know, and always tried to keep it that way.

I wanted to avoid her tonight, but I owed her a greeting. Letting out a heavy sigh, I slid open the door to her chamber, and as the glow of candlelight filled my vision, for a moment, I saw Mother as she had once been. A gisaeng of exquisite beauty, and so intelligent that powerful men would come from all around the kingdom to converse with her. One of the men had been my father. *A whirlwind love story, it was,* Servant Mokgeum had once told me. *They could hardly survive a day without each other.*

But the pool of candlelight faded, and I stared at the

mother who'd raised me, with her severely tied hair and a face that looked as empty as a storm-washed sky, eyes so dim they reminded me of a pair of burnt-out wicks.

"Did you eat, eomonni?" I asked.

She didn't respond, staring at the low-legged table before her.

"Dae-hyeon was awake when I came, so I had to put him back to sleep. It was also busy at the palace today," I went on. "There was so much work to be done. I visited the Hyeminseo after. That's why I'm late."

Her silence persisted, and I wondered if she'd noticed my presence. I often wondered if she even loved me, a question that had kept me awake at night ever since Mother had tried to sell me to the Gibang House, to become a female entertainer.

I'd never forgiven Mother for that. But I still loved her. She was still my mother, and I hoped to one day be *enough*. To earn enough so she'd never have to worry about our livelihood again. To rise high—as high as Dae Jang Geum, the legendary female physician, trusted by the king himself—and be enough that my mother and I found respect in the eyes of society.

"Do you want some tea, eomonni?" I asked, walking over. "I could make some now—"

"Sit down."

I hesitated, then knelt before her, studying her face. Something about her tone filled me with dread, and as I watched her light a silver tobacco pipe, I sensed the conversation would be a long one.

"I heard a horse approaching," she said, "and when I looked out, it was to see you with a young man."

I searched her voice for a note of disapproval, but there was none. "You must have heard about the Hyeminseo massacre, eomonni. My mentor has been arrested as the prime suspect. Inspector Seo wanted to ask me a few questions. He found me at the Hyeminseo, and we talked until it grew late." The lies were coming easier now. "One of my ankles felt a little twisted, so he offered me a ride back."

"Did he?" she said, examining me steadily. "You say it was for an investigation, but no yangban aristocrat lends his horse to a cheonmin girl like you for nothing in return."

"There is nothing like that going on—"

"He wants to make you his concubine. It is the trend these days, young nobles looking for uinyeo concubines. Not only can they be their mistresses, but also provide them with medical care."

You don't know me at all. The words lingered on my tongue. "I have no intention of becoming anyone's concubine."

"Good. Then do not associate with him again."

Her remark both startled and angered me. "You don't even know him—"

"It is your father's request. He approached me two days ago, asking that I keep an eye on you, and to remind you of your promise to him."

A cold chill ran down my skin as Father's specter returned. Haunting my mind with his frowning gaze, his measuring eyes. "Eomonni," I whispered, "please don't tell him. I'm not investigating, but Father will surely misunderstand—"

"Your father rightly guessed that Inspector Seo would solicit your help. He told me the young man is a rather controversial figure, butting heads with the commander like he is a police chief himself with fifty years of experience." Her voice was devoid of emotion as she brought the pipe to her lips and took a puff. Clouds curled from her mouth. "Your father seems to think they are all like that at first, these young inspectors. They come in bright-eyed and ambitious, determined to change the world, to die martyrs of justice. But it doesn't take long for reality to put them in their place."

"Inspector Seo isn't investigating out of mere ambition. He has real reasons." My insides burned as though I, too, breathed in smoke, incensed by how misunderstood Eojin was. He was investigating because of his father's brutal murder. *No one* had the right to stop him, or me. "Nurse Jeongsu's life is in danger, and Father doesn't understand that Commander Song is butchering everything!"

Her voice flat, her eyes emotionless, she murmured, "Don't listen to your father, then."

Surprise struck me hard. "What do mean?"

"Your mentor, Nurse Jeongsu . . . she is like family to you." Mother paused. "Better than your own family."

I froze. I had always thought this, but had never known Mother saw it as well.

"You were out till late, and you returned with a young

inspector notorious for his upright spirit. I can only con-
clude that you must be looking to find a way to free your
mentor. I don't believe you were simply answering questions. He wouldn't have walked you all the way here if that
were so. You're helping him, aren't you?"

"Yes," I whispered. I couldn't believe I was confiding
in my mother.

She fell silent, a contemplative look sinking over her
features. A great haze of smoke was floating around her
when she finally spoke. "Do not tell anyone I told you this,
but there is a deeper reason why your father doesn't want
you involved in the investigation."

I waited, feeling a sense of cold dread, yet also intrigue.
Who *was* this woman, this woman I called Mother? We had
lived under the same roof for years, but now I felt like I was
truly looking at her for the first time. What had changed?

"Your father came to visit me two days ago, and can
you imagine what he told me?" she continued. "He told
me about the rumors of the prince being the Hyeminseo
killer. And he said he was *certain* it was not the prince."

She paused, and I waited, holding my breath. There was
a gleam in her eyes that prodded at me, like she wanted
me to *see* something. Then came a frightful thought. "Do
you think . . . Father was involved?"

"Your father had no part in the murder," Mother said
with certainty. "I spoke with his new concubine, and she
told me he was with her until a little before curfew lifted.
Which was around the time the murder occurred. He is
not a killer, but clearly he knows something."

Questions reeled in my mind. "I should talk to Father."

She arched a brow. "You would incur his wrath by doing so."

"But he knows something. What . . . what should I do, then?" I asked hesitantly.

"Be more discreet, child. Do not speak with your *father* . . . but speak with his gatekeeper."

"Gatekeeper Kwon?"

"Servants hear and see everything." She took another puff of her pipe, then studied the table, the dragons inlaid and lacquered. Softly, she murmured, "If you do continue with this investigation, remember this: Everyone must choose the paths they will walk. And when you choose, remember to count the cost. Do not live with regrets."

I peered up at Mother. "What kind of costs?"

She held my gaze steadily. "If what is right, honorable, and just will cost you your father's approval, will you still choose that path? Sometimes—oftentimes—we cannot do both what is right and also please those around us."

"What if I can do what is right, honorable, and just," I said, "and Father would never find out?"

"Count the cost. Do not charge into the future unaware. Remember that, Hyeon-ah. No matter how hard you try to preserve yourself, every important decision in life will come with a price. It will come with regrets."

"What . . ." I hesitated, but I strangely wanted to know. "What would you do?"

She considered my question for a moment. "Who do you wish to become one day?"

Like Nurse Jeongsu, I realized.

As though reading my mind, Mother whispered, her voice tinged with remorse, "Save your teacher, if she means that much to you. It is those you love that make a wretched life worth living."

Her words thrummed within me as I padded back to my room. Something had happened to Mother to have changed her thus. Or perhaps she had never been whom I'd imagined her to be.

Whatever the truth was, she was a mystery to solve another day.

9

A light mist of rain swept across the land the following day. Birds chirped in a loud chorus as I hurried into the capital, hands attempting to shelter my hair, my breathing ragged and panicked. I'd spent half the day waiting out the heavy rainfall, and it had stopped when I left home, the skies clearing. But the clouds had returned, gathered dark above me.

Hiking up my skirt, I gave up on my hair and ran faster toward Father's residence. He would not be in, as he was usually at the Ministry of Justice during the daytime. Gatekeeper Kwon would be at his post—what valuable information could he possibly have? But Mother was right, either way, it was better not to incur Father's wrath. It would be better to gather information from those around him instead.

I slipped out of an alley, then took Donhwamunro Street. Within a few paces, I caught sight of the police bureau, its flared roof rising above the sea of thatched huts like dark storm clouds. I saw, too, a group of young police officers standing outside, speaking with someone. My gaze gravitated toward the tallest officer, a veil of rain dripping from the brim of his black hat. Then he looked up, and a familiar pair of eyes followed me as I continued down the street. Eojin bowed his head, just a slight tilt. I returned the nod.

The sight of Eojin strengthened my steps as I hurried down the road and into the northern district, the residence of the powerful and wealthy, a cluster of black-roofed mansions gleaming in the rain. I finally arrived before Father's home, out of breath and cold, but determined.

I banged my fist on the door until the gatekeeper opened it, his brows shooting up. He immediately recognized me, likely from the times I'd stood before this very gate on my tiptoes, hoping to catch a glimpse of Father.

"Young mistress!" Gatekeeper Kwon said. "What are you doing out in this weather?"

I wiped a strand of hair away from my face, and as pitifully as I could, I spoke in a wavering voice. "I wish to speak with Lord Shin. If he is at home, please inform him that I've requested his audience."

"Young mistress." His worrying eyes looked me over again. "He is not in. He left for work this morning."

"But . . . but I've come all this way . . ." I floundered a moment, then I turned my distressed gaze to him. "There is something urgent I wished to ask Lord Shin, but perhaps you know the answer?"

"Yeh? A question?" Hesitance strained his features. "Of course."

"Did you hear of the Hyeminseo massacre four days ago? Has Lord Shin made any mention of it?"

The gatekeeper quickly glanced around, then he dipped his voice low and said, "We were ordered not to ever speak of it."

"Why not?"

"Please, young mistress. I would rather not—I know nothing!"

It was then I put to use a strategy I'd thought of while lying on my sleeping mat last night. "Someone told me that they suspect Lord Shin," I whispered. "Is that why he wishes no one to speak of the incident?" I shook my head, frowning. "I was worried. As you know, if he is indeed involved, his entire household will be punished. You would likely be exiled, or worse—"

"Wh-who says this?" His frantic eyes locked on to me. "That is preposterous."

"That is what I think, too, and that is why I've come. I'm so concerned, ajusshi. Why would anyone suspect Lord Shin? Do you know? I am trying to convince the inspector to punish the person for spreading such rumors."

"I know Lord Shin is not involved, and Commander Song knows, too!"

My shoulders tensed. "Commander Song?" The name alone sent a flutter of panic through me. "He was here?"

"Commander Song visited to speak with His Lordship over tea. I overheard a little bit. Apparently while Lord Shin was returning home from Concubine Pak's home, shortly before curfew lifted, he witnessed the murderer fleeing—"

"Wait," I said. "How did Lord Shin know it was the killer?"

"The commander asked the same question! The killer bumped into him while running away and dropped something. I'm not sure what. Lord Shin simply said it was covered in blood, and that he did not think to pick it up—and that it was no longer there the following day. The killer then rushed off, too fast for him to see much. It was still dark." He shot another nervous glance around, then he gripped the side of the door, as though prepared to shut and bolt the gate on me. "I should go, young mistress."

My strength had drained away, setting my knees wobbling. "Thank you," I said under my breath, barely audible over the pitter-pattering rain. "You have been more than helpful—"

"Please don't tell Lord Shin I told you any of this!"

"Of course not," I said, and added, "It would be best to pretend this conversation never occurred. But I will make sure that no one questions Lord Shin any further."

As soon as I turned, the gate door snapped shut, and I dropped my mask. For a long moment, I stood outside the mansion, anchored there by what I'd just learned. Father believed he had seen the killer, and it was around the time Crown Prince Jangheon was wandering the capital. Was the prince the suspect he'd collided with? Yet Father seemed convinced of the prince's innocence. Why was that?

My mind stilled before a possible answer: *Could my father be the prince's alibi?*

The rain suddenly stopped as a shadow engulfed me, startling me back to the present—to the unexpected sight of Eojin by my side, holding a large straw cloak over my head.

"Inspector Seo?" I said. "What are you doing here?"

He continued to gaze ahead at Father's residence. Slowly releasing the cloak, which settled around my head, he asked, "What brought you all the way here in this weather?"

"There was something I wanted to clarify regarding my father. My mother told me—"

"Let's find shelter first." He paused as rain pelted down on his police hat, drenching his robe, then he glanced at me. "Have you eaten?"

I blinked. "Begging your pardon?"

He gave the cloak a slight tug, and the entire thing fell over my face, threatening to swallow me whole. I at once pushed it back and caught a playful half smile disappear from his lips. "Why are you here, nauri?" I asked again.

"We had spare cloaks in the bureau, and you looked in need of one. It took a while to find you, though." Casting one last glance at the residence, he turned and strolled away, and I watched him go in puzzlement. "Come, Nurse Hyeon. I'll buy you a warm meal."

"Why—"

"I have questions to ask, things to tell you. And this case won't solve itself if you fall ill."

I sat under the thatched roof awning of a nearby tavern. Determined not to be caught again with the young inspector, I kept the cloak so pulled over my face that all I could see was Eojin's robe, a glimpse of his jaw, and raindrops still falling from the brim of his hat.

"So why did you visit your father's abode?" Eojin asked.

As we waited for our meal, I told him everything I'd learned from Father's gatekeeper, my voice pitched low for Eojin's ears alone. And whenever someone passed by, I paused, then leaned over the table to whisper the rest to him.

"Would you not agree with me, nauri?" I said, a bit too aggressively. "My father is the prince's alibi, which makes His Highness innocent. So my question is, why does the prince not publicize this truth? He has an alibi; he couldn't be the killer."

"I imagine that if His Highness exposes his alibi, it would admit he illegally left the palace that night. Perhaps he is more afraid of the king's wrath than the rumors." A long pause followed, and I could almost hear the wheels of his mind turning. "And your father . . . he has strong connections to the Old Doctrine faction. They are the prince's rival, and your father likely does not wish to be tied to His Highness in any way."

Our conversation came to a standstill when our meal arrived, black earthenware bowls of gukbap, along with side dishes. My stomach grumbled, and I realized I hadn't eaten all day. I ate my favorite meat bits first, then took a spoonful of boiled rice soup, then another, and noticed

Eojin wasn't eating. He looked preoccupied, saying nothing until at last he murmured:

"Was it difficult? Growing up as Lord Shin's daughter."

The spoon stilled in my hand, uneasiness stirring in my chest. "I'm not really his daughter. Well, I am. But I'm a bastard."

"He's still your father. You are still his daughter."

A mirthless laugh escaped me. "I'm nothing but a vulgar commoner, and that's all he sees." When Eojin remained quiet, I regretted how much I'd said, but told myself that I didn't care. It didn't matter what he thought of me. We'd partnered to solve a crime, not to become friends.

"My mother always taught me about 'gong,' that everyone is equal," Eojin said, his voice quiet and distant—as though he were speaking of someone from long ago. "She said that every person is born a child of heaven and earth, that none of us are different. History proves it, too; slaves who fought during wartime could rise to become ministers or generals." A quiet laugh escaped him. "My grandmother suggested that slaves ought to kill their master and burn the record of their slave status, and live free from the whip."

I peered up from beneath the straw cloak, curious about his strange family. Eojin was sitting straight, his shoulders drawn back, the look of perfect composure, and yet his lashes were downcast.

"I never knew, until Mother passed, that she was a cheonmin, a vulgar commoner. Father had eloped with her, since intermarriage between classes is prohibited. When she died, our wealthy relatives came to slander and celebrate her passing. Father broke every pot and bowl in outrage . . ." Eojin turned a hand over and stared at the little scars littering his palm—scars that made me wonder whether we had more in common than I'd first imagined.

"I apologize if I offend, but I never liked your father very much," he said under his breath, now holding a pair of chopsticks. "I've watched the way he's mishandled appeals; he's corrupt and unfair, prone to accepting bribes. I wouldn't care too much about what he thinks of you."

I sat very still, afraid to move, afraid to feel the weight of his words.

Afraid to agree with him.

I'd never thought of Father in Eojin's perspective before—as a man who fell very short of what was good and honorable.

Eojin used his chopsticks to pick out the delicious bits of meat from his untouched soup and move them into my bowl. Like I was someone he cared for. But of course he cared for me—his informant, his only source of palace intelligence.

Casually, he switched the stream of our conversation. "I'd like to question your father about the Hyeminseo case. But only if you're comfortable with me doing so."

"You may . . ." I said, trying to reorient myself. "As long as he doesn't connect me to you."

"Of course. I'll inform him that a witness saw him that night."

"Inspector!" A frantic shout pierced the air, cutting our conversation short. "Inspector Seo!"

It was a police officer bolting through the rain-soaked crowd. He had one hand clutching the back of his hat, the other wiping droplets from his face. Before he could see who I was, I lowered the cloak even further over my face. In its shadow, I listened to his footsteps splashing through the puddles, halting right before us.

"Inspector! Thank goodness I found you!" he cried, out of breath. "The entire bureau is looking for you!"

"What is it?" Eojin asked, his voice sharp.

"Commander Song and other officers have gone ahead. I was ordered to find you at once." He paused to collect his breath some more, and then he spoke on, his voice trembling. "Two men were fishing on Han River when they found a body. It is another palace woman!"

Eojin slapped his hand onto the table, leaving coins behind. "Do not follow. Too many will notice you," he quietly said to me. Then he disappeared into the blue of falling rain.

I obeyed Eojin for only a few minutes, then rushed to my feet. I had to see the dead woman with my own eyes, for who knew what the commander might do? He might bury the dead before the dead could even speak.

Thick mist hung over Han River, obscuring the huts clustered along the riverbank as well as the long wooden boats docked along the shore, their bamboo sails piercing the sky like hundreds of needles.

I discreetly followed the three silhouettes—Eojin, the

police officer, and a damo carrying a stretcher. My thighs burned from the work of stepping in and out of ankle-deep mud. I'd slipped a few times already. The hem of my skirt was soggy brown, and somehow blobs of dark slush had flicked onto my face. The grime slid against my palm each time I attempted to wipe aside my soaked hair.

More human figures soon materialized in the gloom ahead. I heard Commander Song's voice before I saw him, directing officers to split up into four directions and to travel by foot and by boat to search for evidence. When I drew close enough, I only saw him for a moment, his strong stature and white beard. Then he was gone, his back disappearing through a shroud of fog.

"This way, nauri." The officer led Eojin and the damo to a boat manned by a weather-worn fisherman. "The corpse is on the other side."

I hurried closer, and I was able to glimpse the damo's face. A pair of wide-set eyes met mine. I knew this girl.

"Sulbi-yah!" I called out.

"Uinyeo-nim!" she cried, and her distraught face lit up. Eojin snapped around just then. "What are you doing here?" she asked.

Picking up my skirt, I pushed my legs harder until I stood before Sulbi. "Sulbi-yah, I heard what happened. Do you need assistance—"

"Who are you?" the officer growled. "This is a police matter!"

"I couldn't help but overhear, sir, that a palace woman

has been killed." I fixed my unwavering gaze on the man, trying not to look at Eojin, whose eyes I could feel boring into me. "I may be of help, as I am a nae-uinyeo."

The police officer scoffed. "You absolutely cannot—"

"She may join us," Eojin said.

"She—she may?" The officer stared, blinking like a fish. "Her?"

"Yes, her."

Without further delay, we made our way to the boat, and my stomach rocked the moment my feet stepped inside, the wooden floor so unsteady it was like I was attempting to stand on shifting waves. But I managed to keep my balance and found a seat next to Sulbi at the far end, while the men sat at the head of the narrow but long boat.

"Who is the victim?" I whispered.

"I don't know yet," she replied. "And neither do the officers, I'd gather. They only know she was a palace woman by her dress. They haven't searched her for an identification tag."

"Why not?"

"You know the law. Confucian etiquette. Police officers are forbidden from touching women suspects and victims." Sulbi rubbed her palm furiously against her skirt. Under her breath, for my ears alone, she said, "I am so sick of touching dead women, but women are killed all the time."

Silence, along with the blue mist, hung over us and the inky black waves. Silence, except for the water rippling around the oars.

"Do you know how she died yet?" I asked my companion, flicking a glance at Eojin. His shoulders looked tense, his face slightly turned our way, like he was eavesdropping. "Or whether she might be connected to the Hyeminseo massacre?"

"I know she was bludgeoned on the head and discovered lying on the riverbank with her face in the water," Sulbi replied. "The anonymous handbills were also found again, pasted onto public walls nearby."

"There!" cried the fisherman. "I see them."

The fog parted like hazy curtains, unveiling a small crowd of police officers huddled on the riverbank, their figures hiding the corpse from my view. All I could see was the top of her hair and the tips of her feet—one with a shoe on, the other bare.

The moment we docked and the men heaved the boat onto shore, Sulbi held my hand to keep my balance steady. As soon as my feet hit the mud, I looked up, and this time the human wall of officers had parted, just enough for me to catch a glimpse of a silk skirt, turquoise blue. A blue so distinct that my chest tightened and breathing became difficult.

It wasn't just a palace woman.

It was a palace nurse.

My steps quickened, and as the police officers stepped further back for Eojin, I found myself staring down at the body of a young woman, still lying on her front, her face in the mud. No one had flipped her around. *Confucian etiquette,* Sulbi's explanation echoed in my ear.

"Help me turn her," I said, and Sulbi nodded.

Together, we managed to turn her onto her back, revealing blue-tinged skin covered in mud. I crouched and touched her wrist—and a jolt of alertness ran through me.

A faint pulse, a real pulse, beat under the pressure of my fingers.

At once, I tilted her chin and head back. I leaned over her, placing my cheek near her mouth, and looked along her chest.

"She's still alive," I gasped.

A shadowy figure crouched right next to me, close enough that the side of his robe brushed along my arm. Eojin.

"She's alive?" Frowning, he reexamined the victim. "How could she be? Someone held her underwater until she drowned. There are fingermark bruises on her neck."

"Well, she didn't die," I snapped. "The killer must have mistaken her for dead, when she had only lost consciousness."

"What should we do?" Sulbi asked, looking overwhelmed.

"Could you find out who she is?" Eojin asked.

"Yeh." Sulbi crouched on the other side of the woman, her trembling hands wandering along the white apron. Hand slipping into a pocket, she then drew out a wooden identification tag. "She is indeed a palace nurse. Her name is Nurse Kyunghee."

I had never heard of a Nurse Kyunghee. She likely worked on the days alternate to mine. And if we didn't act soon, we would lose her. But how did one deal with a near-drowning incident?

A rush of anxiety nearly blanked my mind, but I held tight onto the threads of my attention and focused. I flipped through the pages of all that I'd learned, all the pages I'd memorized in my studies. "We need to fully revive her breathing. At once," I finally said.

Sulbi nodded eagerly. "I can assist with that, uinyeo-nim." With skilled movement, she pinched the nurse's nose, then sealed her mouth over hers, blowing into her lungs.

I kept my fingers on Nurse Kyunghee's pulse, listening closely, and after a long and excruciating few minutes, her body heaved, and a gasp exploded from her mouth. Violent coughs ensued, pink froth foaming at her lips. Agony ripped her expression as she clutched at her chest, struggling for air, like she was still drowning. Sulbi and I remained by her side, trying to calm the wild panic in her eyes.

"What is g-going on?" Nurse Kyunghee cried. "W-w-what happened?"

"You were attacked," Eojin said gently. "Do you have any memory of what occurred?"

For a long moment, the nurse broke into a fury of coughs, and when Eojin asked her the second time, she at last replied.

"I—I only remember waiting for Aram." The words rattled as she struggled to breathe. Her red-rimmed eyes darted around. "We always travel to the palace together. I don't remember anything other than that . . . Waiting for Aram."

Aram. The name was so familiar . . . but why?

"Where is Aram, then?" I asked.

"I—I don't know."

"Perhaps she either ran to escape the attacker," Eojin murmured, "or she never left her home in the first place."

A ripple of whispers erupted among the officers, five of them in total, standing around us.

Eojin slowly rose to his feet and placed his hand on the hilt of his sword, which hung at his side. "Damo Sulbi, do all you can to stabilize Nurse Kyunghee." He glanced at the other officers. "Two of you, keep guard of the victim; nothing must happen to her. And the rest of you, continue to search for the killer. I will go to the home of Nurse Aram."

"If you wish, nauri, I will direct you to Nurse Aram's home," came a hesitant voice. It was the fisherman. "She lives not too far away."

"Does she live alone?" Eojin asked.

"Yeh, most of the time. Her father is a fellow fisherman who is almost always out at sea."

Eojin turned his gaze to me, as though attempting to ask, *Do you know her?*

I rose to my feet and, dragging up my mud-damp skirt, trudged over to Eojin. Under my breath, face slightly turned to the side so that the officers couldn't read my lips, I said, "I don't work on the same day as Nurse Aram, yet her name is familiar to me. I'm not sure why."

"Come with me, then," Eojin replied, his voice as quiet. "Perhaps she is still at home."

———

"I know both of them, Nurse Kyunghee and Nurse Aram." The fisherman scurried down the riverbank alongside Eojin and me. "We made an arrangement, you see. Every other day, they would meet me at my boat, and I would bring them over to the other side."

"They live quite a distance away from the capital," Eojin observed.

"It isn't unusual," I pointed out. "Many nurses are too poor to find housing in the capital."

"This way, nauri." The fisherman gestured away from the river, toward a small path that led inland. At the end of the path was a thatch-roofed hut with yellow clay walls, and beyond it, pine trees and the undulating hills.

"So, you saw the two nurses every other day," Eojin continued. "You must have caught snippets of their conversations when they rode in your boat."

The fisherman's steps slowed, and a look of consternation clouded his brows. "The strangest thing is, nauri," he whispered, "they never once spoke on the boat. Each time I looked at them, they seemed stiff with terror, like I was rowing them to the slaughterhouse." He shook his head, quickening his steps again. "They weren't always like that, though."

"What do you mean?" I asked.

"I remembered them to be such bright and cheerful

young women. They used to sit in my boat chatting about their studies, tests, and noblemen who had taken interest in them. And then, one day, they suddenly went quiet. Like the light had been blown out of them."

"When was this?" There was a sudden gruffness to Eojin's voice, along with a sharpened focus to his eyes.

The fisherman pinched his brows. "When was it . . . Let me think . . . Around last year? Sometime early last year."

"Perhaps around the new year?"

"Likely, yes."

Eojin shook his head, as though in disbelief—as though the fisherman had said something profound. I was itching to ask his thoughts when our guide hurried forward and said, "We're here, nauri!"

Eojin and I stood before the lone hut. Nothing looked amiss, except there were two tracks of footprints in the mud, both heading toward the hut, then away from it. Following the trail, we arrived before the hanji-screened door. Eojin rapped his fist against the door frame.

"Nurse Aram. Are you in?" His voice was firm and resounding. "I am Inspector Seo, come from the Capital Police Bureau."

We waited.

No sounds came in response. No shuffling, not even a rustle or a murmur.

"It seems no one is home?" I said.

Eojin held the brass door handle and gave it a little tug. The door moved. "Yet her home was left unlocked," he added.

He slid the door aside, wood rumbling as it opened onto a single room filled with shadows. The gray daylight flooded in and illuminated the back of a young woman slumped facedown over a low-legged table, arms limp by her sides.

"She's asleep?" The fisherman joined us to peek in, then took a stumbling step back. "She—she must be asleep?"

The frigid darkness lurking within the hut leaked into me, drip by drip, until my blood felt cold and I could hardly move. "We should go in," I whispered to Eojin.

In one smooth motion, he drew his sword from his sash belt, flicked the hilt out from the scabbard, blade gleaming as he stepped inside. I held my breath, waiting for a sudden motion, a killer leaping out at him. But everything remained still within—the woman slumped over the table, the unlit candle by her side, the baskets hanging on the wall. Everything was lifelessly still.

Eojin crouched before the woman, and I at once slipped off my wooden rain sandals and stepped inside. "Is she alive, nauri—"

I froze. Wetness soaked through my socks, pooling around my toes. My wide-eyed stare adjusted to the darkness, and it was then that I saw it. The black trail of liquid that flowed from the woman's form and pooled right under my feet. *It is just blood,* I said to myself as my heart pounded. *You have seen blood a thousand times before.*

"She is dead," Eojin whispered, his face half silhouette, half grayish-blue light.

I slipped off my socks, then proceeded in, barefoot and cautious. I cracked a screened window open—more gray light poured into the room, enough for me to see the turquoise blue of the dead woman's uniform. She had been dressed for work, yet something had stopped her from leaving the house.

Eojin motioned for me to come closer. "Would you help me get a better look?"

He had placed the hilt of his sword under the corpse, attempting to lift her, as he could not touch—though he had touched me before, I suddenly remembered, when he'd helped me over the Hyeminseo wall, and when he had helped me mount his horse. I hurried over to assist, holding the woman's shoulder as I lifted her head up by the forehead, grimacing at the cold sensation of her skin. She was dead; I didn't need to feel her pulse to know. A cloudy film had developed over her eyes.

And someone had slit her throat open.

"Who would do such a thing?" I whispered. The same question that had haunted me at the Hyeminseo. "What kind of monster would do this?"

"I'm not sure," Eojin replied, both of us staring at the corpse. "But of one thing I am certain: Nurse Aram knew her killer. She unlocked the door and permitted the culprit to enter. And she prepared tea for herself and her guest."

On the table was a teapot I hadn't noticed earlier, along with two drinking bowls. Both of them were still filled. A whitish substance lay at the bottom of one of the bowls.

"May I lay the corpse back down, nauri?" I asked.

Eojin withdrew the hilt of his sword, and nodded.

I returned the body to its original position. My hands free, I picked up my norigae chimtong and and opened it. I slipped out a silver needle, then picked up the drinking bowl containing the odd substance. I dipped the needle in and watched as a black stain crept up the silver point.

"She was poisoned," I whispered.

His gaze remained unwavering on the corpse. "How do you know?"

"We use this method often at the Hyeminseo. When we suspect a patient was poisoned, we insert a silver pin into the patient's mouth." I held out the needle to him, which he took and examined closely. "Silver tarnishes when exposed to sulfur. And sulfur-based sayak is the poison most easily obtained in the capital."

"So Nurse Aram was poisoned . . . likely slipped into her tea when she wasn't looking. And once she was debilitated—" Eojin motioned at Nurse Aram's perfectly combed hair, only slightly disheveled at the back—"the killer grabbed her by the hair right here, and raised her head to slit her throat."

"Three palace women attacked," I said, feeling sick to my stomach. "Three attacked, two killed, along with at least three witnesses. And the anonymous handbills accusing the prince have spread throughout the capital again, I am told."

"Yes. I believe these acts of violence are all connected somehow."

"But how . . ." The answer seemed so close, just beyond the veil of shadows, and I wished I could tear it down. I wanted to *know*.

I slipped my hand into the nurse's apron, pulling out her identification tag. She was indeed Nurse Aram.

"Why is her name so familiar?" I whispered.

Frustration gnawed at me. I rose to my feet, and crossing my arms, I stared blankly ahead, trying hard to remember. I had never met Nurse Aram or Nurse Kyunghee before, as we worked on alternate days; we would never have crossed paths. Someone must have mentioned her name to me, then . . . but who? A memory flickered, brushing along the edge of my mind.

Before I could grasp it, a whisper came from the door. "She is dead?"

Eojin and I jolted around to see Nurse Kyunghee, dripping with river water, her black hair clinging to the sides of her face like seaweed. Her skin still bluish, her eyes as wide and empty as two fresh graves. Sulbi appeared by her side, out of breath.

"I apologize, Inspector!" the damo said. "She insisted on coming. She started screaming, and the officers ordered me to bring her to you."

Eojin walked over to Nurse Kyunghee, and I watched

as a tremor shook her hands, then crawled up her entire body. Her eyes were fixed upon the corpse slumped over the table. Her friend.

"I know why she is dead." Her voice shook, and then she covered her face with her mud-stained hands. "And I know why I must die, too."

10

The lingering scent of death soaked deep into my thoughts.

What horrible rage could possibly drive someone to bludgeon a woman, and then hold her head beneath the water until she drowned? What had kept the culprit from hesitating, from extending mercy as Kyunghee must have thrashed in the water, desperate to come up for air?

The thought that the truth was finally within our reach left me jittery. Nurse Kyunghee knew the answers; the investigation would soon be over.

I pulled a dry straw cloak from the storage room wall and stepped out into the yard, only to see two police officers backing Nurse Kyunghee against the wall. Their arms were crossed, their voices sharp and demanding:

"So? Who did this to you?"

"You must remember *something*. Man or woman? Tall or short?"

The cloak nearly fell from my arm as I rushed over to the river-drenched nurse. Stepping between her and the two officers, I bowed my head and politely said, "Please, this woman isn't well. She needs to be brought to the Hyeminseo, and perhaps you can question her afterward."

The two men hesitated, then grumbled as they stalked off to guard the brushwood gate.

"Here." I wrapped my straw cloak around Nurse Kyunghee's shivering figure. The rain had stopped, but I was troubled by the sound of her breath still rattling in her chest. She had not drowned, but I knew of patients who had died afterward from resulting complications. "Come, you should sit down."

I led her to the raised platform, a low wooden structure where her friend had likely eaten her meals on sunny days, and never would again. We sat down, and in the quiet that fell between us, I followed the direction of her gaze—it went beyond the yard and back into the hut, where the silhouette of the dead still lingered.

"There is no need to speak until you're ready," I whispered.

Kyunghee remained unresponsive, her staring eyes glazed over and her pale lips slightly parted, her breath continuing to rattle in and out. Expecting another hour or more of silence, I sat up straight and crossed my ankles, prepared to wait.

Eojin had left with Damo Sulbi for some reason, but it wasn't long before I saw him reappear down the path. His arms were folded and his brows furrowed as he stepped into the yard.

"Nauri," I called out as he approached. He flicked a glance my way, his brows lifting. "Nurse Kyunghee needs medical attention."

"Yes, of course. I've sent Damo Sulbi to inform the commander," he replied, "and to prepare transportation on the other side of the river. We will bring her to the Hyeminseo as soon as they arrive."

I glanced at Nurse Kyunghee, wanting to reassure her, and was surprised to see her turning her head, her stare latching on to the inspector.

"I am ready," came her voice, a scratchy whisper. "I'm ready to talk now."

Eojin and I exchanged a frantic glance. He walked over, though not too close, then gathered his hands behind his back. "I know this is difficult to talk about," he said, his voice low-toned and as gentle as he could make it. "You can take your time."

Kyunghee nodded stiffly.

"Could you tell me more about what you meant?" he asked. "You said you knew why Nurse Aram died, and that you, too, ought to die."

She clasped her hands together, wringing her fingers like they were secrets that needed to be twisted out of her. "It is in the mountain somewhere—" She gave me a nervous glance. "Our secret."

"You can tell us this secret," I whispered. "If it is what

155

led to your near death, perhaps sharing it with us will lead to your safety."

Staring down at her white knuckles, she said, "Court Lady Ahnbi, Nurse Aram, and I . . . we were witnesses."

I tensed as a prickle ran down my back.

"Witnesses to what?" Eojin asked slowly.

Her shoulders rose and closed in around her, as though she wanted to disappear. "A . . . a murder." A note of devastation twisted her voice, and her features crumpled. "He was in a fit of rage over his father, and . . . he took his anger out on an innocent nurse. The Crown P-Prince . . . d-decapitated her . . . and rode off with her head."

Nausea stirred in the pit of my stomach. The prince wouldn't do such a thing. I had seen him holding a puppy so gently in his arms, and he hadn't at all looked like a murderer. Lady Hyegyoung had also assured me of his innocence, and I *trusted* her. Yet Eojin's expression only tightened, and a focused alertness lit his eyes. He believed her.

"Then what happened?" he asked.

"We ran away and hid. We knew the prince had seen our faces. He knew we were witnesses." Kyunghee dug her trembling fingers into her eyes, perhaps trying to blot away a vision. "Court Lady Ahnbi left to seek advice for us. We didn't know what to do." A shuddering breath escaped her as she shook her head. "Oh gods, I wish we hadn't listened to her."

"What did she tell you to do?"

"Court Lady Ahnbi returned and ordered us to—" Her voice shook. "To pretend we saw nothing. She said that if we did not, there would only be more blood. *Our* blood! If we didn't wish to die, too, we had to make it so that nothing had happened."

My mind had gone blank, unable to process what I was hearing. It was one thing to hear rumors about the blood-stained palace, whispers carried in the roaming wind, and quite another thing to hear an eyewitness testimony—if Kyunghee was telling the truth. But why would she lie?

"When did this occur?"

"Last year," she said. "On the first lunar month."

A shadow dropped over Eojin's face. "What happened to the victim's body?"

A cough-ridden sob escaped her. "I . . . I don't know. Someone hid the corpse somewhere . . . It's not my fault! What were we to do? I am a mere servant. No one in my position would dare go against the Crown Prince." Her eyes whirled to me, wild with guilt. "You wouldn't, either. You wouldn't have tried to stop him!"

"Of course not," I whispered, and a part of me believed it.

"Ever since that nurse's death," Nurse Kyunghee went on, "we've *tried* to find the body. To give her a proper burial. Aram and I . . . we searched the mountains several times, but she was nowhere to be found."

The weight of Nurse Kyunghee's testimony pressed in around us, the horror of her tale prickling like icicles against my tender skin. "What was the nurse's name?" I asked. "The one whom—" I couldn't finish my sentence. *The one whom the prince killed.*

"It was Nurse Hyo-ok."

I shook my head—I'd never heard this name before.

"Nurse Kyunghee." Eojin's voice was quiet, almost protective. "Is there anything else you want me to know?"

"I . . ." She stared down at her hands. "I remembered lending Nurse Hyo-ok my handkerchief. I didn't want the crime to be traced back to me, so before the body disappeared, I ran back and searched her pockets, and I found a note."

"A note?"

"It . . . it was a note to Physician Khun."

Shock jabbed under my ribs. "Physician Khun?" I whispered.

Kyunghee sent another glance my way. "Nurse Hyo-ok was his mother."

"What did the note say?" I asked.

"I d-don't know. I burned it at once."

"You do know," Eojin said. "You must know. You would have read it first, I'm sure."

She hesitated, her gaze darting around, then at last she said, "It was an ordinary note."

"What did it say?" Eojin pressed.

It took a few moments, then finally Nurse Kyunghee replied, her voice so low I could hardly hear her. "She wrote, *Khun Muyeong, I am concerned for you since you have not talked to me for a while. You avoid me in the palace, ashamed to be seen with your own mother.*" A faraway, haunted look fogged Kyunghee's face. "*You say you are a grown man now, and do not wish to be seen as a mother's little boy. Yet, like a child, you keep company with childish friends who enjoy the practice of drinking and womanizing. I warned you not to befriend such people* . . . And that was it."

I tilted my head to the side, sensing something important lurking under these words. But I couldn't put my finger on what that was.

"Do you and Nurse Aram know Physician Khun?" Eojin asked.

"Yes," she replied. "Although not well; we've only seen him once or twice, since we work on alternate days. But Court Lady Ahnbi always spoke of him when we were together."

"Do you know Nurse Inyeong? The one who reported the massacre?" I asked, then quickly added, "Or my mentor, Nurse Jeongsu? She works at the Hyeminseo."

Kyunghee paused, a frown knotting her brows. "I don't think so. Neither of their names are familiar to me." We all fell silent, and at the sound of rippling water, I looked over to see the silhouette of approaching police officers in two boats.

"They're here," Eojin said.

"Please!" Kyunghee jolted up onto her feet. "Do not tell the commander about the prince. I have heard of peasants being killed for defaming a royal—"

"I will not." His voice was firm, a promise. But when Kyunghee stumbled away, moving toward the brushwood fence, he uttered under his breath, "Not yet."

I glanced at him, and he read the question in my eyes.

"If what she said is true," Eojin said, for my ears alone, "then the prince must be stopped."

"But how?" Not even speaking in a whisper seemed quiet enough. "What if the king chooses to dismiss it? The Crown Prince, killer or not, is still his son. It would look bad for him and his family."

A resolute look hardened in his face. "The Old Doctrine. They are the leading faction, and desperate to rid the kingdom of the prince. His ideas are too revolutionary for them, and he is too determined to distribute their consolidated power to the other factions. Should I provide the Old Doctrine with infallible evidence of His Highness's violent crimes, they will devour him alive. To turn the king against his son, we will have to move those around His Majesty."

I didn't like this. I ran a hand over my throat, wishing suddenly that this was just a nightmare. I had begun the task of assisting Eojin thinking I could find the truth without being scathed. Yet now Lady Hyegyoung's warning hung over me, too close to my skin. Her plea that I not disturb the royal family.

It was at the brink of my tongue, a remark about how I no longer wished to assist, that this investigation was getting out of hand. But then a memory gasped to the surface of my mind. "I remember," I whispered. "I remember why Nurse Aram's name was so familiar."

Eojin frowned. "Why?"

Lady Hyegyoung had mentioned her to me. "She was Madam Mun's spy as well." My heart thrummed fast; I was afraid, but unable to look away from the gleaming thread that connected the women. "Court Lady Ahnbi and Nurse Aram, they were both her spies."

The look on Eojin's face told me that he was thinking the same thing: The death of one spy might be a coincidence, but the death of two?

I picked up the hem of my skirt and hurried over to Nurse Kyunghee. She was staring out at the river.

"Uinyeo-nim." I sounded breathless. "I have one last question. Did Madam Mun use you as her spy?"

Her lips thinned, and a bitter look darkened her eyes. "She blackmailed us into spying for her. Somehow she knew what we had done—or, rather, had not done."

I barely managed to hold in my gasp. Madam Mun had a knack for blackmailing. And for some reason, I was certain that when the prince had killed and decapitated the nurse last year, Court Lady Ahnbi had run to her mistress for advice. And Madam Mun must have immediately wondered how she could use this tale of horror to her own advantage.

———

"Wait for me at the inn."

I glanced at Eojin. He was staring past the crowd of ailing peasants at the Hyeminseo, at the seventh sliding door to the right. It was the room we had settled Nurse Kyunghee in, guarded now by police officers.

"I need to report back to the commander," he said under his breath, "but once I am done, there is something I need to tell you."

I ran an uneasy hand over my skirt. The last time he'd spoken to me at the inn, he had revealed that he was not a servant as I was, but a police inspector. I wondered what else he hadn't told me. "Very well," I replied. "I suppose the inn is to be our command post."

His lips twitched: a near smile. "I suppose so."

We went our separate ways, and I quickened my steps, desperate to be away from the market chaos. When I finally stepped out of the fort and onto the silent road, I took in a deep breath. After days of what seemed like finding only a trail of bewildering questions, we had finally caught a glimpse of the truth. A truth so crisp and clarifying, it was like having spent days with fog in my eyes, only to finally rub it out for the barest moment to truly see. And I wanted to see more.

We were one step closer to the truth.

Stretching my arm up to the sky, I reached for it with my other hand to loosen the knotted tension in my back.

A faint rustle shuddered through the reeds next to me, and I froze.

I glanced behind me only to find an empty road that curved out of sight around a field of tall grass, and mist that rippled like restless spirits.

"Just the wind," I murmured, lowering my arms, my heart thrumming at the memory of the peasant who had died out here.

I took another step forward, then heard it again—the rustling of grass, then the squelch of mud under footsteps. Someone had stepped out of the reed field behind me.

The footfalls continued toward me, closer, and everything in me whispered, *You were followed*. Grabbing my skirt,

I quickened my steps, long strides that turned into a run as I heard the person behind me pick up speed.

The thick, wet ground slipped under my feet, and when it stole my shoe, I risked a glance over my shoulder. A gasp escaped me at the sight of a gentleman—for he was dressed as one—wearing a tall black hat, the wide brim lowered over his brow. A red scarf was tied around his face.

And he was garbed in a crisp white robe that was streaked with blood.

Run! my mind screamed, and I managed to turn and bolt forward.

Numb with terror, I couldn't tell how far I'd run, or why I was scrabbling on all fours, or when I'd left the road. I shoved aside feathery plumes as I dashed across the field, and when I glanced behind to see if I was alone, a hand shot out, grabbed my collar and threw me down. My shoulder hit the ground, and I rolled onto my back in time to see a blade gleaming above like a bared fang.

A whimper escaped me. I squeezed my eyes shut as I waited to feel the hard steel slice through me. But then I heard a loud thud and a grunt. When I opened my eyes, I saw nothing but the swaying reeds and the pale sky.

Scrambling onto my unsteady legs, I glanced around until my gaze arrested upon a tall and familiar figure. It was the young inspector, his chest heaving as though he had sprinted all the way here. There was no time to wonder how he'd even found me, for the attacker rose to his feet, the side of his robe covered in mud from having been shoved away, pushed onto the ground.

Eojin unlocked his sword, a whisper of cold steel. "Stay back."

The gentleman remained wordless and, with graceful ease, angled his own sword horizontally, aimed at Eojin's heart.

"Hide," Eojin whispered, and I knew he was speaking to me, though his gaze remained unwavering on the culprit before him.

In one smooth motion, Eojin drew his sword out and tossed the scabbard aside. Both hands on the handle, he rushed forward with startling speed, closing the twenty feet of grass between them quickly. His blade flashed as he struck, but the gentleman parried, steel clashing against steel. The brilliant ring reverberated in my bones. Everything was happening so fast I could hardly follow. I lost all thought of hiding as I watched the explosion of fleeting movements; one moment they were hilt to hilt, the next they were staggering back, and a second later, they were in the air, robes billowing, swords clanging.

Suddenly a strip of blood spurted through the air, followed by a moment of silence and stillness. *Whose blood was that?*

The gentleman staggered, and right then, Eojin lunged forward to strike. The attacker's sword whirled off and disappeared into the undulating sea of tall grass.

"Who are you?" Eojin inched toward his opponent, blade angled at the ready. "Tell me now."

The gentleman remained silent, motionless as he seemed to be staring at Eojin, taking in the sight of him, remembering every detail of his face. Then he turned and ran in the direction of his sword, snatched it up, and continued to run, his shoulder gleaming bright red with blood.

Once the gentleman vanished, I raced over. Reeds whipped my face, and I was out of breath by the time I stood before Eojin. He was bent forward, hands on his knees as sweat gleamed from under the brim of his police hat.

"Shouldn't we catch him?" I asked.

"Can't risk it," Eojin rasped. "He could slip back into the field and hide. The moment I leave, he'll come back for you."

"But I could follow you—"

My attention froze on the slash across Eojin's robe. I'd thought only the attacker had been injured, but I watched as a dark stain blossomed on the blue silk, along his lower leg. My heart hammered against my chest; Eojin could have died, and the thought left my knees weak.

"You're—you're bleeding," I choked out.

"I'm fine. A small cut." He wiped his brow, then drew himself up to his full height. "I should have wounded him somewhere more visible. A mark to search for on our suspects." He staggered past me, brows furrowed in concentration as he stared at the nearby forest where the man had disappeared. "One thing is certain about the culprit. He knows how to fight."

It was difficult to focus on anything else besides Eojin's bloodstained robe billowing in the breeze.

"Has Physician Khun ever mentioned learning how to wield a sword?" he asked.

It took a moment for his question to register. I dragged my gaze away from Eojin and onto the forest ahead. "No, but Physician Khun had a book on military arts in his home. He could be a self-taught swordsman."

"And a very skilled one at that. It seems unlikely, but if it is true, Khun does have motive," Eojin murmured. "His mother was killed, and the women recently murdered were witnesses to his mother's death."

"But they were only witnesses . . . They helped cover up the murder, yet it wasn't done out of malice."

"We don't know the full story yet. I have a feeling there is more to this than what Nurse Kyunghee told us."

I glanced back down at his slashed robe, hesitated, then asked, "Do you want me to inspect your wound?"

"It's growing dark. It would be unwise to linger out here any longer." Staggering off, he searched for something in the reeds, then returned with his scabbard, his sword now sheathed and hanging by his side. "We should leave."

I walked close by his side, ready to offer him assistance, and as we waded through the vast field a question resurfaced. "How did you find me?"

"I saw your shoe." He continued to survey our periphery, to ensure that we were alone. "And your tracks disappeared into the reed field."

"But you went to the police bureau."

"I changed my mind." His voice grew hesitant. Then looking at me from beneath his lashes, he murmured, "I wanted to make sure you arrived at the inn safe. I'm not so thoughtless as to have left you alone right after a new murder."

Bewilderment tugged at me as I followed him out onto the road where my shoe still was. He crouched despite his wound and pulled it free from the mud; I gingerly held his shoulder for balance as he slipped the wooden namak shoe onto my foot.

"You need to be more careful," he said, rising to his feet. He looked over his shoulder once again at the reed field, in the direction the attacker had escaped. "Whoever it was knows how to wield a sword, and knows that you are involved. It won't be the last time they come for you."

"Or you," I said. "You're in as much danger as I am."

At last our eyes met. "I suppose so," he whispered.

"But never fear. Next time it will be my turn."

"Your turn?"

"To watch out for *you*."

I'd spoken without thought. But he didn't laugh my words away, rather seemed to be soberly examining my offer. "Is that a promise?"

I blinked and hesitated for a moment. "It is."

He held out his hand. I stared at it, never having made a pact with anyone before. A handshake was done between soldiers on battlefields, as a promise to be comrades. Still, I reached out.

His warm fingers wrapped around my hand, his scarred palm pressed into mine, and we shook.

"When the time comes," he said quietly, holding my

gaze the way he held my hand. "You watch out for me. And I will always watch out for you."

———

Rain pelted against the hanji screen of the inn room. We'd made it inside just in time.

"So," I said, sitting down. "What did you mean to tell me before at the Hyeminseo?"

The beads that hung around Eojin's hat swayed as he sat down before me, and as he shifted his leg, he winced slightly. His wound clearly stung more than he let on. "A year and a half ago, I became an assistant to an amhaengŏsa," he said.

"A secret royal investigator," I whispered, frowning. "Is that why you were dressed as a peasant when we first met? You were undercover?"

"No." Quietly, he explained, "Working with a secret investigator taught me with what ease information can be gathered when disguised. Commoners are reluctant to speak freely to an officer, and so I was dressed as I was in order to gather information for a case, of which I am about to tell you." I waited as he paused, emotions flitting through his eyes.

"My father was the amhaengŏsa . . . When he received his assignment in '56, I went with him. It was a daring move, asking me to follow him, but he was concerned for me. Ever since I passed the exam at a young age, I became too proud, and I found myself accepted into the company of the wealthy and corrupt. He was afraid for me. He wanted me to love justice, to love the people, as much as he did. So he took me with him.

"Father's task was to simply investigate the Pyongan Province magistrate." Eojin lowered his gaze, a faraway look glazing his eyes, as though he'd disconnected himself from the memory. A memory too painful to bear. "I managed to be hired as a servant in the magistrate's office. There I intercepted a letter claiming that the Crown Prince had secretly left the palace to stay in the village, but the magistrate was too afraid to report it, too afraid to report the prince to the king. That week, a villager was found slain, and later in the forest, I found the decapitated head of a woman."

Nurse Hyo-ok, I thought at once. *The prince's victim—*

"And my father, stabbed to death."

Digging my nails into my palm, I could only stare at him; how still he sat, like he was carved out of ice. His face was now expressionless, his eyes devoid of tears, and I wondered how Eojin could speak of such horror with a straight face.

"I'd thought her to be a local nurse by the garima fixed to the crown of her head. But none of the nurses at the local medical office recognized the sketch of the woman's face. They told me she had to be a palace nurse, for her garima was made of silk."

"And then what happened?" I asked softly. "Your father was murdered. Did the magistrate conduct any sort of investigation?"

A gleam in Eojin's eyes sharpened. "He did all he could to bury the whole affair. He bribed the local police chief and witnesses, and they used a man with a criminal history as scapegoat. Blamed him for Father's death. The king believed the report, and with my father gone, I felt powerless.

"When I finally returned to the capital a few days later, I was appointed police inspector, and I questioned as many palace nurses as I could. My hope was that in finding the truth behind Nurse Hyo-ok's death, I'd uncover enough evidence to overturn the magistrate's lies. But no one would tell me anything."

"Until now," I whispered.

"Yes," he replied, his voice just as soft. "Nurse Kyunghee's testimony matches what I discovered on my own. A palace nurse, allegedly beheaded by the Crown Prince in the first lunar month of last year . . ."

I had hoped, so hoped, that the prince was somehow innocent. I had hoped this for Lady Hyegyoung's sake, and for the sake of our dynasty's future. But now I saw that hope had been naive.

"Do you truly think the prince killed—" But before I could finish my sentence, the door slid open and the scarred-lipped servant stepped in with the salt water I'd requested, along with a clean cloth and binding material. And just like before, she gave me a wink. Only this time she also asked how many children we intended to have together. At our dead silence, she awkwardly scuttled off, shutting the door behind her.

The room suddenly felt very small, the air a little too charged.

Eojin rubbed his brow, then glanced away, looking flustered.

I cleared my throat, and in a very official manner, I said, "Before we continue our discussion, I should tend to your wound, nauri."

"I can tend to myself—"

"There's no need to be embarrassed. This is my job."

"I'm not embarrassed," he mumbled, then reluctantly gestured at me to proceed.

Men wore white trousers under their robes, and where the sword had swiped at Eojin's leg, a bloody cut peeked out from beneath the slashed fabric. The discomfort of the moment slowly eased away, and my mind steadied as I examined his injury.

"The wound looks awful at a glance," I said as I dabbed away the blood with salt water. "But it's shallow and should heal on its own, if no infection occurs. You should still visit a physician later."

Once his wound was clean, I reached for the strip of fabric and wrapped it carefully around his lower leg. "As I was saying earlier," I said, to keep the both of our minds occupied, "do you really think the prince killed Physician Khun's mother, Nurse Hyo-ok?"

"I do," he replied. "And I'm not surprised. Many in the government—including my father—have sensed that the prince is prone to violent rage. It began ever since the Daerichungjung."

I bowed my head in acknowledgment. I remembered how bewildered everyone had been to hear the announcement that the king had appointed Crown Prince Jangheon as regent, even though the king was healthy enough to continue ruling without assistance.

"The prince is to be seen as ruler, but no one in court treats him like one," Eojin said. "When the prince makes a decision in court, the king vetoes it. And when the prince stalls and turns to his father for advice, he is rebuked for being a fool unable to make up his own mind. Since then, I've heard that the Crown Prince's temper has turned brittle. His anger will soon explode. Or perhaps it already has."

"Then do you think prince is also behind the Hyeminseo massacre?" I asked.

"No," he said, firm. "The anonymous handbill going around . . . I have a feeling he is being framed as an act of revenge. Even more so now that we know how the violence may have been triggered by Nurse Hyo-ok's murder."

"Then Physician Khun has to be involved. Everything is pointing to him, isn't it?"

"We need more evidence in order to convince anyone— whether it be Commander Song, the king, or the Old Doctrine faction."

I ran a finger across the old callus on my thumb. The longer I stared at Eojin, the more vivid the death of his father became in my mind's eye. Of a son holding his father, his entire world bleeding out in his arms. "But you know now, at least," I whispered, "that it is the prince who likely killed your father . . . What will you do?"

I waited, hanging on to his silence. He should say, *To seek revenge*. Filial piety was the backbone of this kingdom.

"Why are you looking at me like that?" he asked.

I blinked. "How am I looking at you?"

"As though I'm a pitiful mutt."

I hesitated before saying, "Because I know what you will do. You're going to seek revenge against the Crown Prince or die trying."

"Revenge . . ." he said under his breath. "In Li Chi's *Book of Rites*, we are told that children are duty-bound to murder their parent's killer, even if in the middle of a public road. But I have no intention of doing so." He held my gaze, his eyes lucid and clear as his conscience. "After Father's death, I realized that everything we hold dear can be taken from us, except for one thing: the lessons learned. The things Father has taught me." A pause. "Before he died, he told me to seek justice—not revenge. I have turned over this plea for more than a year, and serving at the police bureau, I realize there is indeed a difference—a fine difference—between the two."

My brows furrowed, examining the two words for myself.

"Revenge begets revenge; the anger is unquenchable. We become the monsters we are trying to punish. Justice, however, brings closure, and that is what I want. It can only be achieved by remaining sober-minded and rational. And, in the end, it is not my place to punish the prince. It is the king's, and only the king's. All I can do is find enough evidence to make the truth undeniable."

I let out a breath, the weight of the investigation settling heavy inside my chest.

"But don't worry about that," he said, his gaze dropping away from mine. "Don't concern yourself any longer about the Crown Prince, or about the other suspects."

"What do you mean?" I asked.

"About what occurred in the field . . ." He continued to avoid my gaze. "I've given it more thought, and I fear this investigation is growing too dangerous. It would be better if you no longer involved yourself."

I frowned. "You want me out of the investigation?"

"I regret dragging you into this in the first place. From now on, keep your head low and avoid traveling anywhere alone." Holding the wall, he struggled up to his feet, and I followed him up. "It's late. I'll escort you home—"

I sidestepped and blocked his path, peering up at him and refusing to look away. "You need my assistance," I pressed. "Everything about this case is pointing to the palace, and without me, you might as well walk off a cliff's edge blindfolded."

"I know you are right," he said. Then an edge sharpened in his voice as he added, adamantly, "But I also know that you could lose everything, including your life. I can't allow that to happen—"

"But it is *my* life." My chest prickled with both anger and confusion. "I said I would help you, and I mean it. Why would you risk an entire investigation to spare me?"

He frowned as he peered down at me, as though confounded by my stubbornness. "I saw you nearly die today. I watched a man hold a blade over your *throat*." A muscle worked in his jaw, his face ashen. "You are smart, capable, and you have a dream. Jieun told me all about it. So please, listen to me and don't let this investigation ruin you. I'll do all that I can to assist your mentor, so just—" Rawness chafed at his voice as he whispered, "Promise you'll stay out of this case from now on."

I had never seen Eojin appear so distressed, and for a moment, I wanted to concede, if only to wipe the concern from his face. But I knew myself too well. I knew that I would not stop until all my questions were answered.

"We made a pact," I reminded him softly. "We'll watch out for each other. No one is going to get hurt. No one is going to lose anything."

"You know that isn't true," he warned.

"Well . . ." I continued. "The reality is, either you allow me to assist you, or you cut me lose and I'll find the truth on my own. What shall it be, nauri?"

He stared, a line forming between his brows. Then with a shake of his head, he murmured, "You must have been a general in your past life. A most irritatingly stubborn one."

I offered him a faint smile. "I promise I know how to take care of myself."

He let out a breath as he sunk back down onto the floor, a look of utter defeat descending on his features. Leaning against the wall, he half stretched his long legs, his arms resting over his bent knees. In the silence that followed, I could feel his gaze on me, studying me for so long that a blush spread across my chest and crawled up my throat.

"We witnessed a man's execution, and we've known each other for the span of another five murders." A grim smile tugged at the corners of his lips, devoid of any mirth. "We are in a case that will likely kill at least one of us, yet neither one of us intends to leave. Does that make us friends?"

I was suddenly filled with the urge to burst into laughter. Laughter over the terrifyingly ridiculous situation I'd found myself in, and from the sheer sense of wonder that the darkest time had brought a friend into my life.

———

We continued to discuss the investigation well into the evening. We turned questions over, trying to find answers to lingering ones. One moment I would be walking in circles, arms crossed, and the next I was sitting and he was pacing around.

Eojin had borrowed scrolls of hanji and writing equipment from a scholar next door, and with the paper spread out before us, we connected the lines. Pointing here and there to add more notes. Our heads nearly touching, so lost in the moment, so consumed that I could not tell where he began and where I ended. We seemed to have, in that moment, merged into one mind with one purpose: find the killer, find the truth.

Time moved differently in this room, like it was a rushing current of water. It was evening, and then suddenly the sky was pitch-dark and the moon round in the sky. My eyes itched, exhausted, but I wanted to keep talking to Eojin.

"It's late," he said. "Shouldn't you return home? Your mother might worry for you."

I shrugged. "My family isn't the type to notice my absence."

He hesitated, looking confused.

"There is still work to be done." A stubbornness settled over me, the stubbornness that had kept me awake all night during my studies for exams. I could not rest until I had finished my portion of work for the night. "We still haven't talked about Physician Khun."

"You have work tomorrow," he said.

"I've stayed up all night before," I replied.

He finally relented. "I visited his hut to question him again—but he's nowhere to be found. I interviewed the entire village, and no one has seen him since yesterday."

I frowned. "Perhaps he's gone to visit a family member?"

"It's possible. My officers have only just begun searching for him. And once he's found, he'll be arrested. I can't have him disappear like this again."

"And then Commander Song will torture him . . ." Biting my lower lip, I whispered, "And the young student nurse, Minji?"

Eojin sighed. "Still missing, and her parents continue to insist that they have no idea where she is, as do her relatives."

A feeling of helplessness settled around me, heavy and oppressive. I dipped the brush into ink and wrote out the details of our conversation, desperate for movement in this investigation that felt stagnant once more.

"If only I could speak with Nurse Jeongsu. Surely she must know something . . ." I said, half to myself. Then my gaze flew up to Eojin. "*Is* there a way I could speak with her?"

He shook his head. "The commander rarely leaves the bureau during murder investigations. Whenever he does leave, it is so sudden I will have no time to summon you, and he's usually only gone for a short time, anyway."

"You could sneak me in! He doesn't even need to find out."

"Everyone would notice that you are not part of the police bureau. His men would immediately notify—" He paused. "I could disguise you."

I straightened, hopeful but confused. "As an officer?"

"No, as a damo." His gaze was already a thousand li away, already strategizing. "Tomorrow night, right when the great bell rings, meet me outside the small entrance of the bureau. That is when the buildings are most empty, as officers go out to patrol the streets during curfew. And even if you are seen, they will only see a harmless police damo."

With a rush of energy—spurred by the hope that we might finally gain more important information tomorrow—we returned to the map of suspects we'd drawn out, and the collected notes of all that we knew, no longer encased within separate minds but written out onto sheets of paper.

We continued to talk until my mind burned out, nothing but smoke curling up from the wick. I tried to concentrate, but when Eojin began nodding off, I told myself I'd rest my eyes for a bit. I laid my head down on the table and must have drifted off, for I woke to find pre-dawn shadows slumbering in the gray room, and very dim light streaming in through the hanji screens.

As my mind reoriented itself, I noticed I wasn't alone on the table. My head lay resting on my folded arms, my brows pressed against Eojin's, our noses nearly touching.

I watched as his eyelids flinched, moving around in a dream, or perhaps in a nightmare. But not for long. As though sensing my stare, his eyes slowly blinked open, and I was too tired to be flustered when he held my gaze.

"I wonder what time it is, nauri," I whispered.

"You don't need to keep calling me that," he replied just as quietly.

I closed my eyes again. Outside, a woman yawned as her footsteps crunched across the yard. Further off, a dog barked. I would address him properly in the morning.

But just for now in these in-between hours, just for now before the sun rose and everything returned to its rightful place, I whispered, "All right . . . Eojin."

I finally woke to the door sliding open and a blanket I didn't remember placing around my shoulders slipping onto the floor. Blinding sunlight shot through the doorway, and I shaded my eyes with the back of my hand. How long had I been asleep?

It wasn't Eojin who came in, to my disappointment. It was the scarred-lipped servant.

She crossed the room with a tray of steaming soup and side dishes. "Your husband left for the capital as soon as the fortress gate opened, and asked me to wake you at first light."

My husband? It took a moment for me to collect my thoughts, then I glanced out the door. I had just enough time to return home, fetch my uniform, and head to work.

"He also told me to give you this."

The servant set down the tray of food, then scurried to the door to fetch something from the other side. She returned with the familiar cotton sack that I carried my uniform in—I wouldn't have to return home after all. How had Eojin managed to get this?

I opened the sack, and there lay a note: *I asked your servant for your uniform. I informed her that you were assisting the police with the death of Nurse Aram. She agreed not to tell your mother yet, lest it worry her.*

The skin under my eyes felt worn and heavy. Without needing to go home first, I had enough time to eat without rushing. Eojin had chosen the most nourishing dish for me: sullungtang, rich and milky beef broth, a hearty soup that was delicate in taste.

I paused, spoon halfway to my mouth, as a fuzzy memory surfaced.

The grayish blur of pre-dawn light. Eojin reaching out to touch the fallen strand of my hair, just long enough to tuck it behind my ear . . . and then he was gone.

A memory . . . or a dream?

11

Was it a dream?

Each time the thought of Eojin drifted into my mind, I beat it aside. He wasn't the mystery I needed to be solving at the moment.

I continued to remind myself of this as I made my way to the palace. Once inside, I focused on the tense faces around me, searching for clues—a hint of guilt, or perhaps cold indifference. I was certain that the killer was among us, for the murdered victims were witnesses to the Crown Prince's crime. And so it could not be a mere coincidence that on the night of the murder of the first witness, Court Lady Ahnbi, the prince had also happened to be roaming outside the palace walls.

It had all been staged.

The culprit had *known* the prince would sneak out that night. And who else could know such secrets except someone within the palace, their ear pressed against the network of spies?

"I can hardly breathe in here," Jieun whispered, interrupting my stream of thoughts. I glanced at my friend—who looked more tired and haunted than before—as she walked alongside me toward the Royal Apothecary. "I dare not look anyone in the eyes for too long."

I reached for her hand and gave it a little squeeze. "The killer targeted two nurses who work on days alternate to ours. Perhaps it means the culprit isn't even here today." I wasn't so sure about this, yet it seemed possible enough.

Jieun's gaze remained lowered, fixed fearfully on the ground. "I have this deep dread in me that one of us will be next."

"Jieun-ah . . . Don't think like that—"

"We became false alibis to the—" Jieun darted a glance around. "To the Crown Prince. A murder occurred on that night. For some reason, I can't stop thinking about this. That somehow we've got a target on our backs."

"I don't think anything will happen to us," I said, and meant it. "Eojin would tell you the same."

In the large room where nurses were slipping into their uniforms, Jieun and I changed slowly, both of us studying everyone. And everyone seemed suspicious of each other, speculation circulating in a hum of whispers.

"There is a rumor going around," one whispered, "that Nurse Aram died because she was a palace spy."

Another nurse shook her head. "No palace woman becomes a spy by their own choosing. We are all blackmailed into doing so eventually."

The others agreed. "I don't know what Nurse Aram did,

but it couldn't have been her fault. Spies are puppets for those in power—"

"So if you are told to leap off a cliff by your master, will you?" came a familiar and sharp voice—Nurse Inyeong's. "No, you will not obey if that means self-preservation. But if it is to harm another, in exchange for your life, I'm sure you wouldn't think twice in hurting others." She clucked her tongue. "Perhaps you all should reconsider your professions as uinyeos. How could any of you call yourself a protector of lives when all you are is a puppet?"

My thoughts lingered on Inyeong as she walked off. She seemed unwell, pressing a hand against her stomach, pausing now and then to lean her shoulder against a wall; but with a killer of women on the loose, everyone within the palace walls was likely feeling rather nauseous.

I stepped out of the building, wanting to examine more people—and one in particular.

"Excuse me." I stopped a passing clerk. "Do you know if Physician Khun has returned for work today?"

He paused. "I think I saw him heading toward the medicinal garden. He's *finally* returned to work."

Thanking the clerk, I rushed off, wanting to lay my eyes on Eojin's and my prime suspect. I ducked past the little connecting gate and wandered into the medicinal garden with its vast stretch of rolling fields. I looked around until my gaze rested upon a figure stalking down a narrow dirt path, his gaze burning into the distance, not once noting me. There was a bloody cut at the center of his mud-stained forehead. The knees of his uniform were muddy, and so were his hands. The ground was still wet from last night's rainfall; perhaps he had fallen? Yet how had he ended up with such a strange wound?

I closed the distance between myself and Physician Khun. If he was indeed the assailant from the other day, how would he respond at the sight of me? Would he wince with pain if I bumped into his arm, where Eojin had slashed the attacker?

"Uiwon-nim," I called out.

He glanced over his shoulder at me. "What do you want?" His voice sounded hoarse, as though from overuse—the voice of a man who had been yelling or weeping for too long. There were also telltale signs of heartache haunting his face—the red and puffy eyes, the flushed cheeks.

I pointed to my own forehead, watching him carefully. "You're bleeding, uiwon-nim."

"What does it matter to you? Leave me alone." He roughly wiped his brow, and he didn't seem uneasy at the sight of me. His indifference only hardened. If he was the attacker, then he was a skilled actor as well. "I said *leave me.*"

I remained where I was, anchored there by all the questions reeling in my mind. "Nurse Jeongsu is my mentor. She has been accused of committing the murders at the Hyeminseo," I said, watching as he picked up a garden tool abandoned on the ground, its sharp blade gleaming in the skylight. It looked deadly in his grip. "And I was hoping you might assist me in proving her innocence."

"What makes you think I'd be of any help?"

"I heard rumors that one of the victims, Court Lady Ahnbi—" I hesitated. "I heard that she was your secret wife."

His brows furrowed, and a glint of fear flashed through his eyes. I waited for him to deny the accusation, to scramble for self-preservation, but instead, his brows lifted. "If you are intending to blackmail me with this intelligence," he whispered, "it will not work."

"I wasn't trying to—"

"Everyone is trying to blackmail everyone here in the palace."

I had reached a dead end. Wracking my mind, I considered my options and remembered the strategy that had worked on Father's gatekeeper. Fear loosened tightly sealed lips. "Wouldn't it be better to tell the truth freely, than to confess the truth through torture?" I asked.

"What do you mean, torture?" he snapped.

"Haven't you heard?" I held his gaze. "The police are searching for you." *Inspector Seo in particular,* I didn't add.

Panic welled in his eyes, and for a moment he looked as though he'd drown in it. Then he shook his head and let out a cold, mirthless laugh. "What does it matter? I don't care what happens to me. I wish she'd taken me with her," he said, his voice gruff with emotion. Perhaps it was anger, grief . . . or remorse. Glancing down at his reflection in the blade, he whispered, "I would have gladly traded my life for hers."

Observing him, I could almost imagine why Court Lady Ahnbi had fallen in love with this young man. Everything else must have faded away when she was with him, if he loved her so—the loneliness of palace life, the thousands of palace rules, the eternal, unchanging future. She was the king's woman, was to commit her entire life to him and him alone, though she knew him not.

"You really loved her," I said under my breath.

"Of course I did," he rasped, his gaze now falling on mine, clinging to me like a man desperate to be heard. "That is why I—" He faltered. "That is why I sent Ahnbi a note, asking her to run away with me. I went to the fortress early in the morning to wait for her. She'd said she would leave the palace a little before curfew lifted, to meet me at the gate."

"But the palace wouldn't have opened until then. How would she have managed to leave?"

"There are ways to sneak out of the palace that only court ladies and rebellious royals know." He let out another distressed sigh. "But she never came, and I thought it was because she'd changed her mind. Or because she had been caught. But then I learned she was . . . gone."

Gone. The word sent a cold breeze through me. *Murdered.* "I heard you fought with her the day before her death."

A snarl curled his voice. "It is Madam Mun's fault. She learned that the prince might leave the palace that night, so tried to pressure Ahnbi into following after His Highness. Ahnbi was planning to do so, but I convinced her otherwise, and we knew Madam Mun might reveal our relationship as punishment. That is why I asked Ahnbi to run away with me. To escape that evil woman."

His dark mood struck me as too coincidental. Why, on the very day after two new attacks, did he look like he was falling apart?

"Why are you telling me this now?" I asked cautiously.

"Because . . ." His hand drifted to the wound—likely caused by a blow to the head, as though someone had slammed his face into something hard. Or he had done so himself. "Because now I think to myself that . . . perhaps . . . perhaps I could have prevented her death."

"How?" I whispered.

"By having never known her in the first place." He spoke in despair-ridden murmurs, as though talking to himself. "I've been filled with so much regret. I tried to escape it, all the memories of her. I went to stay with family, hoping my family might help keep me sane—" The air around him slowly changed, freezing as if he had stepped into a winter's night, and the color drained from his cheeks. "But no matter what anyone tells me—my conscience speaks the loudest. I brought death upon Ahnbi. It is my fault."

"What do you mean?" I pressed, and panic fluttered in me at the sound of footsteps. A quick glance over my shoulder revealed the gleaming green robe of an approaching eunuch. His attention was fixed on me. I sensed I was running out of time, that if I did not pull the secret out of Physician Khun now, I never would.

I took a step closer to the young man, close enough that he finally looked up at me.

"Why do you think you caused her death, uiwon-nim?" I pressed.

"I am the son of a murdered palace nurse—"

"I know," I said. "Nurse Kyunghee told me everything."

His stare shifted away from me, to the approaching eunuch. A wild darkness flickered in his eyes. "Then you must ask yourself—whether it was by chance or not, that I fell in love with one of the three witnesses to my mother's murder."

My mind raced. I had never thought of it until now, but it was indeed quite the coincidence. Did this mean he'd intentionally sought Court Lady Ahnbi out? Had he gotten close to her in order to gain her trust, to uncover the secret she was hiding? That she had witnessed his mother's death, then perhaps had helped bury her body?

"Nurse Hyeon," came the reedy voice of the eunuch. I turned to stare at the man, whom I finally recognized. It was Eunuch Im, the old man who had played the prince on the night of the Hyeminseo massacre. "His Royal Highness summons you."

For an instant, I wanted to blurt out some excuse as to why I could not follow. Anything to remain in the medicinal garden, to chase after Physician Khun with my questions. But caution stilled me. I dared not cross His Highness.

I at last bowed to the eunuch, and slowly, a new thought rose to the surface. Perhaps, just perhaps, it was the Crown Prince who had the answers to my every question.

———

Eunuch Im remained quiet and three steps ahead of me, his head lowered, his hands gathered in his wide sleeves.

But his strides slowed to a halt, and I fell still behind him when I noticed the curious sight of three government officials, their robes as red as blood stains. They stood crowded before a gate, peering through wooden double doors—spying into the Crown Prince's residence.

"Give me an account of last night, detail for detail," came a sharp and commanding voice from within the courtyard, beyond the gate. It was the king's voice. "You say you strolled around the palace at night. Which guards did you pass? What time did you return to your quarter?"

Long silence stretched, and a chill coursed through me. The king was interrogating his son. He suspected him of yesterday's attack. "Why do you say *nothing*?"

I imagined the Crown Prince, the future king, standing frozen with the eyes of a frightened child. Then, from the tense stillness came the prince's voice, deep and nearly impossible to hear: "Whatever I say, whatever I do, I will always be at fault."

The air tensed with prickling fury.

"I don't want to be king. I will never be good enough," the prince continued, a desperate note trembling in his deep voice. "I only ever wanted to be your son—"

"Pathetic," the king snapped. "Always whining like a pampered mutt. One can never hold a proper conversation with you."

His Majesty's cutting words echoed against the lonely walls of Joseung Pavilion, and then the spying officials hastened away as the gates flew open. The king and the attendants filed out, and the eunuch and I both bowed low.

"Perhaps I should come another time," I said carefully, once we were alone again.

"The prince has summoned you," Eunuch Im said, his voice unnervingly calm. "Follow me."

Holding my hands tight, I reluctantly followed, stepping past the gate. The courtyard was empty; the prince must have stormed off to his chamber inside Joseung Pavilion. *Joseung* meant the "House of the Future King," but also sounded like the word *Afterlife*. A sense of doom oppressed my spirit as the surrounding shadows seemed to hold echoes from the otherworld.

"Do not speak until you are spoken to," the eunuch whispered as we proceeded into the residence. "Always keep your head lowered. Never look the prince in the eye." He spoke as though he'd recited the words a thousand times. "And no matter what, if you value your life, do not say *anything* to upset His Highness."

Screened doors slid open, drawn aside by servants. I treaded cautiously into the vast inner chamber. Its floor was patterned with squares of sunlight imprinted by tall, latticed screens. The whole space was covered in robes and books. Gaze fixed on the piles, I waited, my pulse racing as I sensed his presence—darkness that flooded every corner of the room.

Was this the aura of a killer? Had he indeed decapitated Nurse Hyo-ok? Had he wielded his sword since then?

"I'll speak with her alone, Im," came a deep, reverberating voice.

The eunuch withdrew, and when the doors slid shut

behind me, I waited for the prince to speak again. He did not. I glanced up from beneath my lashes. Prince Jangheon's back was turned to me. He was taller and larger up close, and the stories I'd heard of his military prowess spoke true as I quickly examined him. His silk dragon robe—so dark blue it gleamed almost black—smoothed over his athletic figure like water over mighty rocks. His broad shoulders whispered of strength, and the ability to kill many with one strike.

"Tell me." His voice dipped low. "Are you a spy?"

My muscles tightened as my mind raced. I couldn't understand why he would think I was. Then I remembered how I'd followed him from Lady Hyegyoung's residence all the way to the king's office two days ago. "I am not, Your Highness."

"All spies say they are not." He slowly turned and moved toward me, until I found myself staring at the hem of his robe, his great shadow looming over me. "I shall kill you if you are."

Cold sweat dampened my back. "I am not a spy, Your Highness. I am—" I licked my dry lips, my mouth parched with trepidation. "I am your alibi."

"Alibi?" he whispered.

"On the night of the Hyeminseo massacre," I rushed to say, "Lady Hyegyoung summoned me and a few others to tend to Your Highness. And I have since assured everyone that you were indeed in your chamber that night, indisposed."

"Ah." A note of understanding lit his voice. "That night."

I remained still, very still, my skin prickling with the awareness that I was being watched. Examined. Like a detailed tapestry that held a secret.

"And whom do you suspect of the killings? Do you think it is I, as does everyone else?"

"Your Highness, who am I to wonder such things?" I tried to make myself as small as possible. So small that I might slip free of him, as a mouse might from a tiger's claws. "I am but a mere servant."

The silver dragon emblems on his robe gleamed. Chillingly, he said, "Your name is Baek-hyeon, I am told. Nurse Jeongsu's former student and the bastard daughter of Lord Shin."

I swallowed hard. My voice nearly slipped as I replied, "I am, Your Highness."

"More reasons to spy on me, I am sure."

Stomach knotting, I clutched my hands tighter, feeling as though he had seen straight through me. He knew my father, and perhaps even considered him a rival. Yet they had somehow ended up near the crime scene—an alibi to each other. Based on Gatekeeper Kwon's testimony, the possible killer had bumped into Father, and I wondered now whether the prince had seen the culprit as well.

Curiosity rose, sharpening my senses, drowning out my fear. I paused to piece my question together. There was no possibility that His Highness would tell me anything—but perhaps he would tell his dead sister.

Never look the prince in the eye.

I mustered enough courage to lift my gaze to a pair

of eyes as dark as the night, and hoped it was true, what everyone had said of my face. That I looked almost identical to the prince's dead sister.

His favorite sister.

Almost at once, Prince Jangheon's eyes widened. A flash of surprise illuminated his gaze, followed by a stab of agony. Frightened by the power my face held over him, I quickly lowered my gaze again.

"I only glimpsed you from far away," he said breathlessly, as though struggling for composure. "You look so much like her."

I took in a few steadying breaths, not knowing how to respond. It seemed, at least, that he'd forgotten his initial suspicion of me.

"Look at me again."

What have I done?

But I obeyed, gazing up into the night, a darkness so bewitching that I forgot all the deadly tales about him and could only see the pain in his eyes. It was a pain that could not be performed—I had seen it too often in the eyes of the dying, and those left behind.

"The dead never remain dead for long," he murmured to himself. "They never leave. Do you believe that?"

"I do, Your Highness," I said for his sake—and for mine. "I believe they remain close by our sides. I believe spirits even cohabit the bodies of the living."

"Then my sister must be near?" he rasped. "Have you heard her?"

I faltered, hearing the desperation in his voice. And

his eyes searched my face, perhaps the same way his eyes scoured through occult books, looking for a comfort that this vast and empty palace could not provide him with.

"I have," I lied. "I have heard her, Your Highness. And the voice made me follow you that one time. I didn't mean to spy, Your Highness."

As though unable to look at me any longer, he suddenly left my side. Silk rustled as he sat behind his low-legged desk, his robe pooling around him like a pitch-dark grave. He remained still, his elbow resting on the table, his hand over the silk band tied around his head. Not a strand of hair strayed from his perfect topknot, leaving his face open and clear—and shadowed with a troubled look.

"You may go, but, tell me . . . is there anything you need?" He glanced up, his gaze only reaching the collar of my uniform. "Would you like some ornaments or dresses?"

I bit my lower lip hard. I felt sorry for the prince, for it was clear that he'd cared for his sister very much. It seemed monsters still bled. Killers still had hearts, if only for a particular few.

"There is something on your mind," he pointed out. "Tell me what it is."

I hesitated, and it took a moment to find my voice. "My mentor, Nurse Jeongsu . . . she was falsely imprisoned for the massacre."

A pause. "What is your request?"

"Your Highness," I said cautiously, "if you have any information regarding the massacre, anything that might help the police find the real killer—I would be forever indebted to you." I held my breath and waited as my question hung in the air between us.

"The day of the massacre . . ." He said at last, and relief slid through me, only for it to be dashed away as he spoke on. "Your father was out early, smelling of liquor and perfume, and he saw me wandering the street an hour or so before dawn."

I stood with shoulders tensed. This matched what Father's servant had told me.

"A figure rushed out shortly after the massacre and collided into us. It was too dark to see him, but he dropped something in his hurry. A bloody object . . ." His gaze drifted to a mother-of-pearl cabinet to his left. "Do you want it?"

"I . . . I do, Your Highness," I barely managed to say.

"Then we can exchange favors. I haven't requested this of anyone, for I do not know whom to trust. But I am growing desperate." Prince Jangheon ran a hand over his face, and suddenly, he looked like he hadn't slept for a thousand years, kept awake by too many demons. "Perhaps you could help procure for me a medicine. Something to alleviate the oppressive mood I feel."

I stayed quiet, waiting for him to elaborate.

"When anger grips me, I cannot contain it. And this anger keeps me awake at night, a darkness that I've held in for too long. Every little thing leaves me in a state of rage." His teeth clenched. The mere thought seemed to trouble him. "It is exhausting, this anger that will not leave me— not even for a moment."

"I'll procure the medicine," I whispered. "I promise."

"After that, you ought to reconsider your position in the palace. I would, if I were you." He remained still, such a weight over him. "Heed my advice, Nurse Hyeon, if you have any care for your life. You may go."

I learned later that the king had removed Prince Jangheon from the list of those who would attend Queen Jeongseong's memorial service. Everyone of importance was going, joining the king's entourage to travel out of the palace to the burial mound.

Everyone, except for the king's own son. A son who now refused to eat, refused to drink, devastated by this humiliating news.

The prince would need his anger-alleviating medicine more than ever. I wanted desperately to visit the library to search for the right concoction, but there was work to be done and Physician Nanshin was nearby; I couldn't slip away without his noticing.

My mind thus preoccupied, I meant to cut through a bundle of herbal plants and instead felt sharp pain shoot through my hand.

"Damnation," I whispered, looking down at my fingers. Blood streamed from my wounded thumb, down my palm, and onto the cutting board. Memories of murder gleamed red in my mind.

Panic thrummed in my veins as I looked for a towel, then turned in the wrong direction, stumbling into a pot of precious medicine. There were gasps and gawking eyes, but the crowd of faces fogged. I'd never made so many foolish errors at once before.

Then a hand whirled me around. "Mistakes like this could get you demoted," Nurse Inyeong said. She eyed Physician Nanshin, who was now walking off, away from the scene I'd made.

Letting out a sigh, she snatched something from my hand. A blade. I hadn't realized I was still holding the cutting tool. Putting it aside, she slipped out a handkerchief, tore a strip off, then bound it around my thumb. "What is the matter with you?"

"My mind was preoccupied," I whispered, my heart thrumming. Physician Nanshin was out of sight now, and the nurses around me left me alone. Or perhaps they were simply avoiding Nurse Inyeong. "I'm not usually like this."

"I know you're not." Nurse Inyeong shook her head as she bound my finger with another tight layer to stop the bleeding. "But I can imagine why you must be flustered . . ."

"What do you mean?" I asked.

A pondering look clouded her face, then she took me aside, leading me to a shadowy spot behind the apothecary. "I saw you leaving the medicinal garden earlier with the Crown Prince's eunuch." She held my gaze. "Why?"

I shifted uneasily on my feet. "He simply wanted to ask me a question."

"About what?"

"About—" I paused. "May I ask why you are so interested, uinyeo-nim?"

Silence fell, as chilling as the shadows enveloping us.

"There is something I must tell you," she said, her voice tense. "Perhaps I ought to have told you sooner. You've only served at the palace for less than a month, so you are unaware of all the secrets hidden—" She winced as she moved carefully, pressing a hand over her stomach, and when I looked at her worrisomely, she said through her clenched teeth, "I can't sleep with all that's going on, so I've been drinking too much. It's left me with the most awful stomachaches—"

Again, she paused, nausea draining the color from her cheeks and lips. She didn't look well, not at all. Panic flitted through me as she pressed her lips tight together, like she was on the verge of vomiting.

Before I could examine Nurse Inyeong's symptoms further, she took in a deep breath and spoke on, her voice forceful enough to distract me. "These are dangerous times, Nurse Hyeon, and if you want to survive, you must avoid Prince Jangheon."

Dread snapped my attention back to the matter at hand. "What do you know, uinyeo-nim?"

Turmoil stirred in her eyes. Her mind seemed to jump back and forth between *tell her* and *do not*. Then at length, she said, "You are a good woman, Nurse Hyeon, and if I entrust this secret to you . . . you must guard it as though you are guarding my life."

"I promise," I said, and I meant it.

"Several months ago . . ." she began hesitantly. "A cursed shamanistic pendant was discovered in the Crown Prince's room."

My lips parted. This was a crime of great magnitude. Shamanism was banned, and to practice dark magic against a royal family member was punishable by death. "Who ordered such a thing?"

"Madam Mun," she replied as the hair rose on my skin. "When the prince's mother and his wife tracked the pendant back to the source, they summoned Madam Mun and had every intention of exposing her. I overheard everything. I was certain Madam Mun would be expelled from the palace, but then she threatened them. She said she would reveal to the king a truly horrible secret." Inyeong paused, a frown forming between her brows. "That the Crown Prince is planning to assassinate the king."

Her words sat in my chest like a shard of ice. A part of me was convinced that I'd surely misunderstood.

"Madam Mun said the Crown Prince is secretly amassing military weapons. She said she has evidence." Glancing around, she then looked at me once more, her frown deepening over a pair of solemn eyes. "So stay away from the Crown Prince, Nurse Hyeon. Those that associate with His Highness will all surely die alongside him."

***

During my break, I made my way toward the medical library and caught myself staring at the stone walls of the palace, wondering how many secrets they held in. If the walls were to fall down, would horror and death spill out in a river of blood?

"I'll help you find the medicine," Jieun said, accompanying me up the library steps. "But who is it for?"

"The medicine is for . . ." I dared not tell her that it was for the prince; the less she knew, the safer she'd be. I, myself, was distressed by my unwavering decision to concoct a medicine—despite what Nurse Inyeong had told me.

Before I could find an answer, Jieun said, "Is it for your mother?"

"Yes," I quickly replied. "She's always angry at Father, and I want to find something to alleviate her mood."

We stepped into the quiet establishment surrounded by large hanji-screened windows, beams of light filtering through the rows of open shelves. After collecting a few books, Jieun and I sat down at the table in the far back. I went through one book after the next, my concentration sharp, my shoulders heavy from the weight of responsibility. I needed to provide the right medicine in exchange for the murder weapon.

Jieun elbowed me, jolting me out of my thoughts. "My cousin," she whispered, eyeing me, "he never returned home last night. Do you perhaps know why?"

Her words didn't register at first. Then slowly, the memory came into focus, of Eojin and me in the small inn room, our eyes locked in the pre-dawn light. A blush crept up and burned my cheeks—betraying me to Jieun, whose eyes widened.

"No," I said, horrified, trying to beat down her imagination. "It's not what you think—"

"You spent the *night* together?" She could barely speak, her face turning bright red. A mixture of surprise and delight danced in her eyes. "What does this mean? Are you in love? Is *he* in love? Oh gods, tell me *everything*!"

"Jieun-ah, I mean it. It's not what you think." My heart felt too heavy for this, my mind aching from the events of today. "I need to focus on finding the medicine—"

"I specialize in medicine making, I'll find something for you. And then you must promise to tell me everything."

"I—"

Jieun pulled a stack of books toward her, then flipped through each, her fingers moving with quick and practiced ease. "Ondamtang," she said, finding an answer so soon that, despite my grim mood, admiration swept through me. "This is the medicine you should use."

"You found it so fast . . ." I read through the passage she pointed out to me and was startled to find how perfect the concoction was. I looked over the ingredients, memorizing it at a glance, and decided that I would brew the medicine for Prince Jangheon and sneak it to him tomorrow. It was too late now—

"So," Jieun chirped. "Tell me everything!"

I shook my head. "We were simply discussing the investigation. We accidentally fell asleep, woke up, then went our separate ways. That is all."

"That *can't* be all," she insisted.

"Well, it is, Jieun-ah. Not every servant girl is Chunhyang, and not every young lord is Mongryong. Life isn't always like romantic literature." Avoiding her gaze, I rose to my feet and busily gathered the books from the table, returning each to their rightful place on the shelves. All the while, Jieun's gaze followed me, and when the blush burned hotter on my cheeks, I could feel her smile widen.

"Hyeon-ahhh," she said teasingly, joining my side. "Are you meeting your lover again tonight?"

"He is *not* my lover, and I am not meeting him—" I faltered, remembering. I *was* to meet Eojin again tonight. I'd seen him every day since the massacre, and a part of me had grown accustomed to our rhythm of encounters, the cadence of his presence . . .

What would happen once the investigation was over? Would I turn and find him gone?

A hollow sensation sunk into my chest, and I couldn't understand why.

"I'm your friend," Jieun said as she watched me closely, her voice gentle. The teasing glint had faded from her eyes. "You've trusted me with your deepest secrets before. You know you can confide in me about anything."

I shook my head, trying to push away the ache, telling myself that I didn't care. Yet my hand unconsciously drifted to my hair and my fingers smoothed over the memory of Eojin's caress. Or perhaps it was just a dream after all.

"He touched my hair," I confessed. My pulse thundered, embarrassed that I was even saying such a thing. But I hated this uncertainty, this feeling that I was dangling over the unknown. "Does that mean anything? Or do you think I imagined it?"

"What do you wish it to be?" Jieun asked softly.

My stomach tightened into a knot as I wrung my hands and forced my gaze onto the floor. But I couldn't refocus myself. My guard fell away like a sigh of defeat, and I admitted to myself a truth that made my ears burn.

I wanted to love and be loved.

I wanted to be known.

I wanted to be understood and accepted.

And being with Eojin slipped unwanted shadows into my head, dreams of what that might feel like—to be cherished, like in the love stories in Jieun's personal library.

Yet I was not so naive as to believe that I, a servant girl, could be anything more to Eojin than what Mother was to Lord Shin. And I was not so desperate and foolish as to want anything more.

I had his friendship. It was enough.

It had to be enough.

12

I waited before the Bosingak Pavilion, a majestic two-story building with open sides that stood on a stone foundation. Its torchlit shadow engulfed me as I craned my head back, watching as the silhouette of a guard appeared before the massive bell, and in smooth motions, it was struck. A great rumble echoed down and reverberated into my bones. The fortress gates would close now. It was two hours before midnight; curfew had fallen.

It was time to face Eojin again.

The streets of Hanyang were dark and quiet as I made my way to our meeting place. My mind whirred, replaying the conversations with Jieun and Nurse Inyeong, then stilled when I felt the prickling sensation of being followed.

I glanced over my shoulder and saw two patrolmen, their beady eyes fixed on me, their faces blazing in the torchlight.

They're only patrolling the streets, I told myself.

Still, I turned sharply into an alley, then hurried down

the labyrinth of narrow paths. Glowing lanterns hung from eaves, swaying from strings in the evening breeze, illuminating my way until I finally slipped out onto the main road.

My anxiety eased when I arrived before the police bureau, illuminated by fire blazing in the iron braziers and the knowledge that Eojin had to be somewhere nearby. Darkness returned as I slipped around the walls enclosing the bureau, shadows so deep that I felt formless. I ran my hand along the grimy stone walls, my finger tracing the grooves, waiting to feel the wooden frame of the small gate used by servants. My hand brushed up against warm fabric, and I froze, realizing that it was silk under my touch.

"Baek-hyeon?" came a familiar deep voice.

My eyes adjusted to a tall silhouette before me, standing very still, as though my hand were a branding iron on his chest. I quickly snatched myself away. "I'd prefer you not call me by that name."

Eojin quirked an eyebrow. "But it's your given name."

"A given name I do not like. Have you the damo uniform ready for me, nauri?"

He kept motionless a moment longer, and I couldn't tell whether he was staring down at me or off into the distance. "It's inside. Follow me."

The dirt crunched under his steps as he continued down the wall, and I hurried behind him, nearly walking into him when he suddenly stopped. We'd arrived before the small gate, which he opened onto what appeared to be the servants' courtyard.

I glanced up at Eojin, and all the flutters of silly emotions from earlier vanished at the sight of his brows pressed together. "What's the matter?" I asked, a ball of dread knotting in my stomach.

"It's about Nurse Jeongsu, but I'll tell you later."

Before my concern could spike, he led me into a storage room. "You'll find the uniform inside," he said as he shut the door, just enough to allow me some privacy, but not so much as to block out the torchlight.

Quickly, I removed the garima fixed onto my head and undid my braided coil. It took me a moment to remember how damos styled their hair. With some struggle due to my wounded thumb, I plaited my hair down the back, then tied the end. I slipped out of my uinyeo uniform, folded it, and set it aside. All the while, I whispered through the door to Eojin, relating what I had discovered that day.

"I learned two important things today. First, the prince confirmed that my father was his alibi on the night of the massacre. He also hinted to me that he has the murder weapon in his possession."

"The seja-jeoha told you all this?" There was a note of uneasy surprise in his voice.

"Apparently I look like his dead favorite sister, so he opened up to me easily."

Eojin remained quiet, and through the crack, I caught a glimpse of his tense shoulder. I'd thought he would be more pleased by what I had told him, but I could sense a lecture coming instead, perhaps another warning against associating with the prince. I moved to my next point.

"Nurse Inyeong told me something interesting, too." I turned to leave, then hesitated. I dared not leave my identification tag or my acupuncture case behind, so I slipped both into a pocket. "She said that Madam Mun blackmailed the Crown Prince's mother and wife. Apparently she found evidence to suggest that the prince is planning—" I leaned close to the door, the hair on my skin rising. "To kill the king."

Eojin continued to say nothing, then in a heavy voice, he murmured, "I've heard these rumors before. Perhaps Madam Mun is the one who circulated them in the first place."

I stepped out. "She seems so determined to crush the prince—"

Just then we heard light footsteps and the voices of a man and woman chatting lightly, likely a servant and a damo.

"We should leave," Eojin whispered.

Together, we hurried across the courtyard, our long shadows moving swiftly against the pavilions. I thought he would lead me to the prison block, but instead, I found myself approaching a kitchen.

"There are herbs inside," he said. "Do you think you could make a disinfectant? Nurse Jeongsu requires your assistance."

A frantic beat pulsed inside me. "What happened?"

"While I was away, Commander Song conducted another public trial and tried torturing a confession out of Nurse Jeongsu. She would say nothing at all."

I bit down my panic; there was no time for it. I followed him into the kitchen and headed straight for the clay hearth. "It's too dark in here to work." Sitting on my haunches, I peered into the smoky hole. "The furnace needs to be kindled."

"Here, let me." Eojin crouched next to me, his fine robe pooling on the dusty floor. He picked up a nearby kindling fan and began stirring the embers awake, illuminating the kitchen with a dim glow.

As he did, I could tell he had more to say.

"What is it?" I pressed. "Something else is bothering you."

At first I wasn't sure he would tell me, but after a grim moment, he said, "Nurse Kyunghee is dead. The nurses at the Hyeminseo say it was due to the blunt force trauma to her head. She fell asleep and . . . didn't wake up."

The weight of this news pressed sharp against my heart, but I couldn't say I was shocked. Some patients looked well on the outside, when they were already fatally broken on the inside.

Another palace woman was now dead.

My body trembling, I hurried over to a cabinet filled with tiny drawers—within each was a cotton pouch stuffed with dried medicinal herbs. Damos may have been failed nurses, but they were nurses all the same, so it was not a surprise to me that they kept ingredients so well organized. I slipped out a pouch labeled *Baekgib*, and double-checked by taking a whiff of it: dried orchid root. I tossed it into a bowl and found a pestle—I'd need to grind the root into a powder, to be sprinkled onto wounds to stop bleeding, decrease inflammation, and accelerate healing.

"There is something I've been meaning to ask," came Eojin's quiet voice, breaking my concentration. The ground scraped under his boots as he walked over, and I could feel his gaze drop to my face. It felt so bare under his close inspection. "Why does Nurse Jeongsu mean so much to you?"

I glanced outside the kitchen, as though I was looking out for danger in the courtyard. Not a single murmur or shuffle disturbed the empty dark. "I wouldn't have become an uinyeo without her," I whispered in reply. "She mentored and tutored me throughout my years at the Hyeminseo."

"She has mentored and tutored others, too. Yet I do not see any of her other students risking their lives to save her."

"I suppose I'm just stubborn." I pounded the wooden pestle against the root. "I like completing tasks."

"Surely that can't be all."

I frowned up at him. "Why do you wish to know?"

He gave a little shrug. "I am curious."

"My mother once abandoned me outside the Gibang House," I said. I rarely confided this to anyone, but I felt a sudden need to bare my shame. Maybe to douse that glint in his eyes, like he'd glimpsed a shining pebble under shifting sand. "The madam wouldn't take me in." And then I added, for good measure, "She said I was too bitter, my temper too out of control. I was not raised to be kind, considerate, and honorable."

He continued to watch me, his gaze unwavering.

I cleared my throat awkwardly. "So . . . Mother told me to wait outside, to beg until I was let in. But the madam never let me in, and Mother never came to retrieve me, even as night fell. That's when Nurse Jeongsu found me, nearly frozen to death. She's the only one that has ever truly cared for me."

I waited for a look of pity to pinch his face. Instead, he held his hands behind him and tilted his head slightly to the side, a puzzled frown weighing his brows.

"Who informed Nurse Jeongsu that you were freezing outside?" he asked.

I blinked. "Who told her . . . ? A passing pedestrian, I assume."

"You never asked?"

"No . . ."

"And Nurse Jeongsu never explained herself?"

"No, she—" I paused. "When I did ask once, she told me something I couldn't understand." Something I hadn't even bothered to think of until now. *She does not know how to love. It does not mean that she does not love at all.*

A silence fell over both of us, but I shoved my sudden confusion aside. I didn't want to think about her words, or what they meant. "It should be done now." I set the bowl on a tray, to look as much like a servant on an official errand as possible. "I'm ready."

"Keep your head ducked. Let no one see your face."

Whenever an officer stopped in his tracks to bow to Eojin, I, too, lowered my head to hide my face. No one seemed to notice me, though—a mere damo, the lowest of the low—even when we arrived before the prison block. Not a single question was asked when Eojin ordered a guard to permit us entrance.

The moment we stepped in, I was struck by the foul stench of blood and rotting flesh. Groaning prisoners filled the wooden cells that marched down the long hall, their gaunt faces shuddering in and out of view to the rhythm of the flickering torchlight.

"Suspect Jeongsu is in that cell over there," the guard said. He led us deeper into the prison block, the keys jangling by his side, and then cast a quick glance my way. "She is . . . faring poorly."

I gripped my tray of herbal medicine until the edges bit into my palms. What had compelled Nurse Jeongsu to remain in this godsforsaken place? If she was innocent, surely all she had to do was testify, to offer Commander Song an alibi. Any explanation *other* than the testimony she'd given the first time—that she had gone to the Hyeminseo at midnight, then had slept through the massacre.

The guard halted. "We're here." His keys jangled louder, and then the wooden gate of the cell creaked open. I dared not look up, not yet.

"Go tend to her," Eojin said, his voice turned my way, cool and indifferent. Perhaps had we met under any other circumstances, he would have used such a tone with me as a matter of course. Then he turned to the guard. "I'll speak with her alone now, Officer Choi."

"Yeh." The guard bowed.

I remained still, staring down at the tray as I listened to the guard's footsteps recede down the hall and out the main door, keys jangling all the while. Letting out a nervous breath, I tried to look up, but found that my chin would not rise. It had been easy until now to detach my emotions from the investigation, to be driven by a sense of what was right and wrong. My mentor had, after all, been hidden within the police bureau, out of sight and thus out of mind for the most part.

But now she was right before me. And I was afraid of what I might see.

"I'll wait nearby and keep watch," came Eojin's soft voice. "Go tend to your teacher."

Finally, I lifted my gaze. The space was hemmed by wooden bars, and in the corner beneath a small window, a silhouette trembled. She appeared smaller than I remembered, so thin, and as I stepped closer, my heart clenched. I could hardly recognize her. She was all bones and sharp angles, her wide cheekbones now like two daggers protruding from her cheeks. Her kind and fearless eyes were gone, replaced by a frightened stare. Commander Song had broken this woman.

"Uinyeo-nim," I whispered. "It's me, Hyeon. Baek-hyeon."

It took a few moments before her eyes focused on me. "Hyeon-ah?"

Her voice unlocked a memory—I was eight again, a child half frozen from waiting outside the Gibang House. Nurse Jeongsu had crouched before me. *Where is your mother?* she'd asked, and I had shaken my head. *Then where is your father?* My head had sunk low, tears leaking down my cheeks. She'd then cupped my face with the warmest hands I'd ever felt. *You aren't alone now, I promise.* She'd dusted off the snow that had collected on my head and shoulders. She had wrapped me in the thickest cotton blanket, lifted me onto her back, and then had carried me all the way to the Hyeminseo. Never once stopping to catch her breath.

She had been the age I was now. Eighteen.

She had changed my life, and I wished I could save hers.

I knelt before her, setting the tray down. "I'm here—" My attention caught upon her blood-soaked skirt. Her hands, too, were soaked in blood, like she had been pressing them against a wound that wouldn't stop bleeding. "How many times were you struck?" I whispered, my voice twisting in an attempt to remain composed.

"I lost count," she replied.

"May I?"

After she nodded stiffly, I peeled her dress up. Her undergarment was ripped, shredded from the flogging. Her legs were inflamed and smeared with blood. Her skin was torn so deeply, the white of her bone was visible, cracked and protruding through her flesh. It shouldn't have shocked me. We had treated several patients returned from police interrogations, their legs shattered in such a way. Yet I needed to close my eyes to still my stomach.

"Why are you here?" she asked.

"To tend to you," I replied, then glanced up, "and to ask you for the truth."

She remained silent for a long moment, and I feared she would turn me away. Instead, she nodded, slowly and weakly. "I want you to understand. I don't care what others think."

"Let me first disinfect—"

Nurse Jeongsu touched my wrist. "There is no time."

"Please, uinyeo-nim." I couldn't think about the investigation, not with all the blood and bone. I touched her brow; it was burning up, as I feared. "We have time. If I leave you like this now, I don't think you'll survive—"

"*Hyeon-ah.*" It was a plea. "I need at least you to know the truth."

Truth. A word Eojin and I had been chasing after for days, but now that it was right before me, I wasn't sure I was ready to accept its cost.

"I was not at the Hyeminseo at the time of the killing, nor before that," she said. "But the only alibi I have . . . I dare not expose him to the police. It would be too cruel. He is a baekjeong and has seven children to protect."

An iron ball of disbelief struck my chest hard, and angrily I pointed at her brutalized legs. "And so you would endure the cruelty alone? You'd risk your life for a man who belongs to the lowest class? Save yourself, uinyeo-nim. *Please.*"

Somewhere outside the prison block, I heard the angry thud of footsteps, and a voice boomed, "Where are they?"

I stiffened; I knew Commander Song's voice as well as I did the rumbling sound of thunder.

"No matter how many I save, the dead still haunt me, Hyeon-ah." Nurse Jeongsu turned my hand so that it lay palm up. I could feel her trembling as her bloodstained finger traced along the lines of my hand. "I will never forgive myself for having allowed Commander Song's wife and child to die. It was easily preventable, yet I was too proud to seek help on their behalf."

She held my gaze and my wrist for one long, heart-rending moment. "Remember what I always told you: We must value the lives of others. And those that are most vulnerable are the most precious of all. We are uinyeos, Hyeon-ah. We must protect." She released my hand. "Go now. And do not worry about me."

"But—" I reached out for the bowl I'd prepared for her.

She quickly pulled the tray closer to her leg and threw her skirt over it. "I will tend to myself. You must leave *now*."

"I'll come back for you. I'll make sure nothing happens—"

"I don't need saving." She held my gaze one last time; it felt like a farewell. "I made a decision, and it may result in my death, but I do not regret it. Take care of yourself, Hyeon-ah."

"Please—"

At that moment Eojin bolted into the cell, snatched my

arm, and pulled me to my feet. I felt disconnected; my mind was still kneeling before my mentor, yet my body was hurtling through the shadows, anchored to Eojin's side, down the narrow and endlessly long prison block.

Fresh air burst against my face as we stepped out through an alternate door. We hurried across the courtyard and past the kitchen, then dashed into the storage room just as the air cracked with the commander's voice, somewhere off in the distance: "Idiots! Where *is* that meddlesome nurse?" The sharp barking of a dog seemed to echo his words.

The commander was searching for *me*. My heart pounded with bruising force as I stared out through the crack in the door, Eojin close behind me. His hand held my shoulder, his grip protective.

"What did she write?" he asked. "Nurse Jeongsu, she was writing something on your palm."

I turned my hand around and stared down. Two rust-red Hangul characters gleamed on my skin as though carved there: *Yong-dal*.

"Yong-dal . . ." Eojin muttered. "I know that name."

"You do?"

"That's the name of the culprit who committed a burglary on the night of the massacre. He's notorious among the police," he added. "The first time he was caught, his face was branded, and the second time, his nose was sliced off. He was quiet for a while, then a few days ago, he broke into a nobleman's rice storage and stole two bags. I hear he will be sentenced to death this time."

"Where is he now?" I rasped.

"He escaped, but I believe he was wounded . . . Wait here," he said. "I'll go find the report and return shortly."

And then he was gone. I quickly changed back into my nursing uniform, making sure to retrieve my identification tag and acupuncture case, which I slipped into my apron pocket. I returned my attention to the name painted in red on my palm. Yong-dal. So, he was a petty criminal, one among thousands who had turned to robbery in order to survive the famine. There was a reason why the phrase *mok-gumeung-i-podochung* was so commonly used. It was a saying among the poor that, in order to feed oneself, one would have to become a criminal.

I paced the dark storage, in and out of the beam of torchlight slicing in through the crack. Now it made sense, why Nurse Jeongsu refused to confess the name of her alibi. It was a choice between her death or his—and that of his seven children.

Footsteps crunched outside, interrupting my stream of thought. Eojin had returned. I strode across the storage room, the floor creaking under my weight, and just as I reached the entrance, a wintry cold fell over me. Through the crack, torches blazed, and a dog slowed right before the storage room.

Please go. Please. I held my breath and kept my eyes on the hound, wishing I could will it to leave. But the dog turned his nose in the air, sniffing in my direction, and I suddenly wished I hadn't drawn so close. I should have hidden in the far corner.

The dog barked once.

My heart pounded in my ears as the officers gathered around. I took a step back, but my legs buckled, and I stumbled to the ground just as the door was flung open.

My stare slammed into the sight of Commander Song, two officers, and Damo Sulbi.

"Is this the rat I've been searching for?" The commander's lips curled with disgust. To Sulbi, he said, "Fetch me that girl's identification tag."

Head lowered and face pale with shame, she crept up to me and held out both her hands. "Please, uinyeo-nim."

I couldn't move. My hands were frozen.

"Please," Sulbi tried again, a note of apology in her voice.

I felt feverish and faint as I slipped my shaking hand into my pocket and pulled out both items, my wooden hopae and acupuncture case. The latter clattered to the ground as I fumbled to hand over my tag. The commander's icy stare fell upon it, and when he looked up at me, I felt as though a blade were being pressed to my heart.

"Baek-hyeon, a vulgar commoner." He tossed the identification tag at my feet. "You are the illegitimate daughter of Lord Shin. As I always say, the illegitimate will burn our kingdom to the ground, so rebellious and disobedient as they are. Leave at once and stop causing more chaos."

He was letting me go? I had to restrain myself from scrambling out of his sight, and instead, I took the time to bow, to calmly pick up my tag and make my way out of the storage room, past his shadowy figure. My ears strained as he murmured to the officer by his side.

"Inform His Lordship that his bastard intruded into the police bureau."

My breath hitched in my throat, my steps slowing. I turned to face the commander, eyes wide. "Please," I whispered. "Do not tell my father."

He folded his arms across his chest. "Why? Do you suddenly regret your actions?" A long pause ensued and, perhaps observing the terror in my face, his eyes gleamed bright. "Let us make a deal, then. I intend to petition for the young inspector's removal, and if you will testify—if you will tell me whatever you know about his clandestine investigation against the Crown Prince—I will forgive your transgressions."

I gripped the wooden tag, the crescents of my nails digging into my palm. I had witnessed and felt too many things over the past week to betray Eojin. My voice remained steady as I said, "I don't know what you speak of, sir."

"As stubborn as the jongsagwan himself." Commander Song motioned at Sulbi. "Take her to the prison block, and make sure Inspector Seo does not find out." Then to me, "If your father does not come for you, then I intend to keep you in custody until Nurse Jeongsu's ten days are up. I have enough trouble to deal with."

Ten days . . . ? I stared, my pulse hammering in my ears.

A cruel smile stretched across his lips at the question in my eyes. "It is the national code: a verdict must be passed within ten days of torture. And I intend to charge Nurse Jeongsu for the massacre."

It took a moment for his words to register. When they did, I felt as though I had swallowed a block of ice. I had only ten more days to keep Nurse Jeongsu from being executed.

And most of one was already gone.

13

I shut my eyes and opened them again, and the cell door was still there, locked by a key that now jangled against an officer's waist as he strode down the dark prison hall.

I wasn't angry. I was calm. But I wasn't sure what to do now.

On either side of me were cells that held strangers, and they were whispering, "Isn't that a nurse? What is a nurse doing in prison?" Their voices were amplified in the stillness. I tried not to listen, but that was impossible.

"Maybe she poisoned someone?"

"She doesn't look like a killer to me."

"Killers rarely look like killers."

I sat down and drew my knees up against my chest. A heavy question loomed over me as I listened to the beat of my uneasy heart. *Will Father come?*

I couldn't say how long I'd been sitting there when Sulbi tiptoed into the prison block. I stiffly rose to my feet, a warm surge of relief at the sight of a familiar face.

"Inspector Seo is searching for you," she whispered through the bars of my cell. "I was told to inform him that you'd left for Gaekji House. And he seemed to believe me, since that's where nurses stay when they're stuck in the capital." She hesitated. "I didn't want to lie to him, but the commander's servant was spying on me. If you wish me to inform the inspector of your whereabouts now, I will."

If Sulbi notified the inspector, the commander would find out. I'd caused her enough trouble.

"No," I whispered. "I wish to be alone . . ."

Crossing my arms, I paced the cell, a restless undercurrent prickling through me. Then I paused, seeing that Sulbi was still waiting on me, as though she thought I had something more to say.

And I realized I did.

"You were at the Hyeminseo a year ago, I remember that," I whispered quickly. "Did you perhaps know a student named Minji?"

"You mean the girl that escaped the massacre? I did. In fact, I've been assisting Inspector Seo with the search for her."

My pulse leapt. "You have?"

"I've been tasked with questioning all her relatives that live here. I also have a growing list of her family and acquaintances that live outside the capital—places where Inspector Seo believes Minji could have fled to.

"Apparently Minji's father disappeared for an entire week right after the massacre," she went on. "Inspector Seo believes he escorted Minji to a hiding place and now her family is too terrified to reveal where she's gone. He thinks they're afraid that once their daughter is found, she will be locked up and tortured like Nurse Jeongsu, so he is trying to gain their trust."

Who knew how long that could take? Nurse Jeongsu had only nine days left.

"There is something I need you to do for me."

She nodded. "Anything."

"Go to Nurse Oksun for me. Tell her I no longer need help searching for Nurse Jeongsu's alibi." I had to honor my mentor's wish for me to stop searching for Yong-dal and his seven children. "Tell her instead to ask everyone she knows about Minji's father, and where he went on the week of the massacre. He might not have trusted Inspector Seo enough to tell, but surely he must have let slip his travels to people he knows."

"I'll go to her right now," Sulbi said, her gaze determined. "I know where she lives."

"Thank you."

Once she was gone, I waited in the silence, listening for the striking of the great bell marking the end of curfew. I thought surely Father would come for me soon.

As the hours stretched by, a cold dampness crept across the courtyards and tumbled into my prison cell. My toes were frozen; pain shot up my legs with each step. I paused now and then to crane my neck, to try to catch a clearer glimpse of Nurse Jeongsu far down the line of cells and wooden bars. But she remained curled up on the ground, out of sight—consumed by fever, I feared.

When the bells struck, I was still waiting, listening.

No one came for me.

———

The jangling of keys startled me awake. I must have fallen asleep sometime after dawn—the light outside indicated it was nearing midday. Rubbing my eyes, I blinked ahead and every limb in my body fell still.

Father stood outside my cell as a guard unlocked it. He stared down at me, his hands gathered behind his back.

I staggered up, and I could hardly breathe as I bowed my head low. I'd rehearsed lies all night long, lies to shield me from his wrath and disappointment. But at the moment, my mind remained blank with fear.

"I received an urgent message in the middle of the night," Father's voice droned. "When I arrived at the police bureau, the commander told me how much you have meddled. He informed me that you intruded into the police bureau last night."

His watchful eyes seemed to say, *Defend yourself now . . . if you dare.*

"There must have been a misunderstanding," I said in a bare whisper. "I snuck into the police bureau hoping to tend to Nurse Jeongsu. Nothing more—"

"So, you are not only a meddler, but a liar, too."

Pulse hammering, I dropped my gaze to the floor.

"The commander informed me that you snuck into the crime scene of the Hyeminseo massacre. You thoughtlessly touched the corpses, likely tampering with the evidence.

Then you again thoughtlessly interfered with the examination of a corpse near the Han River. He believes you must be sharing palace secrets, too, with Inspector Seo."

"I'm sorry," I said, attempting to sound sincere. "I will not meddle again—"

"What has Inspector Seo promised in return for assisting him?" Father asked. "Or are you allowing him to use you simply because you are besotted?"

My simpering pretense fell away, and I shot him a look from beneath my lashes. "No, that is not why. He is not using me. We're friends."

"Friends?" he scoffed. "A man and a woman cannot be friends. Friendship exists only among equals. You are a vulgar commoner. When this is over, the most he'll offer is for you to become his concubine. A man with his family ties would never deign marry one such as you."

I grit my teeth. "I have no intention of becoming a concubine, Lord Shin."

He shook his head, clearly not believing me. "Whatever the case, you have humiliated me before the commander. And what is more, you have deliberately disobeyed me." He fell terribly quiet, and in his silence, I could feel the weight of his contempt. "Did I not instruct you *not* to get involved?"

My petulance withered away, and now I wanted to sink into the earth. "You did," I whispered.

He let out a breath and shook his head again. "When I learned you had become a nurse, I was proud of you. But now I see I mistook you for something you are not. You are just like every other bastard in this capital: a trouble-maker and a lawbreaker."

As his disappointment bored into me, I remained frozen, gripping the folds of my skirt until my knuckles burned.

"I cannot ignore Commander Song's words. He is lower than me in rank, yet was so outraged by you as to say to me, 'How can a Minister of Justice ensure that there is order within the capital when he is unable to bring proper order to his own household?'" Father reached out and tapped a finger against the wooden bar; each tap seemed to jab into me—a countdown to whatever punishment brewed in his mind. "I have sent word to the palace of your improper conduct. I have requested that you be demoted."

My lips could hardly form the question: *Demoted?*"

"Stripped of your title as a nae-uinyeo, for a nae-uinyeo is, first and foremost, a palace woman. Secrets are meant to be guarded, yet I have no doubt you have been leaking information."

"But I—" I struggled to speak as panic trickled into my veins. Slow and steady, cold and painful. "I worked h-half my life for this position—"

"Samgang oryun," he said, his voice brusque. "Heaven endowed each person with a specific role according to his or her position. The lord should act like a lord, a servant like a servant, a father like a father, and a son like a son. And you, a daughter like a daughter."

Ice crept into my heart. I had entered the Hyeminseo, had studied late into the night, surviving on as little as three hours of sleep, my nose bleeding every day, all in order to become this daughter of which he spoke. A daughter he could take pride in.

"But you have broken this harmony." The lines in his face hardened. "And now you must bear the consequence—"

"You are my father, yet never acted like a father." My voice cracked, my words trembled, but I had spoken and I couldn't stop. The unfairness of his words was too outrageous for me to keep silent. "So why *should* I act like your daughter?"

Father's face turned ashen with silent fury. An anger I had never before witnessed, like the absence of sunlight and of human warmth, a dark void filled with only wintry cold.

"Who taught you to be so rebellious?" His voice had thinned into a chilly whisper. "So crude?" I could almost feel him counting the number of my bones he wished to crush. But I wasn't prepared at all for the depths of his cruelty. "By the end of this full moon, you are to leave my residence. You, your brother, and your mother—let our paths never cross again."

My eyes watered as though he'd struck my cheek. "But it is *our* home—"

"Nothing you have belongs to you," he snapped with startling ferocity. "Your *home* is *my* property." The snarl in his face lingered, then he took in a deep breath, smoothed a hand over his silk robe, and he was once again the proper Minister of Justice with his grim and composed countenance. "But if you beg for forgiveness, if you swear upon your mother's life that you will not meddle anymore, I will reconsider your home at least. I will not take that from you."

His words stripped the flesh off my bones. These were not things a father should say. I took a step forward and my knees buckled, but I caught myself in time. *Beg,* a voice in my head whispered. Mother's voice. *Please, don't turn him against us.*

Tears trickled down my cheeks. Father's gaze darkened as I reached for the cell door and opened it further. "I'm sorry." I struggled to speak. "But the investigation isn't over yet."

He seemed too stunned to follow me as I staggered down the corridor, then out of the bureau.

———

It was evening by the time I stopped wandering around the empty fields and found the courage to return home. The sky was purple, the land a silhouette, and in between, a crack of orange light shimmered in its dying descent. As the shadows stretched, I felt as though my world had come undone, falling back into darkness, emptiness, and nothingness.

I should tell Mother. The voice in my head hummed as I stumbled up the steps and onto the wooden terrace. I pulled open the door and drifted inside. *I should tell her everything.*

I made my way to Mother's chamber, slid open the latticed door, and found it empty. I remembered that she usually put my little brother to sleep at this time. In the next shadowy room, I found them both asleep, my little brother's head nestled in the crook of her arm.

Mother stirred awake on the mat, her blanket shifting as she rose on her elbow to glance my way. She looked so exhausted.

"What is it?" she whispered.

I should tell her.

"I had a difficult day." I swallowed hard, wondering what Mother would say if she knew what I had done. Would she be angry? Would she say to me what Father had said? *Let our paths never cross again.*

"Can I—" I clenched my chattering teeth. "Can I sleep here?"

She stifled a yawn, looking too tired to be confused. "There is an extra blanket in the corner."

I hobbled my way across and gathered the blanket, then returned to Mother and my little brother—my only family. I lowered myself onto the sleeping mat and lay frozen, staring at her back. One of my childhood dreams had been to fall asleep next to her, safely sheltered in her arms. But I'd always felt too afraid to ask, too certain that she didn't like me very much.

And once she found out the truth, she would like me even less.

I closed my eyes, trying to stem the growing pain in my chest. Mother would never forgive me. She would leave me behind, just as she had ten years ago.

When morning came, I returned to my chamber and wanted to bury myself under the blanket, but Servant Mokgeum arrived with a freshly washed nursing uniform. She thought it was my workday, and it was, even though I feared the palace gates would not open for me.

"You look as though you've seen a ghost," Mokgeum said, shaking her head. "Are you ill?"

She passed me a bronze mirror, and I stared at my reflection, the events of yesterday hanging over me like a specter. I had lost everything in a single moment. Should I have prostrated myself before Father, begged for his forgiveness, however long it took? Should I have bowed with my forehead pressed to the ground until it bled, until my knees ached and my palms were chafed raw?

Unconsciously, I rubbed away an imaginary bruise on my forehead.

"Will you change into your uniform here?" Servant Mokgeum asked. "Or in the palace?"

"I will change here," I murmured, then paused.

A thought lurked in the far shadows of my mind. Raising the mirror again, I stared at my reflection—at my forehead—and tried to understand the uneasiness stirring in me.

"One moment, young mistress. I see a little tear in your uniform." Servant Mokgeum rushed off to find her sewing kit.

In the emptiness of my chamber, I continued to stand still, watching as a memory slowly surfaced onto the bronze mirror. The vision of a forehead marked by mud and a fresh wound. A gasp slipped from my lips as a thought clicked into place.

The odd marks on Physician Khun the day before . . . they were signs of a man who had prostrated himself in the mud—the marked forehead, the dirtied hands and knees. And an emotion, a fit of desperate grief or uncontrollable rage, had driven him—or someone else—into smashing his head on the ground.

Servant Mokgeum rushed back into the room, fussing over my uniform, a blur in the background as a question roared in my mind: Who had Physician Khun been bowing to?

14

I stepped into the palace, half expecting to be thrown out, but everyone seemed too distracted to pay me any mind.

A crowd of nurses talked of the Crown Prince. The king had changed his decision, permitting his son to accompany him and his entourage on the homage trip to Queen Jeongseong's royal tomb for the memorial service.

"When will His Highness return, uiwon-nim?" I asked my superior, remembering the medicine I had promised to bring the prince. I had to do so discreetly, as it was forbidden to administer medicine to a royal without officially recording it. I could have made it sooner, too, if not for the prison incident.

My thoughts came to a standstill at Physician Nanshin's prolonged silence. "Uiwon-nim?"

"You shouldn't be here, Nurse Hyeon." A frown knotted his brows. "Not anymore."

"I'm not sure I know what you mean, uiwon-nim," I said, even as a dreadful weight sunk into my chest.

"Lord Shin . . ." he whispered, a note of worry edging his voice. "He has demanded your removal, and he has many powerful connections within the palace." He then held out his hand. "I am sorry, Nurse Hyeon, but I must ask for your palace identification tag. You no longer serve here."

A surge of grief rose in my chest, followed by panic. The murder weapon was still within the walls. "May I finish assisting Nurse Jieun? I said I'd help her make medicine today," I lied.

Hesitation crumpled his face, then he cast a pity-filled look my way. "Very well, but you must still return the tag."

I blinked fast as I reached into my apron pocket and handed the tag to him, and I felt like I had handed over the only dream I ever had. I was nothing now, had nothing— except a murder case to solve.

"I do not know what happened, but I am sorry to see you go."

Physician Nanshin's words stung, and if this had been weeks ago, I would likely have crouched somewhere to cry alone. But I rallied all my thoughts on the task at hand. To make Crown Prince Jangheon's medicine and await his return.

Following the instructions I'd memorized, I prepared a small iron firepit and a boiling pot of water, then poured in the ingredients I had scavenged. Roughly cut-up baek-bok-ryung mushroom, which looked like chunks of rotten wood; dried jishil citrus; and a handful of other dried ingredients and roots.

Hiding from Jieun—for I knew she'd notice my distress at once—I crouched in the shadow of the Royal Apothecary with my back hunkered over the small pot, fanning the flame beneath. I needed just the right amount of heat to allow the herbs to simmer for a good hour.

Now and then, passing groups of nurses paused to glance my way, whispering among themselves. The word must have spread that I had been demoted. I lowered my head even more. I was a nobody; I didn't want to be seen by anyone.

Then the clouds gathered, dark and rolling. The shadows in the courtyard grew. I glanced up, wondering if it would rain, and right then, a droplet plopped into my eyes. I flinched and dashed the water away.

I was running out of time.

Quickly lifting the lid, I peered into the pot. "Thank heavens," I whispered. The liquid had simmered down to what might fill one small bowl. It was enough.

Gathering my apron around my hand, I picked up the black pot, its spout pointing out, as I escaped from beneath the open sky. Rain began to pour in earnest just as I dashed toward the nearby pavilion.

Across the courtyard, a line of nurses had stopped in their tracks despite the weather, bowing to a tall gentleman. My own steps slowed at the sight of his police hat and the unmistakable crescent of his face. A sharp tremor shot through me.

I rushed back into the shadows, the rain falling heavier now. I hurried down the terrace then hid behind one of the large columns upholding the roof high above me. My heart thundered so loud I could hear its pounding echo in my ears. Setting the pot down, I wiped the sweat and rain-water from my brows, my insides trembling.

"Why are you hiding from me?"

I whirled around to find myself face-to-face with Eojin, his expression taut with pained confusion. "Where did you disappear to last night?" he asked.

I gathered my hands behind my back, curling my fingers into a tight knot. "To the Gaekji House, where nurses can stay overnight." I glanced around—anywhere but at the young man before me. We were alone behind the apothecary, isolated behind the veil of rain dripping from the green-painted eaves.

I swallowed hard, trying to sound unaffected. "What are you doing here, nauri?"

He stood still—his eyes downcast—a tired and haggard look on his face. "This is all my fault. I was too reckless." He took my hand, and, unfolding my fingers, he placed an object in my grasp. It was my silver acupuncture case.

"I questioned Damo Sulbi when I discovered this," his voice rasped. "She told me what occurred. And the other prisoners told me what they'd overheard between you and your father. That you are to lose your position here because of me."

He was still holding my hand. I at once pulled myself free.

"It's not your fault. I asked you to sneak me into the bureau—"

236

"I'll make everything right again." A note of determination hardened his voice. "I've prepared a report for the Old Doctrine faction."

Dread cinched around me. "What report . . ."

"We haven't yet found solid evidence, but . . . I intend to bring all we've discovered before them. And in return, I will ask that they put Commander Song out of power and return you to your position."

My head shook slowly. No one who involved themselves in court politics tended to live for very long. "Not yet, nauri. It's too soon to hand everything over to the Old Doctrine." I picked up the pot, still hot in my grasp. "There is one more thing I need to find. One last thing I can do for the investigation—for your report. The Crown Prince knows something, and I have a way of finding out."

His brows pressed together. "How—"

"I'll tell you more next time, nauri. But you must promise to do nothing until then." I bowed, wanting to rush off before Eojin could protest. "If you will excuse me."

"Hyeon-ah, wait." He reached out for me, but his hand dropped away as I turned. "When all this is over . . ." His gaze bored into me—that familiar searching gaze, as though he were leaning in to peer beneath the surface of who I was. As though he actually saw something worth looking for. "Come with me to the Lantern Festival."

I blinked as a burning sensation spread across my chest. We had only ever visited crime scenes and our command post to hold discussions about corpses and clues. The thought of going anywhere outside of that—the thought of our partnership existing outside of it—it was so hard to fathom. It was hard to imagine being an ordinary young man and woman, without the bonds of death holding us together. It was hard to imagine whether he would even want to remain friends with me then.

"But . . . why me?" I asked, breathless.

Eojin stepped close and whispered, "I like being with you."

I clutched the pot tighter, the only thing separating me from his towering figure. He hesitated, then ran a finger down the side of my cheek. I stopped breathing as I found myself unable to break my gaze from his. At that moment, I forgot where I was. It seemed we must have both forgotten, for he leaned down and pressed his lips against my cheek.

So quickly was he gone—taking a retreating step away from me—that I almost wondered if the kiss had even happened.

"I'm sorry," he said, his voice unsteady. "I wasn't thinking. That won't happen again."

My heart pounded, and a feeling like a bruise formed at the pit of my stomach. Father's words echoed in my head, ringing true now and sharpening the sting. I would never be anyone's Greatest Love. I would always be a stolen kiss, a fleeting moment—a mistake.

"You called me bold, so I will be bold, nauri," I said with surprising calm. "I may be a mere servant girl to you, but I will not be your plaything."

"Hyeon-ah," he called, but I'd already turned to leave. He crossed the terrace in an instant and caught my wrist. "Please, you misunderstand me . . . A plaything? Do you think I care for you so little?"

I lowered my lashes, staring hard at the brilliant blue of his silk robe. *He is no different from me,* Father's voice said, as though he stood right by my side. *Eojin may fancy you now, but later, there will always be someone else. Someone worthier than you.*

"I can't afford to be distracted. Not now. Not when—" I swallowed hard. "Not when I've lost too much searching for the truth already. I apologize, nauri. But I can't be distracted by you, and neither should you be distracted by me."

Someone far off cleared their throat.

Snatching my wrist away, I shot a glance over my shoulder to see Lady Hyegyoung and a drenched court lady standing in the yard. The latter was holding up a jiusan parasol by its long handgrip, protecting Her Ladyship from the rain. When had she arrived? How much had she seen?

My mind raced, and these frantic questions pulled me away from Eojin and the look on his face.

"I need to go," I said, and left him there.

As soon as I approached Lady Hyegyoung, she whispered, "Eunuch Im told me that you were tasked with procuring medicine for the prince. Do you have it?"

This was supposed to be a secret, but Her Ladyship didn't look outraged. "I do." I lifted the pot. "Ondamtang."

"Follow me," she said, and I did. "We must prepare for the prince's return. He will be in a foul mood."

"But, my lady, he has left to pay homage to—"

"His Highness is on his way back." She looked at me, and her eyes were full of dread. "It started raining so heavily. The king blamed His Highness for it, saying the heavens were showing their displeasure at the prince's presence. So the prince—and he alone—was ordered to leave."

15

Under the cover of elaborate green-painted eaves, Lady Hyegyoung waited on the terrace, looking out for the Crown Prince, alongside a row of trembling court ladies.

I stepped into the prince's residence, down an empty corridor, and into the inner quarter with a tray I'd quickly prepared moments ago, loaded with a drinking bowl and the pot of medicine. Both were dry, as I'd journeyed here under the parasol with Her Ladyship. *Prepare a bowl of the Ondamtang medicine,* she had ordered. *Serve it to the prince on his return. We must do all we can to calm the seja-jeoha's rage, or blood will flow again.*

Again.

A creeping realization slid into my mind: Lady Hyegyoung already knew of Prince Jangheon's violence, and his beheading of Nurse Hyo-ok. She had known, as had the three murdered palace women; they were all silent witnesses who had closed their eyes hoping to survive.

My knees bumped up against a low-legged table, and

my mind snapped into focus. I knelt down, unloaded the tray, then poured the medicine into the drinking bowl, right up to the brim. Once that was done, I rose back to my feet and looked around, wondering where to stand.

I made my way toward the row of tall lattice screens where gray light filtered through and washed over the spacious floor, which was still cluttered with books and heaps of robes—as if the Crown Prince had thrown them aside in anger. Then my gaze lingered on the mother-of-pearl inlaid cabinet, glowing in the dim light.

I glanced around. No one was in this chamber but myself, and in the absolute silence that swamped around me, an outrageous idea surfaced. My gaze drifted back to the cabinet—the one Prince Jangheon had glanced at while telling me about a bloody object he had discovered on the night of the massacre.

It had to be the murder weapon.

This is your last day at the palace, a thought whispered in my head. *The last day to uncover one last piece of evidence.*

Gripping the tray tighter, I remained still, my heart leaping within my chest.

You lost your dream, your future. You've lost yourself. All for what? The voice circled around me, prickling down my skin. *At least solve this case you gave up everything for.*

I took a hesitant step forward, glanced around again. At the continued silence, my steps grew bolder. Setting the tray down, I slid one of the cabinet's drawers open, then another, my hands moving quicker with every passing moment. I encountered little gemstones, gold pins, rolls of silk headbands—

I stopped, noticing one drawer that looked shallower than the rest, though it should have been the same size. I ran my fingers along the edge until my finger slipped into a little hole, popping up a false bottom.

I raised it carefully . . . and found myself staring at a dagger crusted in reddish-brown down to its hilt.

No, I realized as a gasp filled my chest. It wasn't a dagger.

It was a pichim—a long, thin medical blade used to make incisions.

I had seen its kind used before, often to deal with an infection. It almost looked like a dagger, considering how long the blade was, but it was only supposed to be sharp at the top. This one was sharper than the average pichim; it must have been honed with some type of grinding device.

I picked up the blade and turned it around, examining it. Was this the weapon that had stabbed Court Lady Ahnbi in the chest and throat?

A door slid open behind me.

Pulse leaping, I kept my back turned, hoping my figure would hide me as I slipped the bloody tool back where I'd found it, lowered the false bottom, then quietly slid the drawer shut. I then turned, and felt nausea churning in my stomach at the sight of Prince Jangheon.

Water dripped from the brim of his black hat, strands of his hair leaking down his shadowed face. His silk robe was also drenched, the silver dragon embroidery mud-smeared.

"What are you doing here." It wasn't a question.

"I came to—" My mouth was so parched, the words stuck to my tongue. I swallowed hard and tried again. "I came to bring the medicine as promised, Your Highness."

He did not move, did not utter a single word. Nothing but his shallow breathing and the drip, drip, drip of water falling from his hat disturbed the tense quiet.

"You drink it," he said softly.

I dug my nails into my palm. "It is for you, Your Highness," I said as politely as possible. "It will help soothe—"

"You poisoned it, didn't you?" Water squelched in his boots as he walked toward me. "I saw you closing that drawer."

"I—I saw it open and so closed it, Your Highness, that is all."

His icy hand grabbed my chin, pinching it tight as he lifted my head. "Look at me," he said, and when I did, I saw bloodshot eyes, as though he were burning from within. "The Old Doctrine faction is behind you, aren't they?" His voice thinned into a sharp whisper. "They knew you looked like my sister, so they placed you close to me, to find out my secrets, my weaknesses."

My eyes widened. "No, Your Highness!"

"Your father has ties to my rival faction." His grip tightened, like he was bent on snapping my jaw, and panic blossomed like ice crystals in my chest. "Both of you have

244

testified, haven't you? That I was indeed outside the palace on the night of the massacre? And now you will tell the Old Doctrine officials about this weapon and say that it was mine. That I killed those girls."

"Please." It was difficult to speak with my chin raised so high. "Let me explain—"

"Now I understand." A twisted, humorless laugh escaped him. "That is why my father—in the midst of hundreds of watching officials—ordered me to leave. It is spies like you that have turned my own father into my greatest enemy."

With a snarl of disgust, he dropped my chin, and I staggered back. My mind blanked of any attempts to hold on to etiquette and reeled with only one thought: I needed to escape.

And the only option was on the other side of the chamber—the double doors still partway open, revealing the corridor.

I darted a glance at the prince, who now stood in the corner of his chamber, the shadows draping him like a cloak. Then he turned, half in darkness, half lit by the storm raging outside, and he was holding a long, sleek bow.

My stomach dropped. "N-no," I stammered. "Please, Your Highness. I am *not* a spy!"

In one smooth motion, he nocked an arrow and pointed the gleaming metal tip my way. "That is what the others said, too. Eunuch Hanch'ae, Nurse Hyo-ok, my own concubine, and the others."

My knees buckled as I continued to back away. *There were others.*

"My father is going to kill me, and if I am to die . . ." He drew his arrow back with practiced ease, and I heard the string stretching, slowly, slowly . . . "I will take all my enemies with me."

He released.

Pain sliced my cheek as I dove to the floor, arms raised over my head; a loud thud echoed behind me. With a quick glance, I saw the arrow embedded in the wall—and that I was only a few steps away from the entrance.

While the prince nocked another arrow, I was up on my feet again, dashing for the door. But no matter how fast I ran, the sound followed me.

Bowstring, stretching.

The silence as the prince lined up his shot.

A whistle pierced the air again, pursuing me in my stumble out of the chamber. A powerful thud slammed me to the ground, taking me down by the thick muscle just below my left shoulder, but the pain hardly registered. Of its own accord, my hand moved to snap off the arrow shaft, and my legs kept moving.

Rain and fresh air burst around me the moment I scrambled out of the pavilion and found myself face-to-face with Lady Hyegyoung and the row of court ladies.

"Help me," I gasped. Disorientation dizzied me; my mind couldn't quite grasp what was happening. "Please, help me."

The crowd of women backed away like I was the

plague, whimpering and appearing as scared as I knew I should have felt. Cold reality sunk into my bones, and the past stepped into me. I was Nurse Hyo-ok, staring at the three witnesses—Court Lady Ahnbi, Nurse Aram, Nurse Kyunghee. *Please,* we begged as the Crown Prince approached, *help me.*

"Go," one of the court ladies cried. "Or we will all die!"

Lady Hyegyoung, her face drained of all blood, hissed, "You must leave. Run, Nurse Hyeon. Hide yourself and do not be found!"

At the sound of footsteps echoing down the corridor, I hobbled across the courtyard, colliding with the stone wall that enclosed the pavilion. I made my way along it, slipped through a small gate, and found myself in a maze of smaller courtyards, winding pavilions, and shadows. Where could I hide that I would not be found? Who could I turn to when the palace was full of silent witnesses?

A warm hand clasped my wrist, and the panic that surged through me faded at the sight of a familiar face.

Eojin.

Any shred of resentment I might have held against him vanished. As he rushed me through the yard, through a small tunnel in between buildings, I stole glances his way, at his rain-drenched face. My shudders stopped as the warmth of his grip sunk into mine, my limbs no longer trembled, and my legs strengthened as I ran alongside him.

"We mustn't leave any tracks," he told me.

He quickly hid his muddy boots, and I realized that I had none, having taken my sandals off before entering the pavilion. I wrenched off my wet socks instead, and after throwing them in a bush, I squeezed the rain out of my clothing. We then hurried down a terrace that wrapped around a long pavilion. The moment we found an unlocked door, we ducked inside and slid it shut as quietly as possible. Eyes fixed on the latticed screen, we waited for a silhouette of an archer to appear.

Eojin reached for his side, only to realize that he was swordless. He must have had to remove it before entering palace grounds. "We need to hide somewhere safer."

I glanced around, and my eyes latched upon a large folding screen that bore a decorative painting, opened against a wall at the far end of the room. Holding Eojin's hand, I pulled him along until we were standing behind it, the screen right before our faces, our backs hovering near the wall.

"Our last encounter ended badly," Eojin spoke in the barest whisper, "so I came here to explain myself to you. Then I heard the commotion." He turned to me, then his attention froze on my shoulder. "You were shot—"

I placed a finger to my lips. "We must stay calm."

"Calm?" A shallow breath escaped him as his face turned pale. "You're *bleeding*."

"The more urgent a circumstance," I said quietly, repeating Nurse Jeongsu's words, "the calmer we must be."

Footsteps creaked across the terrace outside.

I held his hands tighter, fear chilling my blood, but this time coupled with the dread that I'd lose Eojin. Even if he had his sword, drawing a weapon against the Crown

Prince was punishable by death. We were trapped, with nothing to save us.

The door slowly slid open.

A damp, crisp breeze tumbled in.

I held my breath—we both did—hands growing damp with sweat.

Wind continued to howl in for what felt like an eternity.

Then, at long last, the door slid shut with a forceful clack, and the footsteps stalked off, heavy and determined. More doors slid open and shut in the near distance. A few moments later, the sound of female screams erupted, followed by the scattering of footsteps, like a crowd of court ladies fleeing from a prowling tiger.

Then, nothing.

Rain pitter-pattered against the hanji screens, and soon, even the rain stopped pouring. The shadows in the room did not move, as though they were painted onto the floor.

"Let me see your wound." Eojin at last spoke.

Reminded of it now, I turned my shoulder to him and became aware of the throbbing pain, like someone had seared me with a burning coal. The arrow seemed to have lodged somewhere between my shoulder and upper arm. The side of my face also stung, and when I touched it, I felt the slippery wetness of blood. Nicked by an arrow. A shudder coursed through me at the memory.

"It's not a hunting arrow," Eojin whispered. "I'm sure of that."

The pain was beginning to become unbearable. Clenching my teeth, I asked, "How can you tell?"

"Because the arrow isn't lodged too deep. I can see a bit of the arrowhead." He grasped my hand, gently. "We need to leave and find you a physician."

We slipped out of the room, treading with quiet steps, pausing every now and then to strain our ears for any warning of the prince's approach. But it was all grave silence. We were near a gate that led out of the prince's compound when I saw it—blood smeared across the yard. The bright crimson stain filled my vision, a haze of red that I couldn't blink away.

When we finally managed to escape out of the palace through Tonghwa Gate, I turned to Eojin and whispered, "It should have been me."

"It should have been no one," he said, his voice tight as he led me to a post where his horse was tethered. "No one should have died today."

"But someone did. And no one will hear of it tomorrow."

"That is the way of the palace. My father warned me of this." He paused, glancing over his shoulder at the small gate. "If you enter the palace, you either die or you survive and become another monster within its walls . . . Come," he whispered, as he lifted me onto the saddle and sat behind me, urging the horse forward. "We need to get you out of the capital."

16

The great bell struck, its resounding ring rumbling down the streets. Massive gates on all corners of the fortress thundered shut, and we narrowly made it out on horseback. Hooves pounded across the earth as the capital and its guardian mountain dwindled into a black-ridged shadow. The distance that had taken me over a half hour to walk, we covered in a matter of minutes; soon, the lights of my home twinkled in the distance.

"We're almost there," Eojin called out over the blast of wind. "I'll summon a physician right away."

Biting my lip hard, I ducked my head over the horse's whipping mane to hide my tears. The pain had sunk in, a thousand blades stabbing into my back, twisting through the flesh and sawing through my bones. Each breath I took felt like breathing in shards of ice, making deep inhales impossible. I sipped in shallow breaths instead, my head spinning; I would have fallen off the saddle if not for Eojin's tight embrace.

As soon as we arrived, Eojin slid off the horse and helped me down, careful not to press against my wound. I had thought the horrors were behind me, but as he helped me stagger toward the glowing screened door of my home, another nightmare descended. A rush of memories from a day ago, of Father standing before my prison cell, of all my hopes and dreams shattering under the weight of his words. This was not *my* home, this was Father's property. And Mother—it was no longer her home, either.

Breathing became more difficult, and I could feel the strength draining from my legs. "I have to tell you," I choked, trying to deflect the pain of loss and the blade-sharp arrowhead digging inside my flesh. "I found evidence . . . in the Crown Prince's chamber . . ."

My head whirled as I stumbled, Eojin's grip tightening in an attempt to steady me.

"Stay with me, Hyeon-ah," he said desperately. "Just a few more steps."

A few more steps and my bones turned to water, my hearing faded, and shadows closed in around my vision. I plunged into a welcome darkness.

———

At first, there were only faraway echoes.

"It is a foamy narcotic powder," said a male voice, ringing as though I were hearing him from underwater. "I will dissolve it into wine. It will ease the pain."

Then the darkness shifted as someone lifted my head

and poured a drink into my mouth, and I was once more adrift in a lightweight void.

When I opened my eyes, I saw a haze of colors that slowly sharpened into familiar shapes. My room lit with the rays of first light. Servant Mokgeum and—to my surprise—Jieun sat against the wall, their heads nodding in sleep.

Then my gaze locked on Eojin.

He was crouched, his sleeves rolled up as he rinsed the side of a silk blanket in a bowl of water, twisted it out, then rinsed it again. The small red stain remained on the fabric. I followed his sunlit shadow to the tray next to where I lay, and on that tray was a bloody arrowhead attached to a broken shaft. The blood must have spurted onto my blanket when the arrowhead was pulled out of me. Water trickled again. Eojin dipped the blanket back into the bowl, his brows furrowed with determination. It was a strange sight, seeing a man dressed in blue silk and a black police hat hunched over the ground, scrubbing away like he was a servant.

Lying still, too afraid to move on my own, I cleared my throat. "The blood is dried in. It won't come out."

Eojin glanced up, and a look of relief washed over his face. "You're awake," he said. "How are you feeling?"

"Aching." I cautiously reached and picked up the arrow, spun it between my fingers, trying to appear unaffected by the incident at the palace. "But nothing I cannot handle."

He rose to his feet and moved closer. Then, helping me into a sitting position, he leaned to the side and inspected my shoulder. "Blood is starting to soak through your bandage. The physician said not to remove it, though, as we need to maintain pressure over your wound. I'll ask the servant to add a fresh layer over the old one." He turned to leave.

"Wait." I caught the side of his robe, then quickly withdrew my hand. "What happened last night, nauri? I don't remember anything after the moment we arrived here."

"Three days have passed."

I blinked, stunned. "Three?"

"Perhaps it was the injury and the shock of the incident combined, but you slept through those three days." He paused. "And you were also given narcotics to cope with the pain, as you requested."

"I don't remember any of that," I mumbled. "I don't remember anything . . ."

Gently taking the arrow, he placed it back on the tray, then pushed it behind him, out of his line of sight. Like he didn't want to remember.

"You passed out, and I managed to find a local physician." His gaze remained fixed on his hand, raw from trying to clean the bloodstain. "I couldn't trust him, though, especially not when he suggested that the arrow be left in. I have seen several cases of such decisions resulting in deadly infections. So the following day I summoned a physician from the capital. He'd treated many arrow wounds before, and extracted the arrowhead within moments. He said that you were fortunate, as the arrow wasn't embedded in bone."

He expelled a breath and turned his gaze to the folding screen open before us, fixed there as though he were appreciating the watercolors. "The wound should heal naturally."

Eojin, I realized, was avoiding my gaze. Something else had occurred in the past three days, something he didn't want to tell me about. "What's wrong?"

A look of hesitation flickered across his face. "I wanted to wait to talk to you, to let you rest. But it seems we are running out of time."

"Talk to me about what?"

"Before passing out, you mentioned that you had found evidence in the Crown Prince's chamber."

Memory of that day surged into my mind. The gleaming black bow, the arrow nocked and pointed at my head. I hid my hands in the fold of my skirt, to hide the returning tremors. "Remember what I told you a few days ago? That the Crown Prince told me my father was his alibi?"

He still wouldn't look at me. "Go on."

"He said the culprit had bumped into him while running away," I continued. "And had dropped a weapon. I saw where he was looking as he said this, and so three days ago, when I found myself in his chamber alone, I . . . I went to see what was inside."

"And then the prince caught you in the act." His expression turned to stone. "And nearly killed you for it."

"It was worth it," I said defensively. I didn't like the way he was talking to me, like I had done something wrong. He was the one who had asked me to assist him with the investigation in the first place.

A tense silence unfolded around us, and I kept my stare on him, waiting for him to ask. When he did not, I gave up and blurted, "Well, nauri? Do you want to know what I found or not?"

He ran a hand over his face. "What did you find?"

"A pichim. It is a kind of medical blade used to make incisions."

An oppressive stillness fell over him. "A pichim? Why a medical tool?"

"I wondered that myself."

He folded his arms across his chest, his brows lowered. At length, he murmured, "The only reason I can think of is familiarity. The killer reached for a tool their hands knew best how to wield."

The most obvious name now surfaced in my mind. "Physician Khun. He's our only suspect with a medical background."

The motive for Physician Khun seemed clear: to avenge his mother's death, murdering the silent witnesses and framing the Crown Prince for it all.

"There is also Nurse Inyeong, the witness," I murmured. I could think of no motive at all for her. Yet I couldn't get over what a strange coincidence it had been to see her at the scene of Court Lady Ahnbi's murder. "What now?"

He stared out the window a moment, then turned just enough to reveal a crescent of his face. "Rest, Hyeon-ah," he whispered. "Until you recover, there is no 'what now.' Let us pretend that everything is well for a few days."

I studied him, greatly puzzled, as he rose and crossed the room.

"Ajumma," he called out, and Servant Mokgeum snored loudly before her eyes startled open. Jieun also shot awake. "The young mistress is in need of a fresh layer of bandage."

"She is awake?" The old woman looked my way, and her eyes shone with relief. "She is awake!"

"Thank heavens!" Jieun expelled a deep sigh.

As both women hurried over, clucking over me like two motherly hens, Eojin disappeared out the door, the sliding doors shutting behind him with a gentle clack. Why was he behaving so strangely? And why did his parting remark bother me so? *Let us pretend that everything is well.*

"Your mother and I were so worried!" Servant Mokgeum said. "We feared the worst—"

"Did anything happen in the three days that I was out?" I asked, still watching the door. "Besides my injury. What else happened?"

"Geulsseyo . . ." She tilted her head to the side, brows furrowed. "I don't know, agasshi."

"I did hear my cousin say that he'd discovered a crucial piece of evidence," Jieun chimed in, "but I'm not sure what. I overheard it so quickly, as he spoke with your mother, then had to hurry off."

Now I understood why his remark had bothered me. He had told me to rest, to pretend as though everything was well for a few days—when there were absolutely no more days to spare. Every single day, every single hour that passed, was critical to Nurse Jeongsu. It could only mean one thing.

He had dropped me from his investigation.

He intended to go it alone.

Struggling to my feet, I said, "Help me braid and coil my hair."

Servant Mokgeum fluttered about in worry at my request, but I fixed her with an imperious stare. She remained tight-lipped with disapproval as she proceeded to style my hair.

"But you can't leave the house, Hyeon-ah," Jieun protested, her eyes darting nervously between my servant and me. "You *need* to rest."

I kept quiet, determined. I would go to the police bureau and demand answers from Eojin; I would go to him not as a wounded bird he felt duty-bound to protect, but as an uinyeo who had staked her life for the truth. I had come all this way, and I wasn't going to let him leave me out now. I had given up too much for this.

I secured the black silk garima to my head, perhaps for the last time, and right then I heard the voice of Mokgeum outside my room. She must have snuck out to tattle on me. "Mistress, mistress!" came her voice. "The agasshi dressed herself and is about to leave the house!"

With Jieun's assistance, I struggled into my silk uniform—dark blue skirt and pale blue jacket—wincing each time the slightest movement jostled my wound. I then added the final touch: jibun powder to the cut on my face. It was then that the doors behind me slid open. I raised my guard, prepared for Mother to try to stop me.

"Men never came to me for entertainment," she said calmly as Jieun quickly left the room and shut the door to allow us privacy, "but rather when they needed to talk. Your father, too, only comes to me when he has something on his mind."

I slipped a glance over my shoulder, bewildered and slightly wary. Mother stood with her black hair smoothed and tied into the perfect knot at the nape of her neck, a silver pin gleaming from it. Her handsome face was, as ever, emotionless as a rock. There was a straw cloak draped over one arm, and in the other, she was holding a straw satgat hat.

"I will make him talk. I have old friends who are influential members of the Southerner faction; they will be eager for evidence that proves the Crown Prince's innocence. They are the faction that will be wiped out if the prince falls."

My gaze dropped to the hem of Mother's skirt, sunk by the sudden weight of confusion.

"I overheard," she explained. "You told the inspector that your father was His Highness's alibi. Such truths ought not to be hidden."

"You would . . . betray Father?"

"If no one speaks the truth, how will you ever rescue your teacher? It must begin with your father. He needs to testify whom he was with during the time of the killing. From there, hopefully, more truths will be unveiled."

I let her words settle in. Even with the confession, it would only be enough for Father to receive punishment; surely it wouldn't free Nurse Jeongsu. But as Mother had said, it was a step in the right direction—and perhaps one of the most difficult steps of all.

"Finding a way to speak to him might prove difficult . . ." I whispered, unable to meet her gaze any longer. "He is furious at me. He ordered us all to leave this house."

I waited for her anger, for her violent rage. I waited for her to turn me away from her presence. To disown me. But when the storm did not strike, I glanced up to see a pair of steady eyes.

"I already know," she said, and a ripple of surprise coursed down my spine, followed by relief. "Prisoners gossip, as do police servants, and gossip spreads fast in the capital. Do not concern yourself about me. Surely I can muster enough courage to leave this house." Her voice softened, her brows knotted. "We must both be brave, Baek-hyeon. But you must be braver. You must save Nurse Jeongsu."

I could hardly believe my ears. Nothing about who Mother was matched my understanding of her.

"Why do you care what happens to Nurse Jeongsu?" I asked. They were words I would never have thought to ask even a month ago, but so much had changed since then. "You left me outside the Gibang House in the middle of winter."

But now, in my memory of that incident, I no longer stood alone before the Gibang House. Now, in the snowy scene of my mind, another figure appeared—a shadow that sat in her frigid palanquin, wide-eyed as she watched me and prayed that the madam would take me in.

"You . . . You watched me waiting outside in the snow," I whispered. "You remained watching even as I was crying."

Not even a flicker of shock registered on her face, except for an ever-so-slight reddening of her eyes. "I have no excuse . . ." Her voice rasped. "I wanted to raise you to be strong, to be prepared for the hardship that awaited you as a woman of your status. Yet I almost crushed you instead, would have if Nurse Jeongsu had not intervened. I am forever grateful to her. She is more of a mother to you than I will ever be."

She walked over to me, closing the great chasm between us. When she stood only a pace away, she suddenly looked too vulnerable, too fragile, like a delicate willow leaf. "If you are going to Damyang County, you ought to hide yourself. You do not know who might be looking for you after the . . . incident at the palace."

She offered me the conical straw hat, and after a grief-stricken moment, I reluctantly removed my garima—my crown, a testament to the highest achievement any girl in my position could hope to obtain. I'd never be able to wear it again. My fingers ran along the silk, my heart filling with memories of how proud I'd felt to wear this, and I was afraid to think of life without it—of who I was without my title.

Swallowing hard, I at last put the garima aside and donned the satgat, lowering its wide brim over my wet eyes, and that was when Mother's words finally registered.

"Damyang?" I whispered. "Why did you say Damyang?"

Her hands paused midair, fingers lifted to touch the brim of my hat. "Did the inspector not tell you?"

"Tell me what?"

"Apparently you asked a police damo to search for information. I do not know the details, but they found where the missing student nurse is. Minji is with a relative in Damyang; the young inspector was leaving for that county."

I glanced at the bloody arrowhead, still on the tray, and my shoulder burned with pain. I nevertheless intended to find Eojin, though now his leaving without me didn't seem so unreasonable—Damyang was almost two days away by horse.

"If you leave now," Mother continued, "you might catch up with him near the shores of Han River."

I would go because I wished to, but I couldn't understand why Mother wished the same of me. "Why are you encouraging me to go?" I asked hesitantly. "Other mothers would order me to stay."

In one billowing movement, she tucked the straw cloak around me. "I watched you these three days, and I listened to the inspector's stories of your part in the investigation. It reminded me of my taemong dream of you before your birth. I dreamt of a black dragon on the walls, and was sure I would have a boy, and was thus so confused when you were born a girl. Still, I gave you the name based on the dream I'd had. *Baek*, meaning 'eldest.' And *Hyeon*, meaning 'virtuous, worthy, and able.' I even named your little brother after you—Dae-*hyeon*."

A strange sensation prickled under my skin, the same sensation I'd felt when Nurse Kyunghee had read the last letter from the beheaded palace nurse to her son, Physician Khun. But I still couldn't put a finger on what bothered me about it.

"I realize now," Mother continued, "that you are quite capable, and I do not think a wound on your shoulder will stop you." She slipped out a cylinder case from a pouch tied to her skirt and pressed it into my hand. The cold of the silver stilled the hum of frustration prickling through me, returning my attention to the present, and I found myself staring down at delicate symbols engraved into the metal.

"It is a jangdo knife manufactured in Ulsan's Byeong-yeong region," she said. "I meant to save this for you, for when you marry."

A knife was the symbol of a woman's duty to fulfill her proper duties in married life. "I see," I whispered, not knowing what else to say.

"But it seems more fitting to give this to you now. A parent gives a knife to their son when he reaches adulthood, so that he might be loyal to the kingdom and fulfill his duty." She paused, letting out a wavering breath. "You are an adult now, and there are heavy decisions that await you. I trust that you will make the right ones."

I pulled the case apart, removing the sheath until a

dagger gleamed in my hand. My grip trembled around the silver handle. I'd never held a weapon before.

"Come back to us, Hyeon-ah." Mother spoke softly, and with that, she left me alone with a weight in my chest. I prayed that I would not need to use this dagger, and at the same time thought, *I would never hurt anyone with this.*

But perhaps this was what the killer had once believed, too—until they had lost the most precious thing in their life.

I wondered what that might be for me.

What it might take for me to end the life of another.

17

I did not find Eojin on the shores of Han River, but while crossing to the other side of the waterway, I caught a flash of blue silk past the crowd of boats and fishermen. I saw him standing with his hands held behind his back, a posture of intense concentration as he listened to a merchant with boxes loaded onto his back. This merchant held a folded fan, which he pointed at different directions in the distance, then undulated in the air as though he were tracing out mountains.

Once I was in hearing distance, the merchant asked in a thick southwestern dialect, "Are you certain you can memorize all the directions, nauri?"

"Once I am informed," Eojin replied, low-voiced, "I rarely forget."

Of course, I thought, as I watched him drop a coin into the merchant's hand. Eojin had passed the civil service exam at such a young age, which spoke of his great capacity to memorize and to understand. Most languished in their ambition to pass the gwageo exam, many studying from when they were five and still failing it at thirty, and even eighty.

I understood that desperate ambition to pass, to rise from anonymity.

Anonymity that I'd never escape now.

My heart ached around the empty hole Father had left behind. He'd taken my dream, my everything.

Shoving my grief down, I sucked in a deep breath of fresh air, then locked my focus on Eojin. He was now heading down the wide, dusty road that seemed to disappear into the pale blue distance. I followed, always keeping several paces behind him, far enough that he wouldn't hear my footsteps. I tilted the brim of my straw hat lower.

After a while, certain he wouldn't discover me, I eased my alertness. My stomach rumbled with hunger. I slipped open the small traveling sack Servant Mokgeum had prepared for me before I left, filled with a string of coins, fresh bandages, and dried squid. I pulled out a tentacle and, while chewing on it, looked around.

Nature whispered to me its age-old promise, as it had at the Segeomjeong Pavilion. I might have lost my position—I might still lose more—but everything would be well in the end. *Look,* the trees whispered, *look how we sway, how we sing and dance.*

I took another bite, my eyes watering.

A part of me feared this promise was meant for everyone but me.

I sniffled and wiped the tears away with my sleeve.

Just then, my feet tripped over something solid, a rock

jutting from the ground, and a short cry escaped me. I at once steadied myself, hands clamped over my mouth. Had he heard? When I looked up, my gaze slammed into the sight of Eojin, who'd turned back at the noise. He was too far for me to see his expression. He drew closer, closer, and his oblique brows and aquiline nose came into view, a stormy look clouding his face. His hand fell away from the sword at his side.

"What—" He seemed at a loss for words, his stare boring into me. Then he ran a hand over his haggard face. "Your mother told you, didn't she."

"By accident."

He shot a glance past my shoulder, and I knew what he would not see—neither the shadow of the capital nor a glimmer of the Han River. We were too far now to justify turning back.

"Come." He stalked past me anyway. "I am taking you home."

I stood anchored. "We've been walking for at least two hours. It'll take another two to escort me back, then another two for you to return to this very spot. The day will nearly be over, and you will have gotten nowhere." Then, solemnly, I added, "We have less than four days left until the verdict drops for Nurse Jeongsu. There will only be two days left when you reach Damyang County. And you will have barely any time to return to convince Commander Song. You have no time to spare."

Eojin fell still, and remained with his back to me, facing the direction that would lead us to the Han River. A stubborn edge cut along his stiff shoulders. "We will have to travel through a dozen villages," he warned, "through rivers and mountains. The journey will only aggravate your wound."

"It doesn't matter; I am an uinyeo, I know how to take care of myself."

He did not budge.

"I chose this path," I said, my voice rising a notch. "This is the only path I can take now, and you must let me walk it."

The tension in his shoulders eased, and turning on his heel, he walked past me without a glance. "You are most irritating," he said when I caught up with him.

"Irritating because I am right, nauri?" I asked, sliding in a note of politeness.

"Yes." A reluctant half smile. "You are right, Nurse Hyeon. You are always right."

We walked quietly, and I kept the brim of my hat lowered to hide the smile that tugged at my lips. With Eojin, the mountains rose high and the fields of swaying grass enclosed us in a small world of our own where it was easy to forget—even for the briefest moment—the direness of our circumstance and the sadness still lurking under my ribs.

"So, you found that Minji is in Damyang," I said after a time. "How did Damo Sulbi and Nurse Oksun discover this?"

"I suppose your mother told you this, too."

"Not in detail."

"Nurse Oksun learned of Minji's father's recent travels through another physician. Apparently, the father was injured on his brief journey to and from Damyang. I thought it odd that he would leave the capital for Damyang so soon after the Hyeminseo massacre, and discovered that he has a relative there, a distant family member. When I approached Minji's father about this yesterday, he turned pale and begged me to keep her out of the investigation, saying that they did not wish to see her arrested and tortured like Nurse Jeongsu. This was enough to confirm my suspicion."

A tingle coursed through me, down to the tips of my fingers. I clasped my hands tightly together. "We'll finally find the truth of what happened that night," I whispered. "And considering how the Hyeminseo victims fought back, surely if the killer was wearing a veil or mask around their face, it would have been torn off."

"That is my hope, too," Eojin replied. "That Minji caught a glimpse of the culprit's face."

"And if not?"

"Then we can ask if she heard the culprit speak. Was the killer a man or a woman? And if not even that, then we will find out something I've wondered since the very start: How did Student Nurse Minji manage to escape the massacre?"

His question lingered in my mind as a light drizzle fell, sunlit rain carried on the wind from the dark clouds gathering overhead. We were on the edge of a storm. As we passed into the woodlands that covered the mountain base and followed a winding trail that many had walked before, worry pinched at me. The path seemed endless, and it seemed an eternity stretched between us and Damyang.

"There's a storm coming, nauri," I said. "When we find a town, we should borrow horses, or else this journey will take far too long." I loosened my traveling sack and pulled out a string of coins, sunlight gleaming off the jangling loop. "I brought enough for that."

"That won't be necessary. Over the mountain is a town with a police bureau," he said. "I intend to requisition horses there." He paused. "Do you know how to ride?"

"I do."

"We'll have a long trip ahead on horseback. If your shoulder hurts, you will be sure to tell me?"

"I will," I lied.

"And you will need something to protect yourself with. There are many bandits and wild animals roaming these parts."

"I have something. A dagger. My mother gifted it to me."

"Do you? Let me see it." He reached out and took the silver case, and when he pulled off the sheath, a look of surprise glinted on his face as he examined the steel. "This blade is from the military region of Byeongyeong, where the greatest types of jangdo knives were forged. For a mother whom you claim cares nothing for you, she went far out of her way to purchase this."

I sighed. "She's not entirely who I thought her to be." A pause beat through me as the memory of her words surfaced. "Mother told me the story of why she gave me my name."

"Indeed?" Eojin said. "I am curious to know why anyone would name their daughter Baek-hyeon. 'Virtuous Elder Brother.'"

Again, like before, an uneasy sensation shifted under my skin as my muscles tensed. A feeling that there was something I should *know*. I massaged my temple and murmured, "It was from a dream—"

I realized when I had felt this way before: It was the feeling of heightened frustration, my mind splintering along the edges, as I found myself so close yet so far from deducing the real illness of a patient. The frustration sharpened from the hours spent weighing the significance of various symptoms. But now the signs were lined up before me:

Mother's story about my name.

Nurse Hyo-ok's letter, which coincidentally began with a name.

Names held significance in our kingdom.

I had thought that Mother had named me out of spite, to name me the boy she wished she had birthed, but no, she had named me based on a dream. And my little brother's name, she'd based on the last syllable of my name. Hyeon. Our shared syllable to indicate the generation.

"There is something bothering me about Physician Khun's name. Khun Muyeong . . . All names are given with meaning," I mused.

"I saw the Hanja characters of his name," Eojin replied. "His name consists of the characters that mean *mu*, for 'bearer of arms,' and *yeong*, for 'hero.'"

"Yeong . . ." I tilted my head to the side, frowning as the image of Khun's wounded forehead came to mind, along with the muddy marks of a man who had prostrated on the ground. "When you spoke with Khun, did he ever tell you . . ." I paused, trying to piece my thoughts together. "Is there anyone Khun doesn't get along particularly well with? Anyone that seems to greatly distress him?"

"There is Madam Mun."

"Anyone else? Perhaps a family member?"

"Both his parents are deceased. He has three step-siblings, though, and he seemed quite distressed when I asked about them. I tried to look them up, but there is no official family record. My guess is that his parents didn't report the remarriage."

"Physician Khun Muyeong . . . Nurse Inyeong . . ." I muttered their names, the only two I could think of who could have carried around a pichim. "The medical tool must belong to one of them. But Inyeong was only ever a witness to us—"

Then it clicked. My mind stepped out of itself, stunned by the possible revelation of the moment. Silence pooled into my head, muting even the sound of birds chirping on the bare branches, flickering under the light drizzle. When my thoughts slipped back into my shell, I felt Eojin's waiting stare on me.

"What are the Hanja characters for Inyeong's name?"

"*In,* for 'benevolence,' and—" He froze. "*Yeong,* for 'hero.'"

"Dollimja," I whispered, still suspended in disbelief. "The very common practice of circulating letters, naming one's children by either the same first or last syllable. It may be a coincidence, but our two suspects share the same last syllable. Physician Khun Mu*yeong* and Nurse In*yeong*. What if they are half-siblings?"

"I see what you mean, but . . ." he hesitated. "As you mentioned, it could be a coincidence."

"Do you not think there are *too* many coincidences?" I said. "She *happened* to be at the Hyeminseo on the night of the massacre. She was in a straw cloak, perhaps hiding the blood and scratches underneath. She could have hidden somewhere to smooth out her disheveled hair. And a little while after the beheading of Nurse Hyo-ok, Nurse Inyeong entered the palace, leaving behind her position at the police bureau."

I decided that it was time to move on when another tragedy struck life, Inyeong had said, the memory returning to me as I spoke. *My mother died, and her dream had always been that I become a palace nurse.*

I continued. "Before that, she was a police damo. She told me she'd chosen not to enter the palace because she was preoccupied with solving a murder. Imagine all she must have learned—wait. How long does it take to be trained into a skilled swordswoman?"

"It would have taken her at least seven years to master the art."

"She was there for nine years, and the inspector was her mentor . . ."

A deep silence fell over us. "Nurse Inyeong completely slipped my attention. I only considered her as a witness."

"Perhaps it is just a coincidence." I retracted my theory, unable to imagine Inyeong as the gentleman who had held a blade over my neck. "She has an alibi, after all."

A look of discomfort darkened his expression. "A drunk father who couldn't even remember what year it was, along with a den full of greedy gamblers. She could have paid them to lie to me. And her father is divorced. He could have once been married to Nurse Hyo-ok—" Eojin pressed his fingers into his eyes, frustration hardening his face. "Damnation. I should have questioned them all more."

"It's not your fault," I rushed to say. "You had to deal with an entire investigation on your own, without the commander's help. Besides, Inyeong was the first witness that ran to the police." I wavered, shaking my head. "What killer reports the crime?"

"Maybe that is precisely what Nurse Inyeong thought," he said, his voice dropping into a chilly note. "It could still be a coincidence, yet as you mentioned, there seems to be one too many. The fifth victim, Nurse Aram, had tea set up for whoever had come to visit her in the early morning—the killer. It would seem unusual that she'd create such an intimate space for Physician Khun, but Nurse Inyeong . . ."

"I used to think Physician Khun was the killer until a few days ago," I added, more thoughts rising to the surface, "the day after Nurse Aram's murder. He told me something strange, that he wished he'd died instead of Ahnbi, blaming himself for her death. When I asked him what he meant, he asked me whether I did not think it an odd coincidence, that he had fallen in love with one of the three witnesses of his mother's death."

A frown deepened over Eojin's brows. I could see his mind racing.

"And there were three marks on him," I added. "Blood on his forehead, mud on his hands and knees. He had bowed to someone . . ."

"If we are to go with your theory," Eojin murmured, "Maybe Nurse Inyeong entered the palace to find out how her mother disappeared. Maybe there were whispers of who had seen her last."

"Perhaps," I added, breathless with a rush of thrill, "perhaps while serving Madam Mun, she discovered that the madam and Court Lady Ahnbi might know something about her mother, so she encouraged her brother to pursue Ahnbi."

"He fell in love with her," Eojin followed along, "but also obeyed Nurse Inyeong's order to retrieve information. On the day he finally does, the Hyeminseo massacre occurs. And Nurse Inyeong hunts down the other two names Ahnbi mentioned: Nurses Kyunghee and Aram."

"And on the morning after," I said. "Maybe he was bowing to *her* . . . to his older sister. To beg her to stop!"

"I've changed my mind," Eojin said. "Once we collect the horses, we will go to Gwangju."

I blinked. "What is in Gwangju?"

"The police bureau Nurse Inyeong once served at; it will end up causing a longer detour, but I think we must. We were so focused on the prince and Physician Khun that we hardly looked into her past."

"Perhaps we both didn't think it possible," I said, "that a woman could be so cruel. Perhaps when she was born, her mother dreamt of dragons, too."

18

Dark clouds rolled low over the sky. We rode into the fortressed town of Gwangju and arrived at the local police bureau—with its faded red pillars and two-tiered pagoda gate—just as rain sluiced across the town in great sheets. An increasing sense of anticipation numbed the soreness of my wounded shoulder.

"Do I know Damo Inyeong?" the officer guarding the bureau entrance repeated after Eojin asked. "Yes, we once had a damo by that name. She was promoted to a palace nurse a year or so ago."

"If the commander is in"—Eojin slipped out his mapae pendant—"inform him that an inspector from the Capital Police Bureau requests an audience."

At once, the officer complied. He returned with a servant, who escorted us under the shelter of eaves to the main pavilion, a long building with columns that soared upward, connecting to a black-tiled roof.

Inside, we were greeted by Commander Chae, a middle-aged man with a long, wispy black beard. Pleasantries were exchanged between the two men as they seated themselves on the floor mat. I took my place far behind them, near the sliding doors, but then Eojin glanced over his shoulder and gestured for me to sit by his side. It seemed the most natural thing to him, but the commander looked startled. His heavy brows twitched, and his gaze darted over to me with curiosity. But only for a moment.

"So, you are Inspector Seo," he said, his voice deep and mellow. "I have heard about you. A young prodigy whom the king favored with a position at the age of eighteen. What brings you all the way here, Inspector?"

"We've come to ask what you know about Inyeong. She was a damo here for nine years before becoming a palace nurse."

The commander let out a long, pensive sigh. "So my suspicions were right." Before we could ask what he meant by this, he said, "Inyeong entered the police bureau at the age of fourteen, a girl with such a bright mind that I decided to train her to become my eyes and ears. To become an extension of me."

"Did this training involve swordsmanship?" Eojin asked.

"She asked me, when a series of murders occurred in the town, to teach her how to wield a sword. I regarded her as a young woman of integrity and decency. So I asked one of the police inspectors to teach her."

"Why did she choose to leave the bureau after nine years?"

"Her younger brother, a palace physician, wrote to her . . ."

"What was the brother's name?"

"I do not know. Her brother left home at a young age to pursue medicine in the capital, and beyond that, she spoke very little about him. It seems she was never close to him. She wasn't close to him or her stepfather . . ." Then his face lit. "Ah! The stepfather! He used to be a military official before being demoted to a servant as punishment for something. Mr. Khun, that was what the people here called him. His surname passed down to his son."

Physician Khun, I thought.

"You refer to Inyeong's father as her stepfather. Does this mean Inyeong's mother remarried?" Eojin asked. "Remarriage is prohibited."

"The lower class do as they wish, and as I said, her family always kept to themselves. They lived quietly together after the mother's divorce, so whether they truly married or not, I do not know for certain." The commander cleared his throat. "As I was saying, the brother wrote home to Inyeong, and that was when she learned her mother had disappeared, last seen alive in the palace. I hadn't even known her mother had become a palace nurse until then; she had worked in the local apothecary for the longest time."

I clenched my skirt to still the tremors in my hands.

"Against my advice, Inyeong took on her mother's disappearance like it was her own case, as though she were the investigator. She wrote to her brother almost every day, asking questions of him, urging him to gain a court lady's trust—"

"A court lady?" Eojin asked.

"Yes, apparently the court lady who was last seen with their mother. After a while, he simply stopped replying to Inyeong. That was when she began poring over medical texts every spare moment she had, often studying through the night. She took test after test at the local apothecary, and each time, her grade rose higher and higher. She was then recruited back into the apothecary, where she stayed for a few months before—and I was quite surprised when I heard this—before she was chosen to enter the palace."

"If I may," I whispered, and the commander glanced my way. He seemed uncertain what to make of me, but he nodded nevertheless. "You mentioned that Inyeong was a woman of integrity and decency. After her mother's disappearance, did anything change about her? Did she exhibit any odd behavior?"

The commander observed me, then looked at Eojin. "Who is she, Inspector?"

"A palace nurse," Eojin replied. "She has been integral to this investigation."

"Of course . . . How else is anyone to know the goings-on beyond the palace walls?" he whispered. He knew something, and as he pursed his lips and furrowed his brows, my back tensed.

"Inyeong became preoccupied with cases that involved injustice," he continued. "Obsessed over them—frighteningly so. Then, one day, when she was tasked with arresting a female witness for giving false testimony, I found the witness . . . in a most disturbing state. Her face battered, hardly recognizable, beaten so badly she never woke up. I closed my eyes to this. Though, I admit, I wonder now whether I erred in doing so."

"I say with utmost respect," Eojin said slowly, and I cast him a nervous glance. "But sometimes too much mercy is as detrimental as too little."

I waited for the commander's blast of anger—Commander Song certainly would have exploded in outrage. Instead, he let out a remorseful breath as Eojin's words seemed to sink in. Perhaps officials outside the capital were not as cutthroat.

"You must have heard of the Hyeminseo massacre, yeonggam," Eojin continued.

"I did. And I suppose that is why you have come." He stroked his beard as his gaze slipped back toward me. In a lowered voice, he said, "I thought no one would come here to ask me these questions . . . Who would believe that a mere servant girl is capable of such violent wrath?"

"You believe Nurse Inyeong may have had a part in the murders?" Eojin asked.

"I do. It was only an inkling, but now, going over the details again, I do believe she was behind it." Commander Chae rose to his feet and retrieved something from a cabinet drawer. A part of me feared he would draw a sword, kill us for having caught on to his error. But it wasn't a sword he pulled out—it was a piece of wood, with his seal carved on it. A tongbu, a warrant that gave officers the authority to arrest individuals.

"I have followed the Hyeminseo massacre case closely, and have seen the chaos it has caused. Making the people question the Crown Prince himself," he said. "When you return, present my seal to Commander Song, and inform him that you have received testimony from the bureau chief of Gwangju. Nurse Inyeong is to be arrested and interrogated."

By the time the rain eased, the sky was a dark, washed-out blue. We'd left the fortress town, hoping to find an inn nearby, but instead we passed by field after field of muddy rice paddies, then a seemingly endless stretch of woodland—a forest of crooked trees and towering green bamboo stalks. Then at last we saw the silhouette of a hut and a pair of candlelit windows, which peered out from the shadows like bright yellow eyes.

"Thank goodness." The words whooshed out of me.

"Let's hope a kind old couple lives there," Eojin said. "And not a lung-feasting gumiho."

He sounded light spirited. We were, after all, near the end of our investigation. Yet I did not feel at ease, not at all, for the woman Eojin now intended to arrest was a nurse I knew. I had spoken with her; I had worked with her.

But nevertheless, I tried to sound cheerful. "For your sake, let us hope that is so. Nine-tail foxes prefer the lungs of men over women."

When we arrived near the hut, which had a small yard

and kitchen adjoined to its side, we tethered our horses and approached. I stood nervously behind Eojin as he rapped his fist on the entrance door. Never in my life had I walked up to the home of a stranger to ask for room and board, but it seemed Eojin had done this many times before—likely when he had traveled with his Secret Royal Investigator father, disguised as peasants.

The door opened onto the wary face of a young woman. She was garbed in a white jacket and a pale yellow skirt, her hair tied into a low coil with a binyeo pin pierced through, marking her as a married woman. She remained wary, even after Eojin explained that he was a military official journeying home with his sister and asked whether she could spare a room for us to stay overnight.

"I have one spare room. You may both sleep there," she said begrudgingly, then stepped aside to allow us in.

A tiny wooden maru—the main living space—was cluttered with stacks of straw baskets. A kitchen knife lay next to a clump of garlic cloves on a low table. She led us across the wooden floor, then slid open a door to an even tinier room.

"There are blankets over there, and I have no spare candles. I will bring you both some water. But I have no meals for you; I barely get by myself."

I was famished, but the snacks in my travel bag would have to suffice.

"I think she is a widow," Eojin said quietly, once we were alone. The woman had brought us two bowls of water, and with that, we freshened ourselves up. "Or her husband is not home."

Once my hands and nails were clean, the sweat wiped from my brows, I ran a hand discreetly under my jeogori jacket, over my bare shoulder, and felt the stiffness of my bandage. I needed to add another layer, but I was reluctant to take off my jacket. At my dilemma, I cast Eojin a sheepish glance.

He quickly looked away. "I will call for the ajumma to assist you. I'll be outside."

He left, and when the woman came in, she gasped at the sight of the blood. But she asked no questions.

"You're not brother and sister," she said instead as she wrapped a fresh layer of bandaging over the old one. "I can tell by the way he looks at you when you are not looking."

I wasn't sure what she meant by this, and when I was alone with Eojin again, the woman's words lingered.

I rolled out my sleeping mat, which I'd arranged as far from Eojin's as possible—which was not very far at all, given how small the room was. I sat on my mat, hugging my knees, as Eojin stretched himself out on his, arms tucked under his head and eyes closed. His sword and a coil of rope were secured to his waist; it seemed he would sleep with them.

"You should rest," he murmured. "We have a long journey ahead of us at first light."

"Are we going to Damyang still?" I asked. "To retrieve the key witness?"

"I'll send other officers to find Minji, now that we know where she is. I don't want to give Nurse Inyeong any chance of running away."

We fell quiet and still, listening to the rustling forest. The hooting of an owl. Wings beating over the woodland.

In the quiet, my thoughts turned to what lay ahead. In a matter of days, the case would be over, and I almost dreaded the idea of returning to a life of normalcy. A life where a different type of mystery awaited me. Who was Mother, really? Did she truly love me? And what ought I to do with my life, the shambles left behind by Father's wrath?

And where did Eojin fit into this?

It was depressing to think of. Yet as I pressed my fingers into my eyelids, in the darkness, I saw floating spots of light, like lanterns in the night.

"The Lantern Festival," I said, lowering my hands until my palms were cupping my cheeks. "You asked me to go with you."

His eyes remained closed. "You called me a distraction."

My cheeks grew warm, stinging my fingers. "I didn't mean it. I was upset by what had occurred with my father."

"So you do care for me."

"Of course," I said softly.

His eyes opened, and he stared up at the shadowy ceiling for such a long time, I wondered what was on his mind. Was he also thinking of where I fit in to his life, post-investigation? Or perhaps he was thinking of a way to turn me down . . .

"I always felt like I was alone until I met you," he

murmured hesitantly, then turned his head the slightest bit. In the dimming light, his eye glimmered with a sincerity that left me breathless. "I find myself wondering if you feel the same way I do."

I was afraid, but I wanted to know. "How . . . how is that?"

He faced the ceiling once more, studying the patterns of light and shadow, perhaps piecing together his thoughts. "When we're together . . . it's as though we are like water in the river, my thoughts flowing through yours, yours through mine. And when we are silent"—a faint smile tugged at his lips—"I forget you are even there sometimes."

"I'm flattered, nauri," I said drily.

"It is the greatest compliment. I dislike being around people for too long. But when I am with you . . . I never feel the need to be someone I am not."

I blinked at him, realizing I *did* feel the same way. When I was with him, I felt as I had at the Segeomjeong Pavilion—as though we'd escaped into another world where only we two existed. There were no rules, no conditions to belong there.

"I think I feel the same way, too—"

A short burst of a noise outside stole my attention. It sounded almost like a high-pitched cry, cut short. Eojin was already bolting upright, hands on his sword.

"An animal?" I asked.

"Sounded like one. I'll be back. Wait here."

"Let me come—"

"No."

Before Eojin could leave, I was on my feet and caught his hand. And his hand was cold. He knew as I did that something wasn't right.

"I'll come back." He gave my hand a gentle squeeze. "I promise."

He said this as though he truly meant it, and I nodded, even though the fear thrummed in my veins. "Of course you will."

When he left, I listened to his boots recede, footsteps over branches cracking outside. At one point, he even passed near the window closest to me, then headed further away from the hut. My heart jabbed against my ribs. Rising to my feet, I hastened over to the window, cracked it open to see Eojin disappearing into the forest of towering bamboos that looked grayish-green in the fading light. He paused to lean a small stick against the shaft. And then he was gone. Swallowed up in shadow.

I waited. I paced. I bit my nails. I looked out the window again before pacing the room once more. I tried imagining his steps as he scouted our periphery. And each time I imagined that he should be returning to the hut, silence reigned. I could hear only the rustling of the surrounding woodland.

Then, what must have been an hour or so later—or perhaps only a few minutes—I heard the outside door slide open, then shut. I hurried out, the relief at his return flooding through me.

But my relief was short-lived. There was no one but the young woman sitting on the maru floor that connected our room with hers. Her back was turned to me, and she had changed into a new outfit. Her white jacket strained against her shoulder. Her dark blue skirt pooled around her, and her black hair gleamed in the candlelight.

As did the blade.

The kitchen knife on the floor. She was trembling, and I caught the smell of something acidic and pungent. The scent of decay—or perhaps vomit? Then I noticed a sliver of red on the side of her jacket, edging into view.

"Ajumma?" I whispered, taking a step closer to her. "Ajumma?"

"The prince is the killer," the woman said, her voice too deadly, too familiar to be the widow. My blood turned to ice with recognition. "Yet here you are, coming after *me*. I have no patience for meddlers."

"How did you find us here?" As I spoke, I slowly reached for my dagger, unsheathed it, then hid it behind my skirt.

"Witnesses. There are always witnesses. People who saw you and the blue-robed inspector." Nurse Inyeong rose and turned, revealing her front outfit torn and drenched in blood. It took me a moment to realize that it was not her blood—there was none pooling under her feet or dripping down her front. "I followed you both, hoping to find Nurse Minji. To get rid of her before she spoke to you. But then you went to Commander Chae and turned him against me."

"And you followed us all the way here and . . . killed the owner of this house?" Then horror struck me again— *Eojin had not returned.* My knees buckled and my voice sounded shrill. "Where is Inspector Seo? What did you do to him?"

"Your friend is dead."

A high-pitched ringing exploded in my ears, growing louder and louder until I could hear absolutely nothing else.

My legs stumbled forward, desperate to bolt out of the hut, but a grip as strong as iron clamped around my arm. Sharp pain exploded from my injured shoulder. Gritting my teeth hard, I glanced over and saw a blade rushing down toward my back.

I had only one thought.

Eojin needs me.

My hands moved of their own accord. My dagger slashed toward the hand gripping me, the blade sliding through flesh, both hers and mine. And then I was free.

Cold air burst against my face as I stumbled out of the hut. A whimper escaped me as I nearly tripped over an object on the way—the widow's bloody corpse. I forced my feet forward. A blur of shadows wrapped my vision, but everything came into sharp focus when I arrived before the last place I'd seen Eojin: The small stick leaned against a bamboo stalk. A trail marker.

I looked back to see Inyeong following, a sword now clenched in her bloody fist.

I passed by the marker, then slipped into the woods that seemed to glow pale blue under the evening sky, the last bit of light before nightfall. Panic crawled up my skin like frost, threatening to petrify me, but I took in deep breaths, trying to grip the lesson I'd learned at the Hyeminseo.

The more urgent a circumstance, Nurse Jeongsu had drilled into us, *the calmer we must be.*

Another deep breath, and I examined my surroundings. There was no point dashing in a random direction. I needed to find the next marker. It took a few moments of scouring my periphery before I saw another stick, longer this time, awkwardly leaned against a rock. I continued on this way, running and stopping, until I found a marker next to a rising slope. After that, the markers stopped.

"Eojin," I cried as I reached the end of the trail. Then I dared to raise my voice a notch as the forest loomed around me. *"Eojin!"*

My calm shattered. I hurried along the slope, and it only rose higher. Branches cut my face, stabbed my arms, snagged on my skirt. And then I came to an abrupt halt, soil crumbling beneath my feet as I stared down a sudden descent, barely visible in the growing shadows—a steep slope that crept downward, the trees tilted, and from below, wind swept up into my face, and an ocean of bamboo stalks rustled far below. My knees wobbled as I stumbled back, tripping over a rock and landing on my bottom, palms sinking into the wet earth. When I raised my hands to clean them, I froze, seeing my hand stained in red.

"Please no," I whispered, inspecting the ground before me. A trail of blood-covered leaves and twigs led over the edge of the precipice. Scrambling to my feet, I considered climbing down, but decided against it as the forest grew darker by the moment. Shadows stretched along the forest floor, rising up the ancient trunks, swallowing everything they touched. One slip, and I'd go crashing all the way down.

Hiking up my skirt, I rushed around, heading downward until my lungs were aching, and upon reaching the lower forest ground, I turned and made my way back to where the drop was, only this time I stood below the intimidating height.

And at my feet was a police hat, and a chinstrap of blood-speckled amber beads.

My heart clenched as I pushed past the tall bamboo stalks. Branches sprouted long, glossy leaves, foliage so dense that I could hardly see where I was going. Fear spiked in my chest at the thought that I might have walked past Eojin, when finally the leaves opened onto the sight of a figure kneeling in a trickling stream, hunched over and shivering violently.

"Eojin!" I rushed forward and crouched before him, my gaze landing on a face mottled with cuts and bruises, and a pair of eyes that stared at me with raw fear. His right hand hung limp by his side, broken at the elbow, and his other hand pressed tightly against his side. Blood streamed down his wrist, branching out into thick rivulets that drenched half his robe.

"Hyeon-ah," he said, struggling to breathe. "It won't stop."

I wiped the cold sweat off my brows. "Let me see."

I tried to appear calm as I laid him on his back, away from the frigid stream. But panic fluttered under the tips of my fingers as I skimmed the front of his robe, quickly loosening it to find a deep slashing cut, a sword wound gaping from his lower left stomach and over his ribs. Nurse Inyeong must have caught him unawares, attacked, and then pushed him off the slope.

"How did she even find us?" I cut off a strand of my skirt and wrapped it around him, binding him with as much pressure as possible. I would not let him bleed to death. And I needed to keep talking—both to help him stay conscious and to keep my own mind from straying to the worst-case scenarios: broken bones, damaged organs, deadly infections . . . "She must have been keeping an eye on one or both of us for a while."

He wasn't listening, staring at me with lackluster eyes. The muscles in his jaw tensed, his hand clenching his bandaged wound as his shivering intensified. His skin was clammy and too cold. *What do I do?* I wished I could turn to a medical professor, or to my mentor—anyone more knowledgeable than I—as I helplessly whispered Eojin's name over and over. All I could do was rest his head on my knee and watch as he curled up in pain.

I don't know what to do next. Please, tell me, I don't know what to do.

Then the woods crackled awake.

Leaves stirred under approaching footsteps.

"Thank you for leading me to the inspector," came a female voice.

Nurse Inyeong appeared out of the dark and stepped into a pale blue shaft of light, a sword in her hand. She seemed so changed from back at the palace. So frail, like a bone about to snap.

"I had hoped he would bleed to death," she growled like a gumiho, her eyes gleaming as bright as her blade, "but now I must finish the deed. You wished to investigate together, and so it shall end for you—together."

19

I remained on my knees, one arm folded around Eojin, the other brandishing a dagger, as though that might be enough to shield him. His head remained a still weight on my lap. He didn't stir, and I was too afraid to look down.

"Leave him alone," I cried, my desperate voice resounding in the empty forest. "Please, just go!"

"I would have left you both alone, if only you had not dug your way into my police bureau. You know the truth now. That is why you sought out Commander Chae." She edged closer. "You shouldn't have tried to stop me. Not even my brother tried to stop me when I gave him his wife's ring, signifying her death. He knew, he *knew*, that it was my right to seek revenge. One cannot live with the killer of one's parents under the same heaven."

A quote Eojin had once mentioned. Li Chi's *Book of Rites*.

"But we are nurses," I countered, my voice hoarse with a surge of emotion. "Do you not remember reading the words of Sun Simiao, right on the first page of our medical encyclopedia? 'Mankind is the most precious of all living things in the universe.' How—How could you kill all those women?"

It was one thing to suspect Nurse Inyeong from what the commander had told us; it was quite another thing, I realized, to see her face-to-face—the last woman I had suspected, the one woman who had seemed trustworthy in a palace full of spies. "I don't understand. How could you do this? Court Lady Ahnbi, Nurse Aram, Nurse Kyunghee—they were only witnesses. They *couldn't* have saved your mother. Even if they'd tried to stand up to him, they would have all been killed, too—"

"You think yourself better than me?" Inyeong whispered, her voice chilly. "That you know what is right and what is wrong, and that I do not? Most of us believe that we are not capable of murder . . . until it happens to us. Until your mother"—her voice strained, a rock of pain lodged in her throat—"until your *mother*, the woman who birthed you, who raised you with the gentlest hand, is beheaded. Until you learn that three cruel women dragged her body out of the courtyard, stripped her naked so that nothing could be traced back to the palace, and then left her somewhere on Mount Bugak. To be forgotten there, to be eaten by wild animals."

Ice expanded in my chest. *Nurse Kyunghee never told me this.* The night yawned open in my mind like a grave—I saw the silhouettes of three women dragging a headless corpse as they traversed deep into the mountain, leaving it in the isolated expanse.

"Then, and only then, can you know whether you are better than I."

Inyeong's voice wavered as she took another step forward, now only a few paces away from the stream between us. "I suppose Nurse Kyunghee did not reveal that part. Neither did Court Lady Ahnbi with my brother. She told him nothing of this, until I lured her out of the palace one night. I threatened her with a medical tool—just to scare her. I never meant to harm her. But then she told me the full truth. And I—I wanted her to *know* what that fear was like. I wanted her to feel what Mother had felt."

"But the student nurses and their teacher," I whispered, "they didn't deserve to die."

"They were in my way," she retorted. "When Court Lady Ahnbi ran into the Hyeminseo, the teacher came out, and she saw my face. I had to kill her. Then all the students saw and started screaming. I had to silence them all. But I did feel guilt when they were all dead. I felt it pierce my bones, the horror of what I'd done. It made me despise the prince even more, the man who seems to feel no remorse for all he's done."

"So you posted anonymous handbills . . ." I said slowly, trying to buy myself time, "to cast suspicion on him and killed the other two witnesses for hiding your mother's corpse—" My throat tightened, panic rising in my chest as Eojin's warm blood oozed through my skirt. He was going to die if I didn't get him out of here now. My gaze flicked around, desperate to find an escape. But everywhere I looked, every possible route of escape, I could only imagine ending in death. The dagger in my hand, no matter how strongly forged, was of little use against a woman who had spent nine years of her life mastering the art of the sword.

"I cannot even *find* her," Inyeong rasped. She was too close now. Stream water trickled past the hem of her skirt. "I cannot even give her a proper burial. This life we live in, Nurse Hyeon, it is not worth living in, anyway."

Gathering Eojin in my arms, I tried to push away from her shadow hovering over us. But escape would be impossible with his weight. I could only hold him tighter against my chest, my head ducked, wishing I could tuck him safely under my rib cage, protected under my bones and next to my heart, no matter what happened to me.

I promised to watch out for you—I squeezed my eyes shut against the burning of tears—*but I don't know how.*

Then the wind blew. I smelled it again—that pungent, acidic odor I'd detected back at the widow's house. I lifted my head, just a notch, as recognition stirred awake. It was indeed the smell of vomit.

"I will make it quick, for all of us," Inyeong whispered. An eerie, metallic noise resounded as she unsheathed her sword, exposing a blade that gleamed in the moonlight. "Our time is ending."

The odor continued to waft by me, now that Inyeong stood so close. My mind turned, the side of my mind that illuminated when I opened a medical text, or when I knelt before an ailing patient. Whenever I played the familiar game of inference.

My gaze slid up the length of Inyeong's tall height. Her

face looked a washed-out blue, but it was likely the fading twilight. Was I imagining it, or were her cheeks slightly swollen? I watched as she gripped the sword tighter, and my gaze ran along her bloody hand, up her sleeve—where I noticed nail-inflicted scratches and scattered pale spots along her throat and the sides of her face, a face usually layered with jibun powder. She had been hiding them since the day after the Hyeminseo massacre.

"Human perseverance often surprises me." Inyeong settled the blade against the pulse throbbing at the side of my throat; I shuddered at the sensation of cold steel against my skin but urged my mind to flip faster, faster through the pages of all that I'd learned. "We rarely die in an instant. But if you stay very still, Nurse Hyeon, you will hardly feel the pain. A blink, and I promise, you will be gone."

Spots. Like raindrops on a dusty road.

My mind stilled, a finger on a page.

Slowly, I craned my head back and stared up at Inyeong. I could be wrong. I likely was wrong. Yet the spots were unquestionably there. And as I thought back to all the signs and symptoms, the truth struck me.

"Wait . . ." I whispered. "You know what's wrong with you, don't you?"

Her grip on the sword hilt tightened, and the slightest fissure cracked the surface of her expression.

"We are both uinyeos; we have been trained to detect signs of death." I dared to place a hand between my throat and the blade, and Inyeong did not budge. "You were poisoned, weren't you?"

"I should kill you," she snapped, with a surge of vitriol. Her sword angled away, threatening to slash through my fingers along with my throat. "I will, if you say another word."

"Who was it?" I pressed. "Who poisoned you?"

The longest silence stretched, a silence so thick it blanketed the rocky ground. The final rays of sundown vanished, swallowing the forest in darkness, leaving only slivers of sight. Slivers of moonlit tree trunks. Slivers of Inyeong's contorted face. A sliver of her sword, still raised and ready to strike.

"I lied." Her voice cracked, and a trembling laugh escaped her. "My brother did try to stop me. Begged me after the first murder. Yet we are family, and he could not find it in himself to turn me in. So he poisoned me."

Her words sliced through me: Physician Khun, her own brother, was her killer. He had loved Ahnbi too dearly, the girl who had become a silent witness.

"You only have a matter of days to live, if you are fortunate," I said quietly. "You are using the last of your life to kill the only two people who can help give your mother justice. The last of your life to have an innocent nurse convicted, a scapegoat for the crown prince. You may be stronger than me now, but you will not be strong enough to scathe the prince. Not in your condition. Your fury is not enough."

I waited, staring at her burning eyes. Then I added, "But it may be enough . . . to create a spark. You are not the only one who lost a loved one. Prince Jangheon killed Inspector Seo's father."

The blade wavered. "His father?"

Clenching my chattering teeth, I tried to sound firm. "The inspector's father was a secret royal investigator, sent to Pyongan Province where Prince Jangheon carried your— your mother's head to. The prince murdered his father, along with another villager there. The inspector told me that if the king will not listen to him, he will report all the prince's misdeeds to the Old Doctrine faction. And if you wish to bring justice to your mother, you need to live long enough to testify."

I held my breath, tensing against the violent shaking of my limbs. I ran my hand along Eojin's face and placed my fingers against his throat, searching for a heartbeat. It was barely there. So faint, like a departing whisper. A hot surge of pain seared my chest.

"Make up your mind!" I snarled, no longer afraid. Anger seethed in my voice as I hissed, "If you want to see your mother in the afterlife without remorse, you need to let Inspector Seo live. If you do not, we will all be damned, and the prince will go on murdering, and then one day he will be king. Untouchable."

Metal clattered onto rocks. Inyeong had dropped her sword. Her hand hung limp by her side. "I thought, maybe once they were all dead, the pain would ease a little . . . My mother was the only one who loved me. She always told me how she loved me since the very moment I was born. And I keep thinking about how no one else in the world loves me as she did."

I was barely listening. Quickly, I removed the coil of rope from Eojin's waist, the rope I knew officers used to arrest culprits. "Hold out your wrist," I said, my breath a whoosh of anxiety. Every second that passed was a second in which Inyeong could change her mind. "If you want justice, you need to turn yourself in."

"I will," she said, then paused. "I will, but I have a request."

"What is that?" I asked. *I'll do anything.*

Inyeong's silhouette moved, then a sound of crinkling paper reached my ear. "I have an old letter from my mother. I have carried it with me always, since entering the palace. Would you bury it with me?"

"I will."

The moon above us was not bright, a chipped skull hanging in the sky, but bright enough to outline the folded piece of paper. As soon as I took it, I carefully moved Eojin aside and stood to wrap her wrists as best I could. Picking up her sword, I cautiously led her to a tree and tethered her to it.

"If I don't live," Inyeong said, her voice now calm as she watched me. "My brother will testify on my behalf. Tell him that his older sister has permitted him."

I hid the sword and rushed over to Eojin, gathering him in my arms. I remembered the question he'd wanted to know since the beginning of the investigation. Glancing over my shoulder, I asked, "Why is Nurse Minji still alive? How did she escape the massacre?"

After a heavy pause, Inyeong replied, "She cried out 'eomma.' When I was about to kill her, that is what she said. *Mother.*"

I swore to myself I'd tell Eojin all of this. But I would make sure he lived first.

Carefully flipping him onto his front, I slid my arms under his shoulders and clenched my teeth as I heaved him onto his knees. I then leaned him onto my back, his faint heartbeat tapping against me. I hunched forward under his deadweight. My injured shoulder blazed with pain, and the bones of my legs felt like they were splintering under me as I rose to my feet.

With each step forward, I feared I might collapse, but I felt Inyeong's haunted eyes boring into us.

I wanted to get as far away from her as possible.

Eojin's arms hung on either side of me, his bloody hands swaying with my hobbling steps. Strands of his dark hair, loosened from his topknot, brushed against the sides of my face and the length of my throat. He was so still, it terrified me—a terror that pierced the dizzying haze of exhaustion as I staggered forward in small, painful steps. I desperately gazed up at the dark shape of the slope I'd walked earlier. I followed it from below until I arrived where my path and the rising slope met, and there was Eojin's trail marker.

As I followed the path he'd left, I also searched every patch of moonlit earth for useful plants. The forest was always a storehouse of medicine, especially as spring had come early. At length, a sprawling bush caught my attention. I paused to inspect it with my foot, heaving for air as sweat seeped into my eyes and my arms trembled under Eojin's weight. The moonlight fell upon yellow flowers and spiky red balls of baemddalgi.

"Hyeon-ah."

At first, I thought it was the trick of the wind, but then I heard his voice again, thick and coarse. "Hyeon-ah."

My heart leapt in a sharp, painful, delighted twist.

"Just leave me here," he whispered.

"Do you not know me, nauri? I am Baek-hyeon." I blinked the sweat from my eyes. With all my remaining strength, I heaved him higher on my back and continued on. I would have to return for the plant later. "Once I set my mind on a task, I will not stop until I complete it."

My voice wavered, and at the thought of losing him, my voice cracked. "Please, just stay alive. Don't let go of me."

Seven years of studying ought to have prepared me for this moment.

Yet I had never saved anyone's life before. I had assisted, but I had never been alone. As I used the last of my strength—a strength I didn't even know I'd had—to lay Eojin down on the floor of the empty hut, I knew there was no time to search for a physician.

I closed my eyes against the tremors creeping up my limbs, and reminded myself what I always did at the

Hyeminseo—when panicked orders flew around, nurses scrambling like headless chickens, as a patient hovered on the brink of death.

A calm and steady hand, Nurse Jeongsu would always remind me, *and a calm and steady mind.*

Her words steadied me now.

I bundled Eojin's cold body with layer after layer of all the blankets I could find, then ran out and returned with the medicinal ingredients. The leaves from the baemddalgi bush and its yellow flowers I separated into two piles before me, to organize my thoughts.

The poultice. I'd make that first.

Taking a bowl from the kitchen, I used the bottom of it to crush the fresh leaves, then applied the soft, damp mass over Eojin's wound, without removing the strip of my skirt already helping to clot the blood. I retrieved fresh rolls of bandage from my traveling sack and used a few to carefully bind his chest and stomach.

Next, I moved to his right arm, where the bone jutted out at an awkward angle. I snapped it back into place, wincing as his face contorted in pain. Then with the remaining roll of bandage, I slathered a thick layer of poultice over it and wrapped it around the arm. All the while, a haunting thought drifted through my mind: His right arm might never function the way it had before.

As I left the paste to seep into the wounds, I dashed into the kitchen again. I fit a small black pot into the hollow of the already-kindled stove, scooped water in, and tossed in the baemddalgi flowers. Once the concoction simmered down, I poured it into a bowl and managed to dribble it into Eojin's mouth. This would hopefully trigger better blood circulation, speeding up his body's natural healing process.

When all was done, when I had spent all my knowledge and I was dried up and trembling, I sunk to the ground before Eojin. It was just the two of us in a small hut, yet the memory of Nurse Inyeong remained heavy over me, like she was sitting right behind me in the shadows. *Remember your promise,* I could almost hear her calling out to me from the forest.

I was too tired to weep, or to think of all that awaited me. Later, I would have to ride to the police bureau to ask for assistance, and hope Nurse Inyeong was still tied to the tree, and had not escaped. Later, I would have to find a skilled physician to stitch up Eojin's gaping wound. Later, I would have to think of what awaited us in the capital.

But for now, I tucked the letter away and curled up next to Eojin and laid my three fingers on his pulse, at the three crucial positions on his wrist. Chon, gwan, and cheok. I closed my eyes, too afraid to keep them open, and listened through the tips of my fingers, to the three beating threads, whispers that told one story:

Of our fragile existence, yet our determination to survive.

Of secret pains, and the yearning for love.

This was the story of all lives, and I felt its dearness so deeply, so painfully, as one faded beneath my touch. Fading, fading, like the pulse of the murdered victims, whose cold wrists I had read. Too many had died, their lives gone like a flash of lightning, consumed by another's rage.

And I swore to myself—*you must always remember them, Hyeon-ah. Never forget.*

Squeezing my eyes tighter, I prayed Eojin's pulse would not go silent on me.

I prayed he wouldn't become one more person I would need to remember.

EPILOGUE

Word of Prince Jangheon's crimes and Nurse Inyeong's revenge inevitably reached the palace. By then, a week had passed since our return from Gwangju, and two days since Nurse Inyeong had confessed and had been found guilty. She had died before her execution day.

With her gone and Eojin still in fragile condition, it was I who was summoned to the palace by members of the Old Doctrine faction. I was to testify against the Crown Prince. In that moment, while kneeling in the courtyard before King Yeongjo, detailing all that I'd discovered while assisting the inspector, I felt perilously close to my end. Truth could easily be twisted into slander, and slander against the prince meant death. But His Majesty had shown me immeasurable grace; he'd called me a loyal subject for sharing what the palace had kept hidden from him.

That night, while leaving the capital, I wondered what lay ahead for Crown Prince Jangheon, and whether Nurse Inyeong and her mother would ever find rest, or if their spirits would forever roam this kingdom filled with han—deep sorrow, resentment, grief, and helpless anger. For now, all I knew was that I had done my best to keep my promise to her.

I paused by the road in which Nurse Inyeong had been buried. For the first time since receiving her request, I unfolded the crinkled letter, to read before burying it with her. Raising the paper to the starlight, I frowned, noting how familiar the writing looked. It took only a moment to realize why: it was the original handwriting that Inyeong had imitated in the anonymous handbill she'd circulated.

> Inyeong—
> I am happy to learn from your letter that all is well with you. When my daughter is doing well, I too am doing well.
> I am sending you my love, along with a bundle of top-quality cotton tightly packed and tied with string. I will pay you a visit during the Chuseok festival. I will stop writing now even though I have so much to say.
> Eomma, twenty-fifth of the fifth moon.

A shallow breath escaped me, the words an iron ball in my chest. It was just an ordinary letter between a mother and daughter. Yet the ordinary, I realized, became like cherished treasure when taken—torn away, stripped, and left to rot in the mountains, like Inyeong's mother.

She ought never to have died.

"I wish you both a better afterlife," I whispered as I dug a little hole in the earth and slipped the letter in. Smoothing the soil back over, I remained still, my heart too heavy to move.

The only consolation I could find was in imagining their life to come. Perhaps Inyeong would open her eyes to find herself a child once more, resting in her mother's arms—a mother with a warm, smiling face, cooing down at her. They would live life, grow old together, and this time—please, just this once—they would choose a different path.

The path that did not lead into the palace.

***

Neither Eojin nor I went to the Lotus Lantern Festival. He had left the capital for the mountainous province of Gangwon, taken there by his worried uncle and at the physician's advice. The hope was that nature would become its own medicine, helping him to heal. And as for myself, I had avoided the festival, knowing that the sight of lanterns would only sharpen Eojin's absence.

He did manage to send me a letter, consisting of three barely legible words: *Wait for me.*

I didn't reply, not knowing what to say. I instead waited for further word from Jieun every day at Nurse Jeongsu's home. I lived with her now, helping her around the house, as she still struggled to walk. She'd invited me to stay ever since we'd lost our house; Father hadn't changed his mind about throwing us out, even after the case was resolved.

Mother seemed quite content without him, though, with her new life as a servant at an inn. The innkeeper, Madam Song, was an old friend, another retired gisaeng like herself.

"No word yet?" Mother asked when I visited her there. "Did the inspector share when he would return?"

"Not yet," I replied.

We sat on a raised platform in the backyard of the inn, next to the kitchen. There were baskets full of vegetables, which Mother had sliced into neat little mountains, and she was slicing more yet. *Chop—chop—chop.* She cut slowly, carefully, still new to this work. Her brows were lowered in concentration, her face bright and full of vigor, her hair loose in the mountain breeze.

It was pleasant seeing her like this, no longer cooped up in a cage of her own making.

She seemed more at ease with herself, and with me, each time I visited her—and with every visit, she also fussed over me more. *Why haven't you eaten yet?* she'd demand, then badger me for an entire afternoon about the importance of eating three meals a day; then on my following visit, it would be about something else. And today, it was about the inspector.

"When the jongsagwan returns, what then?" she asked, glancing my way. "The investigation is over. It will not be the same as it was before."

I reached for a bulb of garlic and aimlessly picked at its thin, papery skin, trying not to let her words bother me. Mother annoyed me at times with her questions, yet it was a strange delight—to be annoyed at all, rather than experience the stiff and formal silence I'd grown up with.

"I just . . ." She heaved out a sigh. "I just don't want to see you hurt or disappointed."

I turned her words over for a moment. "No matter what happens, life goes on, doesn't it?" *Yours did.* "I will be fine, eomonni. Besides, I hardly think about him these days."

Mother arched a brow. "But you wait for news from Jieun every day."

"Only out of curiosity—to see how the inspector is faring," I said, rather heatedly. "Like you said, the investigation is over, and has been for months. He's likely moved on. I've moved on, and I am *fine.*"

"You don't sound fine. Why don't you write to him?" she asked. "Isn't that what Jieun keeps telling you to do—"

"I will not," I said, as the truth bruised me: I had mustered up the courage to write to him once, then had torn the letter into pieces, afraid that he'd forgotten me. And equally afraid that he still cared. "I'm not going to chase after a boy."

Mother shook her head, clucking her tongue as she returned to her work. "I certainly do not miss my younger days," she murmured. "Such chaotic days of unnecessary strife—"

"Ajumma." A young servant girl ran over to my mother, then discreetly gestured behind her. "There's a strange man lingering by the fence. He's been staring at you for so long."

I glanced past the row of glossy brown pots, past the brushwood fence, and there, standing by a tree, was my father. Mother stood at once, and while walking away, she mumbled something about how she never wanted to see his face again. But I remained, watching as the man who'd haunted my life hesitantly walked around and entered through the back innyard gate.

On the day I had been summoned to the palace, I had detailed my investigation—including the truth that Father had been Prince Jangheon's alibi. The king had stripped Father of his title as punishment for withholding evidence. For weeks now, Father had rushed out to the palace gate every day, where he expected the king to order his banishment or execution, waiting in the rain, sun, and wind.

"Hyeon-ah."

Father stood before me now, his gentleman's hat crooked and his robe filthy. He looked no different from a commoner. At last, he sat down on the platform, far enough from me that three men could have sat between us.

"Hyeon-ah," he said again, and a tremor crept into his voice. "The king was so gracious as to reinstate me. He said it was all owing to you. What did you do?"

I peeled off the garlic skin. "The king offered to reward me for telling the truth," I said matter-of-factly, peering up at him. His brows had clouded over, and his pale face had grown even paler. "And I asked that His Majesty be gracious to you."

"But you could have asked for any reward," Father said, searching me, as though he might detect some scheme underneath my words. "You could have asked for your own position back. Why did you ask for *my* reinstatement?"

I silently held his gaze, the man who had always

reminded me of what I would never have: a loving father. The harmony had long been broken between us, and I realized now that hanging on to him any longer would morph into hatred. It would twist me.

"Because," I said at last, "I decided on that day, just that day, I would be your daughter for the last time."

A defeated, remorseful look filled his eyes. He tried straightening his hat, then spoke in a whisper. "I suppose I owe you an apology. I—I am sorry."

My eyes watered, my throat so sore I couldn't speak. His apology had come too late. Much, much too late.

"Hyeon-ah—" There was an anguished, scrambling note to his voice. Then, as though struck by an understanding, he closed his eyes for a moment and whispered, "Nurse Hyeon." He swallowed hard, then looked up at me, a new calm in his gaze. "When I am in need of medical advice, may I come visit you? My health is no longer what it once was . . ."

Pushing down all my emotions, I offered him a small nod. I had parted ways with him as daughter and father . . . but perhaps we could come together as uinyeo and patient.

We sat together like this for a long time, saying not a word. I turned my gaze up to the sky. The ache in my chest eased; the sting passed away.

This was enough. It would be enough.

———

October arrived in a splendor of red maple and vivid yellow ginkgos. Eight months had passed since the Hyeminseo massacre, long enough that the bleeding wound left open by the violence had closed and repaired, and was now pink and slightly tender to the touch.

Physician Khun had barely survived a flogging, his punishment for marrying a court lady, and was working in an apothecary somewhere on the penal island of Jeju. Madam Mun had lost favor with the king, but still remained in the palace. Commander Song continued to stubbornly guard his position in the bureau, still terrorizing the weak, despite the growing rumors that His Majesty intended to replace him. Nurse Jeongsu had gone back to teaching, and Minji had returned to her place as a student nurse. As for Jieun, she had resigned from the palace to join me at the Hyeminseo.

Life seemed almost ordinary again.

I paused on my walk through the marketplace, before a bronze mirror propped up for customers who wished to try on hair ornaments. Leaning forward, I straightened the black garima on my head. The weight of the cotton no longer felt so heavy. It felt as it should—a long strip of black fabric, light enough that it billowed behind me in the wind.

Some dreams, I'd learned, were meant to fade away. And to let go of them didn't mean to let go of myself, but to release the life I'd imagined I wanted. The loss had grieved me at first, but in its fading away—slowly, very slowly—a new dream had bloomed. A dream that was quieter, less desperate, mellowed by the ashes of those who had died in the massacre. But it was also a dream that infused my world with deeper shades and brighter hues, with richer scents and far warmer streaks of contentment.

As I left the stall and continued on my way, I opened my five-stitched book, looking over the text I planned on teaching to a group of student nurses who'd begged me to tutor them. I had finished reviewing *The Great Learning* with them. And now we had moved on to the medical texts, with titles as difficult as their content: *Injaejikjimaek, Tonginch'imhyŏlch'imgugyŏng, Kagamsipsambang, T'aepyŏnghyeminhwajegukbang*, and the *Puinmunsansŏ*. It was the last that I'd be teaching today, which I had spent the past few days reviewing myself. As Nurse Jeongsu had said, a good teacher must teach precisely and with a whole heart in order for a student to be molded into a true uinyeo.

I flipped to the next page and paused, glancing up from the text to the police bureau. It had become a habit over the months—looking, but no longer searching, that way each time I passed by. And out of the same habit, I lowered my gaze to the text, then froze. I must have imagined it, a glimpse of blue silk at the corner of my vision.

I shot a glance back up.

There, across the wide road, stood a familiar young man among a circle of officers. He looked bright and healthy, his skin a crisp contrast to the dark sweep of his brows. At the sight of Eojin, memories swept in, bright and flickering. Our promises whispered within the papered walls of the inn. Our long nights of discussion, questions that haunted us both. The kiss on my cheek, which I'd turned away. The sensation of his heart fading on my back as I'd carried him through the forest.

I couldn't compel myself to leave, my stare fixed on him as crowds passed by, farmers leading wagon-loaded ponies, nobles in their black hats and flowing robes, young ladies hidden under jangot veils. When Eojin chuckled over something, my chest ached and my eyes grew damp. Half of me was convinced that this was a hallucination . . . until he glanced my way, and his smile faded.

Instantly, I turned and hurried away, my fingers ice-cold. I wasn't even sure why I was so afraid.

"Hyeon-ah." Eojin had followed me on the other side of the road, matching my quick pace, his gaze unwavering on me. He hurried over to my side, bringing with him the scent of pine on windy mountains. Like the forests that engulfed the shadowy slopes, his gaze engulfed me.

"Where are you going so fast?" he asked, his voice uncertain.

"I'm going to the Hyeminseo." My throat felt deathly parched. "I work there now."

After a moment of hesitation, he said, "I'll walk you there."

I could feel his hesitant glances my way as we strolled down Jongno Road, before turning right at the intersection. *What are you thinking about?* I wanted to ask him. *What has changed between us? Or has nothing changed?* But a sudden shyness fell over me, and instead I asked, "How is your arm?"

"Not the same," he replied, and that was when I noticed

316

his waist was bereft of a sword; he'd always carried one before. "There's a stiffness to my elbow, and I can hardly feel my right hand." He cast another glance my way. "I wrote several letters to you, but the writing was too illegible to send. Neither did I want to dictate to a servant. I'm sorry for the wait . . ."

In his lingering gaze, I could see what he truly wished to say: *Why didn't you write back?*

I quickly shook my head and said light-heartedly, "No need to apologize. It must have taken you a while to even recover enough strength. You were so badly injured."

A muscle worked in his jaw, then he matched my light-hearted note. "I suppose so." Stretching out his right arm, he stared down at his hand and murmured, "I'm hoping the stiffness will go away with time, or I'll be the only inspector in this entire kingdom that is unable to wield a sword."

"One doesn't always need a sword to find the truth."

"Like you," he whispered.

I blinked up at him. "Like me?"

"That day in the forest," he said, and my body tensed at the memory, "you didn't even raise a blade to Nurse Inyeong. I was terrified she'd murder you right before my eyes. But you made her lower her sword."

Our steps slowed as we arrived before the back gate of the Hyeminseo, near the spot where he'd helped me over the wall when we first met, more than half a year ago. Eojin seemed to be thinking of that day, too, for he gazed at the tile-capped wall, as though imagining me—the

Hyeon who had dangled over, whispering to him, *I highly doubt our paths will ever cross again.*

"The first time I met you, I don't think I quite knew," he said softly, looking back at me, "what a surprise you would become to me."

He said no more, his gaze on mine ever searching—ever waiting—and for a moment, fear split through my chest. I didn't want him to go, but I was afraid of what would happen if he stayed. This kingdom was filled with young women who were far more than I was, or could ever be. More beautiful, more respectful, more charming. Father had always wanted more, and Mother had never been enough. And that was my greatest nightmare—that Eojin would stay and find out that I was not enough.

"I should go," I said, my heart closing up like a clam.

"Will I see you later?"

"Perhaps," I said.

His expression faltered. "Only perhaps?"

Chewing nervously on my lower lip, I could imagine the days ahead unfolding before me. I would bid him farewell, promise to perhaps see him again, then avoid him for weeks, and weeks would turn into months. Growing distant, severing the ties myself before I could get hurt. We would go our own separate ways, and years later, I would see him passing down the street one day and wonder—*Why were you so afraid, Hyeon?*

Why, indeed, was I so afraid?

"So much has happened since we first met," I murmured. "We've solved a string of murders and a palace conspiracy together. We've braved uncertainty, with both our lives on the line. Too much has happened . . ." My voice trailed off as my mind reached a realization—too much had happened to be afraid. Whatever awaited in the future, I had to trust that he would watch out for me, as I would always watch out for him.

At the frown pinching my brows, Eojin must have misunderstood my silence. "I know; too much has happened. But I am still the same, and I thought you were waiting. I had hoped—" His voice rasped, then he ran a hand over his face, the handsome face that had grown so familiar to me. "No, never mind. I do understand . . ." His expression tensed as his back turned to me, and he moved to leave.

"Eojin." I reached out to stop him, gently catching his wrist. He felt my hand and grew very still. "We endured so much together. You didn't let go of me then. Don't let go of me now."

His pulse bounded against my fingers, as quick as my heart beating in my chest. Then slowly he turned to face me, his cheeks flushed, a timidity I'd never seen before now lighting his eyes. "I won't," he said in a bare whisper. "I won't let you go, no matter what."

He moved my hand into his, and as our fingers intertwined, it occurred to me that love wasn't all that I'd feared it to be. I had imagined that it was a wildfire that incinerated everything in its path. Instead, it felt as ordinary and extraordinary as waking up to a new day.

"The Segeomjeong Pavilion," he said quietly. "Wait for me there after work. There's so much I want to tell you."

I nodded, my heart feeling so full and near bursting as he stepped impossibly close. His lashes lowered, his ears bright red, Eojin ducked his head and pressed a soft kiss against my cheek.

"There is only you." His words caressed me, winding themselves around my soul. "There will only ever be you. I promise, Hyeon-ah."

Tiptoeing, I wrapped my arms around his neck, the book I held dangled against his back as I found his lips. He seemed stunned at first, then he smiled against my kiss, and I could hear his thoughts: *You always surprise me.*

I smiled, too. *I know.*

When at last we broke away, our gazes remained locked—half dazed, half startled to have broken etiquette in broad daylight.

"I really should go now," I whispered.

He continued to linger, brushing a strand of my hair behind my ear. "You probably should; it seems you are needed."

Together, we glanced down the narrow road that curved around the Hyeminseo. There was a line of ailing peasants crowding the front of the establishment, waiting for the gates to open; it was astonishing that no one seemed to have noticed us.

I gave Eojin one last look, held his hand a moment longer, then slipped past the back gate.

I tucked my medical book under my arm and made my way—face flushed—to the main pavilion, where the physicians and nurses were gathered, awaiting the start of their duties.

"You are late," came a familiar voice. It was Nurse Jeongsu, now in charge of the uinyeos. She watched me closely as I hurried up the stone steps onto the terrace; it overlooked the vast courtyard and the main gate. "You've never been late before."

"I got distracted, uinyeo-nim," I said, slightly out of breath, as I found my place next to Jieun.

"That is good to hear." After a pause, a smile creased Nurse Jeongsu's lips. She leaned her weight onto the walking stick, a cane made of bamboo that the baekjeong she'd protected had carved out for her, delivered by one of his children. "I've worried, even since you were a student nurse, that you perhaps try too hard to excel at everything. It is good to see you late and rather flustered for once. You seem almost changed."

"Perhaps it is because I've grown a little, since you were away," I said, my voice lowered for her ears alone. My mentor's smile widened, and the servants unbolted the main entrance, opening onto a flood of clamoring patients.

I held my hands together and drew my back straight, my heart rising with the morning sun. "The gates are now open, uinyeo-nim. Our day begins."

AUTHOR'S NOTE

The Red Palace is loosely based on the life and death of Crown Prince Jangheon (also known as Crown Prince Sado), a historical figure I've been fascinated by for a long time. When I finally found the courage to write about him, I tried not to stray too far from historical facts. I studied as much as I could about his life and listened to as many lectures by Korean historians as I could find. But even then, I am aware of my limitations both as a diaspora Korean and as a writer of fiction, and so my goal in writing this book was not to offer a purely fact-based account. For example, Nurse Hyo-ok's murder is a fictional event, based on the real event of the Crown Prince's first documented act of homicide, where he killed and beheaded Eunuch Kim Han-chae in 1757. Ultimately, my goal in writing this book was to tell a story, while being as true to history as possible.

And the history of Crown Prince Jangheon was a very sad one, indeed.

To give some context, the prince's story is remembered

as one of the greatest tragedies in the history of the Joseon Dynasty (1392–1910). At the age of twenty-seven, Crown Prince Jangheon was ordered to step into a rice chest on a hot summer's day, and he was then sealed within by order of his father. He was left there until he starved to death eight days later.

This method of execution was the king's attempt to evade the court rules that forbade someone from harming a royal person and the then-common practice of communal punishment, which would have endangered the life of the Crown Prince's son (the only direct heir to the throne).

The question of what *led* to this tragic event is still a source of controversy. Of the two main theories, the oldest one suggests that the Crown Prince struggled with severe and untreated mental health problems that escalated into violence.

A review of the literature suggests that the Crown Prince did indeed suffer from psychiatric symptoms. However, this is a delicate and complex topic, and so I chose not to focus on this aspect of the Crown Prince's life. I knew I wouldn't be able to do justice to a portrayal of this particular experience without falling into the danger of suggesting that those who have mental health problems are dangerous. This is something I absolutely do not believe or condone.

As for the more recent theory, it presents him not as a "psychotic killer" but as a tragic prodigy whose revolutionary ideas clashed with the Old Doctrine faction, the leading political party at the time. He therefore fell victim to their political conspiracy at the royal court.

However, one thing to note is that even if Crown Prince Jangheon was really a victim of political strife, this doesn't negate his homicidal acts. None of the scholars dispute the fact that the Crown Prince was a murderer, because these facts appeared in too many court documents, such as the *Annals of the Joseon Dynasty* and the *Diaries of the Royal Secretariat*, along with his wife's *Memoirs of Lady Hyegyoung*. The violent acts he committed were ruthless, and he allegedly killed a hundred people in his lifetime.

Whatever the truth behind his execution is, the Crown Prince lived an extremely difficult and painful life and died in 1762 without the opportunity to reign. Many view this tragedy as King Yeongjo choosing his own political life over his son's actual life. And after his son's passing, the king gave him the posthumous title of Sado, meaning "Thinking of with Great Sorrow."

For the rest of his reign, the king strictly banned any mention of the prince's name. It wasn't until many years later that Crown Prince Jangheon's son, Jeongjo, would finally address the tragedy upon ascending the throne by declaring, "I am the son of Prince Sado."

For those who want a more extensive account of Prince Sado's life, I highly recommend the book *Memoirs of Lady Hyegyoung*.

ACKNOWLEDGMENTS

Writing this book was such a joy, and I'm so grateful to a number of people who made this experience possible.

To my dream editor, Emily Settle, thank you for always inspiring me and for having so many brilliant ideas. I wanted to write about Crown Prince Sado for the longest time, but never knew how to approach this historical event until you thought of the Palace Nurse x Royal Inspector pairing. So I owe the existence of this book in part to you.

To my champion (and agent), Amy Elizabeth Bishop, I'm so grateful that I can always turn to you. This publishing journey is no longer so intimidating with you as my agent, and I'm where I am today because of your guidance and encouragement.

Many thanks to my publishing team at Feiwel & Friends, including my fantastic publicist, Brittany Pearlman; my copyeditor, Ana Deboo; cover artist, Sunga Park; managing editor Dawn Ryan and production editor Kathy Wielgosz; my designer, Liz Dresner; and production manager, Celeste Cass.

To the early supporters and readers of this book, Kristin Dwyer, Erin Kim, Axie Oh, Eunice Kim, Cristina Lee, and my sister, Sharon, thank you for reading and boosting my confidence in this book! I also want to thank Kess Costales, my Queen of Romance, for all your wonderful suggestions (I credit the last line of chapter 18 to you), as well as Sarah Rana, for restraining me from deleting too many scenes (the "one table trope" scene is dedicated to you).

My eternal gratitude to all the librarians, booksellers, reviewers, and readers who have supported my works. Your enthusiasm allows me to keep on doing what I love: exploring Korean history through fiction. I'd also like to thank my longtime friends, Janice and Phil; I'll always and forever be grateful for your support of my dream since Day One.

To Mom and Dad, thank you for believing in me and for always cheering me on; your continued support means so much to me. I also want to thank my in-laws, Mr. and Mrs. Tung, for babysitting so I could carve out writing time for me; I would have struggled to meet my deadlines without your help.

A special thank-you to my husband, Bosco; you're my go-to brainstorm partner, and I so appreciate how kind and considerate you are, no matter how prickly I can be, especially when I'm on deadline. You're the best.

I'm grateful for the many resources that made it possible to write this book, especially JaHyun Kim Haboush's translation of *The Memoirs of Lady Hyegyong*, Anders Karlsson's "Law and the Body in Joseon Korea: Statecraft and the Negotiation of Ideology," Bak Yeong-Kyu's 에로틱 조선: 우리가 몰랐던 조선인들의 성 이야기 and 조선 관청기행, The Institute of Seoul Studies' 한양의 탄생: 의정부에서 도화서까지 관청으로 읽는 오백년 조선사, Han Hui-Suk's 의녀(키워드 한국문화 11), 팔방미인 조선 여의사, and Vincenza D'Urso's "Origin and Development of the Female Medical Practitioners' (ŭinyŏ) System During the Chosŏn Dynasty (1392–1910)."

And lastly: I thank Jesus, my lord and savior, for being my anchor.

Thank you for reading this Feiwel & Friends book.

THE FRIENDS WHO MADE
THE RED PALACE
POSSIBLE ARE:

JEAN FEIWEL, Publisher

LIZ SZABLA, Associate Publisher

RICH DEAS, Senior Creative Director

HOLLY WEST, Senior Editor

ANNA ROBERTO, Senior Editor

KAT BRZOZOWSKI, Senior Editor

DAWN RYAN, Executive Managing Editor

CELESTE CASS, Assistant Production Manager

EMILY SETTLE, Associate Editor

ERIN SIU, Associate Editor

FOYINSI ADEGBONMIRE, Associate Editor

RACHEL DIEBEL, Assistant Editor

LIZ DRESNER, Associate Art Director

KATHY WIELGOSZ, Production Editor

AVIA PEREZ, Production Editor

Follow us on Facebook or visit us online at fiercereads.com.

OUR BOOKS ARE FRIENDS FOR LIFE.